PRAISE FOR
AWARD-WINNING AUTHOR
Wendy Rosnau

"Rosnau threads mystery and romance throughout.
She keeps the reader alert and guessing. You'll find
yourself racing to the explosive conclusion."
—*Rendezvous* on *The Long Hot Summer*

"A wonderful read.
The adventure begins on the first page!"
—*Romantic Times* on *A Younger Woman*

"A flair for romantic adventure and
sizzling romance. Wendy Rosnau shines."
—*romantictimes.com* on *The Right Side of the Law*

"Wendy Rosnau's feisty characters and
non-stop snappy banter provide enjoyable
entertainment as an enticing mystery unfolds."
—*romantictimes.com* on *Beneath the Silk*

A Thousand
Kisses Deep

Wendy Rosnau

Silhouette® Books

Published by Silhouette Books

America's Publisher of Contemporary Romance

SILHOUETTE BOOKS

A THOUSAND KISSES DEEP

ISBN 0-373-21821-4

Dear Reader,

Onyxx is looking for a few good men....

Welcome to the first book in my new SPY GAMES
miniseries. Onyxx is a specialized division of NSA
Intelligence. Each team is comprised of a six-man
field team, with a commander based behind the
scenes. These hand-picked agents are an elite breed
of men who have one thing in common—they've
seen hell and survived.

In *A Thousand Kisses Deep* you'll meet Onyxx
agent Sly McEwen. Profile: Six-three, black hair,
blue eyes. His hell—twelve years in a maximum-
security prison. His expertise—diving rescue and
marine navigation. He owns the record for holding
his breath underwater longer than any man alive.

I hope you enjoy Sly's story and come back for
The Spy Wore Red, when Onyxx agent Bjorn Odell
teams up with bedroom assassin Nadja Stefn from
EURO-Quest. Watch for their story in Silhouette
BOMBSHELL coming in February 2005.

You can learn more about future stories in the
SPY GAMES miniseries and my backlist by
logging on to www.wendyrosnau.com.

*The surf pounding the jagged rocks three hundred
feet below told the story. The only way off the Greek
island was the way they had arrived, clinging
cliffside on a rope.*

Welcome to Sly's world....

To aka Jake White, Carol Holmes and Lorie Brown.
With an honorable mention to Marsha Zinberg,
for thinking of me. And to Jerry, Tyler
and Jeni for their love, loyalty
and keeping the faith.

A Thousand
Kisses Deep

Chapter 1

It began like any other mission, with the same calculated proficiency instinctive to the *rat fighters*—operatives who had proven themselves to be natural-born survivors.

They had arrived after dark. Six men dressed in black: special intelligence agents who had survived seven years in the trenches of global espionage. Six Onyxx agents on their last field mission before reassignment. Their last hurrah—as the saying went—before they were disbanded and their expertise took each of them in a different direction.

But on this night in early September something had gone wrong. Terribly wrong. And the question of the hour was, who had sold them out, friend or foe?

Sly McEwen had been asking himself that question from the moment his point man had gone down and he'd lost contact with the other four agents.

The surf pounding the jagged rocks three hundred

feet below told the story. The only way off the Greek island was the way they had arrived, clinging cliffside on a rope. The rescue boat was two miles out. The aqua gliders and scuba gear that had brought them ashore, purposely sunk in the depths of the Aegean Sea to aid in their escape.

"So the predator becomes the prey." Jacy Madox sat wedged between two rocks, his tone as easy as ever, as if his life's blood wasn't flowing from his body with every breath he took. "A failed mission, with casualties. Merrick's going to be an ass about this when you get back. Neat and tidy. No excuses. That's the way he likes it."

Sly had seen it before—the way the half Blackfoot Indian could separate himself from his pain. Some kind of spiritual, out-of-body business, is how Jacy had once explained it.

He stripped off his shirt, ignoring the four-inch knife wound that had laid open his shoulder. It was bone deep, but he dismissed it and tied his shirt around Jacy's waist to slow his blood loss. After cinching it tight, he pulled his Warhawk from the Kydex scabbard strapped to his thigh. One quick maneuver and the razor-sharp blade sliced through his point man's pant leg.

Jacy relaxed his head against the rock and closed his eyes as Sly examined his leg. "Tucking tail isn't our style, but you sure as hell were tucking, ducking and dodging coming out of that compound. I knew you could run, but damn, I don't think I've ever seen you pick 'em up and lay 'em down quite that fast."

"That's because you're usually ahead of me."

"That's true. Which means you should have left me behind where I lay."

Sly ignored the comment, knowing the rules on sanctioned missions and fallen comrades. It was bullshit.

"Now we know why the Chameleon's on the Agency's top five most wanted," Jacy said.

"He's a slippery son of a bitch," Sly agreed, continuing to assess the mangled leg. "I thought we should have taken more time to prepare. Things might have been different if Merrick hadn't been in such a damn hurry."

"You don't prepare for a *wanagi*."

Sly snorted. "The Chameleon's no ghost."

"Then what is he? Just another lucky underground criminal?"

"A damn good criminal," Sly amended. "And why not? If he's an ex-operative, the Agency can take credit for teaching him the tricks of the trade."

"Then you believe the rumors?"

"Don't you?"

"The Chameleon a rogue operative… I don't know. His profile's too sketchy to be an ex-Onyxx agent," Jacy said. "We don't even know what the hell he looks like. Seems to me if Onyxx can pin down the eye color of a gnat on a gorilla's ass in the Congo they sure as hell should be able to harvest a picture or fingerprints of the Chameleon. Especially if he's one of their own."

Onyxx was one of the National Security's most advanced special intelligence agencies. Sly admitted that something didn't smell right.

"This guy's flesh and blood," he said, examining the protruding bone below Jacy's knee. "He puts his pants on one leg at a time, same as you and me."

"Equals, then?"

Sly looked up and gave his friend one of his rare smiles. "I can't say."

"You mean you won't until you're breathing down his neck and have him on the run?"

"How he maneuvers would do it."

"Because then you'd know if he can piss on the run."

The pissing joke had survived for seven years along with the rat fighters. Jacy, Sly and the other field agents had been sent to Brazil on their first mission. Caught in a war with rebel fighters, they had fought their way through a snake infested, hellhole of a jungle for ten hours. To survive that day everything—including pissing—had been done on the run.

"You do manage that with amazing coordination, Sly," Jacy complimented. "Makes me wonder what else you can do with that trained animal in a tight spot. Aaah! Go easy on the leg. Damn. You trying to break it clean off?"

Sly sheathed the Warhawk, rocked back on his hunches. "Your tibia's broken."

"You mean shattered, don't you? They were using P90's with tumblers. The leg's gone."

Jacy was probably right. If the leg could be saved it would take a miracle. But the leg wasn't the worst of it. The second bullet had entered along his spine while Sly was running from the compound with Jacy slung over his shoulder. With the amount of blood he was losing, he'd bleed to death before they got off the island.

The irony was that the bullet that would likely kill Jacy had saved Sly.

Sly seldom allowed himself to get emotionally caught up in the fallout surrounding a mission. But from the moment they'd been ambushed inside the compound his gut had started to churn—emotions butting heads with a strong suspicion that Merrick had sent them on a suicide mission. It was the only explanation for things turning to shit so fast.

"Stinks like a setup," Jacy said around a labored breath.

Sometimes his ability to tap into Sly's mind was downright spooky. "If Merrick set us up, I'll kill him."

Because Sly never talked much unless he had something important to say, his words were never taken lightly. He was the quiet one in the outfit, the *sly one*. His size and natural born athletic ability and intelligence made him unbelievably tough and as deadly as a straight-line wind.

But then manners and popularity hadn't been on Adolf Merrick's list of requirements the day the Agency's commander had seated himself at Sly's table in a little café in Lula, Mississippi. No, Merrick hadn't been searching for a dinner companion who knew how to win friends, or use his napkin.

He'd wasted no time getting to the point, saying in an educated New England voice, "I'm looking for men with nine lives who are living on number thirteen. Men who have seen hell. From what I've read, you've been living in hell since you were born. Men like yourself interest me, Mr. McEwen. I hire survivors, and pay them a lot of money to do what comes natural to them. You interested?"

Sly looked over his shoulder to where Castle Rock compound stood lit up like an amusement park. The alarms were still blaring while three spotlights continued to search the perimeter.

Days ago, from a rented fishing boat, they had gotten their first look at the rocky island in the middle of the Aegean Sea. The compound looked like an isolated monastery high on a rocky cliff, but it was anything but a lamasery for monks. The Chameleon was neither a religious man, nor an ill-bred pagan rebel. But an ex-Onyxx agent? Until he was captured no one would know for sure. All that could be guaranteed was that he was one of the richest international criminals in the country—the richest and the most elusive.

The monastery's exterior bleakness had been pure subterfuge. Inside, Sly and Jacy had found a pleasure palace of sorts, an exotic recreational facility for the Chameleon's league of supporters and thieves in between jobs.

Bjorn and Pierce had gone over the stone wall first, their job to disarm the perimeter. And while Ashland and Sully planted explosives to seal off an underground escape tunnel, Sly and Jacy had scaled the monastery walls and slipped inside to knock out the security system. Only the system had been triggered by sophisticated heat sensors—sensors strategically placed deep within the interior to ensure an intruder's entrapment.

The sound of shifting rocks warned Sly that someone was on the trail below them. He reached for his H&K, slid the short barrel between the rocks, and aimed it at the footpath. Looking through the weapon's night-vision scope, he spotted an armed force of ten.

Long minutes ticked by as the men moved along the rocky path unaware that they were being observed. When the danger had passed, Sly pulled back the H&K and relaxed on his heels.

"You're dead if you don't get going." Jacy's voice was liquid smooth with no hint of the pain that must be ravaging his body. "There's still time. Leave me, Sly. Take off, and don't look back. Go on."

Sly let Jacy's words roll off his back. "Dead or alive, we're leaving together. If you don't have the guts to keep breathing, I'll carry out a dead man. Makes no difference to me. You'll be riding either way."

The sky was black. No moon. No stars. Just rocky terrain, and the smell and sound of the pounding surf below. Sly waited another thirty minutes, then made his move. He pulled Jacy to his feet and hoisted him onto his good shoulder, the action forcing an odd whooshing noise from his point man's lungs. He was out in the open, a hundred yards away from cover, when he heard footsteps behind him. He swung around, his gun anchored against his hip. But there was no need to fire when he heard Bjorn Odell's Scandinavian accent swearing at Pierce Fourtier to slow down.

Seconds later the shadows materialized into men, and Sly saw why Bjorn was cursing. Pierce was moving as swiftly as a low soaring eagle, while Bjorn was hobbling on one good leg, leaning heavily on Ashland Kelly.

Bjorn's bloody thigh guaranteed he carried lead, and Ash had a bandanna tied around his head to keep the blood from flowing into his eyes. As for Pierce, the Frenchman from Louisiana had more visible skin showing on his muscular body than clothing—he looked like he'd been run through a human cheese shredder.

They were one man short. Sly asked, "Where's Paxton?"

"Sully's dead."

Sly could hear the guilt in Ash's voice. The two men had gone into the underbelly of the monastery together, and only one had come out. It was clear in Ash's voice that he blamed himself. Sly understood; Jacy should be on point right now instead of riding his shoulder.

"What happened to the breed?" Bjorn asked.

"Hit twice. Alive, but bleeding like a leaky faucet." Pierce eyed Jacy. "You sure he's alive? He looks dead."

Sly saw Bjorn lower his head. Over the years the man from Denmark and the breed from Montana had become close friends.

He said, "Dead or alive, he's going out with us."

"Damn right he is." Bjorn's head came up fast. "I'll carry him."

"You worry about that lame leg of yours and keeping up. I'll carry Jacy." Sly asked Ash, "Was Sully able to plant the explosives before he went down?"

"I'm not sure. I was forced to fall back when they started unloading tumblers a dozen at a time. I tried to get to him, but they had him pinned down."

"There's ten guns out hunting our asses." Sly looked at Pierce. "You're on point. Get us out of here."

Sly shifted Jacy on his shoulder and the breed moaned. He was still alive—hanging on by a thread. That thread would break before they reached the boat, but dead or alive, Jacy Madox was coming off the rock. Sly would have it no other way.

When they reached the cliffs Pierce quickly lashed Jacy to Sly's body, saying, "If Sully set that detonator those explosives should go off any minute. Buy us some time."

Sly grabbed hold of the rope he'd pinned into the rock earlier. "I'll see you at the bottom. If I get hung up, don't wait for me. Haul your asses out of here." He pinned Pierce with his unforgiving steel-blue eyes. "Make sure Bjorn and Ash make it back."

Washington, D.C.—six days later

"Casualties are always hard to swallow, McEwen. Especially if the mission is written up as a failure. But this one won't be. You were able to verify that the compound exists even if you weren't able to confirm that the Chameleon was there."

Merrick's voice was as cut-and-dried as his manners. Sly hadn't expected different. From the moment he'd met his commander, he'd suspected Adolf Merrick had survived his own hell once upon a time.

He was one chilly bastard, all right. Even his winter-gray eyes and silver hair fit Merrick's code name of *Icis.*

Ignoring the guest chair that his commander gestured to, Sly remained standing. At six foot three, his legs widespread, his back steel-pipe straight, he appeared as constant and unforgiving as Mississippi mud.

"I read your report, cross-referenced it with the others. Too bad about Paxton. He was a good operative. A helluva thing to have happen weeks before he would have been transferred out of field duty."

"A helluva thing." Sly was no longer able to keep the emotion out of his voice. "Sully's dead. Jacy is still in the hospital fighting for his life. That sure is one helluva thing, all right."

Merrick said nothing.

"Was the mission a bogus manhunt?" Sly asked. "Was it a suicide mission? Rumor has it that the Chameleon took out one of our agents in Istanbul while we were being shot to shit in the middle of the Aegean Sea."

"It's true that an Onyxx agent was assassinated in Turkey. We can't prove it was sanctioned by the Chameleon, however. To answer your question, this was no bogus manhunt. We had solid information that led us to Castle Rock. And as far as being a suicide mission, that's ludicrous. Here at Onyxx we don't dispose of our agents once they've maxed out their field service, McEwen. We find them a new home within the Agency according to their expertise."

A field operative's tour lasted seven years, and once the tour was up, the agent was reassigned. Although it was rare for agents to return to civilian life, they had a choice to do so. Of the rat fighters, less than one percent ever left. Not ordinary men, the rats had no reason to leave the nest since the Agency was the closest thing to a real family any of them had ever had.

Sly studied Merrick's face for the slightest sign that he was lying. A subtle twitch. A slight tightening in his jaw. But there was nothing. His boss was as chilly as always, his mouth concealed behind a full gray mustache, and his eyes obscured by a pair of gray-tinted glasses.

"The mission smells sour, Merrick. Like we were set up."

"There's nothing in your report to support that. Are you working on a hunch, McEwen? Yours, or Odell's? Or did the breed have another vision?"

Sly ignored the sarcasm. He wasn't going to apologize because Merrick was a facts-and-data military man, and he was a street survivor who played his gut and had a second pair of eyes in the back of his head.

"All I can tell you is that I received information pinpointing Castle Rock as one of the Chameleon's compounds. The tip needed to be checked out."

"First it was a solid piece of information, and now you're calling it a tip. Which was it?"

"In my report I'll be referring to it as a tip."

The bureaucratic bullshit games the Agency played made Sly sick. "Because the mission was doomed from the beginning, and you knew it."

"No!"

"Then bring your informant forward so he can be questioned."

"That's not how we do things here and you know it. At the moment I'm satisfied with what we have. Proof that Castle Rock is, or was, a compound for the Chameleon's band of criminals. That explosion you authorized blew one helluva hole in that monastery, and our mop crew isn't having much success finding anything we can use to sanction another mission. But we aren't giving up."

"Ever consider that your informant is working for the Chameleon? That he sold you out?"

"I've considered it. I'll be investigating the possibility, but I don't believe for one minute that's the case."

"What about a mole inside the Agency leaking information to the outside?"

"If you have proof of that you neglected to put it in your report."

Sly had purposely left out certain details so he could witness Merrick's reaction to his news. But none of it hinted that Onyxx was harboring a mole. "I have no proof that someone inside is working for the opposition. All I've got is one dead friend, and another one who may never walk again. That is if he lives at all."

"Casualties come with the job. And these two men are not your friends, they are your comrades. Yes, I know that working so closely together forms certain bonds, but you knew when you came aboard that the odds were stacked against all of you surviving. As cold as that sounds, it's fact. Your team has fared better than most. Consider yourself one of the lucky ones, McEwen, and leave it at that."

Sly watched Merrick closely when he said, "Holic Reznik was there."

"What?"

"I said Reznik was at Castle Rock."

"Why wasn't that in your report? Any of the reports?"

"I was the only one who saw him. I thought I'd save it for a private conversation."

"We have no information connecting him to the Chameleon."

"Exactly."

"He's an independent professional assassin."

"Right again."

"Why would he be there?"

"The Chameleon has been steadily gaining momentum. That doesn't happen without gaining enemies. Maybe he needs to thin some of them out," Sly offered.

"That's a good point."

The price on Holic Reznik's head was as high as the

price on the Chameleon's. The only difference between the two men was that Reznik's identity had been confirmed, and the Chameleon's identity was still anyone's guess.

A man with no face, is how the spy world described the Chameleon. In Jacy's words, a *wanagi*.

Merrick leaned back in his chair and stroked his silver mustache. A moment later, he removed his tinted glasses, allowing Sly to see that his commander's eyes were bloodshot.

Either Merrick was drinking again, or he hadn't slept in several days. Maybe both.

"You're absolutely sure it was Reznik?"

"We met in Austria. He was the one who shot Bjorn Odell in the back a few years ago." Sly dismissed Reznik for the time being. "This informant...I'd like to talk to him."

"That's not possible. If there's nothing else to report, this portion of our meeting is over." Merrick closed the file, its significance clear. "Again, I express my regret on the loss of a good agent. Sully will be hard to replace. Onyxx could have used him behind the scenes. Let's hope Jacy will be able to overcome his injuries. Now then, what about your reassignment? Have you given my offer consideration? The job as my assistant is perfect for you. Age-wise you couldn't do better."

"Age-wise?"

"You're thirty-four. One of the oldest field operatives we have."

Sly studied his commander. His silver hair and beard put Adolf Merrick somewhere in his fifties. "And when do *you* retire...*Icis?* When does Onyxx consider the old legend, age-wise, over the hill?"

"I've been asked to stay on for another term. But then I'm a military man with credentials. You are an ex-con who didn't finish high school. Sorry to be so blunt, but facts are facts, McEwen. So, what will it be?"

Sly hadn't needed days to consider Merrick's offer. He'd known what his answer would be the minute he'd heard the words. "I've decided to retire."

Merrick never blinked. He leaned back in his chair and said, "If you were anyone else, I'd try to change your mind. But I won't waste my breath. Over the years I've never known you to straddle the fence on one damn thing. But it won't be easy, returning to civilian life. After twelve years in prison, and seven spent here at Onyxx, what do you know about living free?"

Not a damn thing, Sly thought. Not one damn thing. But then he hadn't known a damn thing about being an Onyxx agent seven years ago, either.

"You're aware of our policy? Two hundred thousand will be deposited into your bank account within forty-eight hours. And of course, if trouble should come looking for you anytime in the future—"

"Onyxx doesn't want to know about it."

"That's the way it has to be, Sly, for security reasons."

Even though they hadn't always seen eye to eye, when Merrick stood and held out his hand, Sly shook it. Surprised when his commander slipped a card into his palm, he asked, "What's this?"

"My private number. Memorize it, then burn the card. In case you need to talk. Good luck, McEwen."

When the door closed, Adolf Merrick sat down and opened his top drawer. He located a bottle of pills next to his laptop computer, took both out and placed them on his desk.

He made a call on his private phone, left a one-word message, then opened the bottle of pills and shook out two white disks onto the desk. In his bottom drawer he kept a bottle of Glen Moray and he pulled it out. Uncorking it, he sent the pills to the back of his throat, then chased them down with a healthy swig of whiskey.

The day progressed as usual. Four hours later, after Merrick had taken two more pills and finished the bottle of Glen Moray, and while resting his head against the leather chair, his private phone rang. Before the second ring, the phone was pressed to his ear.

"Your information led my agents into a trap. What kind of game are you playing?"

"A serious game. I told you it was one of the Chameleon's compounds. A compound is usually full of armed men."

"There was no sign of the Chameleon."

"Did I say he would be there?"

"I don't tolerate half truths," Merrick warned.

"I think you'll tolerate whatever will get you what you want. And what you want is the Chameleon. Am I right?"

"I don't deny that he's become important to Onyxx."

"We both know why he's important...to you."

Merrick felt a chill along his spine. If his informant wasn't bluffing, then somehow there had been a breach in security at Onyxx. His own file was secure in the archives.

"The information I gave you was hardly twenty-four hours old when you sent your rat fighters racing off to Greece. Maybe if you hadn't been in such a hurry, you would have been more successful. Maybe you should learn better how to play the game."

"And maybe you should be concerned with what I do to informants who send me on wild-goose chases," Merrick snapped, wishing he hadn't revealed his frustration.

"You refused me two weeks ago. Do you still refuse me?"

Merrick said nothing.

"I want the file I requested two weeks ago. The one you told me I couldn't have. And in return I'll give you what you so desperately want."

"You tricked me. You gave me false information to—"

"I gave you a piece of correct information. Proof that I am in a better position than you are where the Chameleon is concerned."

"You think I'll play your silly games again after this?"

"I think you'll play on the chance that I know more than you. And if you play, you'll find out that I do. Did you do a background check on me like I suggested?"

"Yes."

"Then you know who I am. Who I really am."

"There's evidence to substantiate your claim."

"Damn right there is."

"You said you know where the Chameleon is going to be in the near future. How do you know?"

"I know, because I know where I'm going to be in the near future, and he's going to be with me."

"Tell me what you're looking for in the file, and I'll—"

"No. I need all of it."

"If I decide to get you the file, how do I deliver it to you?"

"I'm sure you already know where I'm at. Recruit someone you can trust to bring me the data. That is if you want to know what I know. I need the Agency's file on Paavo Creon before the first of November."

When the phone went dead, Merrick disconnected and slid it into his inside pocket. For fourteen years

Onyxx had been hunting for the Chameleon, with no luck. What was he supposed to do, ignore this unbelievable lead that had clearly come straight out of nowhere?

No, of course not. He had remained at Onyxx because he was confident that someday a lead would put him on the scent of his old enemy, and that day had finally come.

Behind him was a wall-size world map, and as Adolf stood, his bloodshot eyes scanned the Aegean Sea. Thousands of islands made up the Greek Isles. The Chameleon was there on one of them. Somewhere on a remote beach sipping wine, or in some plush hotel sprawled naked in a bed with his latest female conquest.

The image of the latter had Merrick swearing violently. The sudden reaction snapped his head back and sent an explosion of fresh pain shooting behind his eyes. Inwardly he groaned as his right eye started to water. He became dizzy, and it was only then that he reached out to steady himself and keep from dropping to his knees.

He closed his eyes, and for the first time in too many years, he began to pray. He prayed that it wasn't too late. Prayed that somehow his fate would be delayed long enough to find his enemy.

Find him, face him and kill him.

He would kill the Chameleon for Johanna. Kill him for the constant pain he'd lived with every day for the past fourteen years. Kill him for the wasted years. For the nights he'd sat frozen in front of the computer screen watching and waiting for a glimpse of Johanna's flawless face.

Kill him for the years the Chameleon had deprived him the scent and feel of Johanna in the dark hours before dawn.

Kill him for the children that would never be born.

Kill him for the sheer pleasure of killing him and watching the life fade from his eyes.

Yes, if Fate was kind, and God merciful, he would find the Chameleon before it was too late, and kill him for Johanna.

Chapter 2

"When the game is over and the predator has caught his prey, what are you thinking about, Eva?"

"I really don't have time to talk today, Dr. Fielding. I'm running late."

"You know the rules, Eva."

"I'm thinking about survival, Dr. Fielding. Only survival. Living isn't for the weak, you know. It's for those who master the game. I really am running late."

"Late for what?"

"I'm off to Greece again. I have a million things to do before we leave."

"We...meaning you and Simon?"

"Yes."

"For how long this time?"

"At least a month."

"Then I think this session is important, don't you?"

"The pills are what's important, Dr. Fielding."

"I planned to discuss your parents today. We haven't talked about them in a while."

"We've discussed them at length many times. It hasn't changed anything. My father is still too busy to see me more than once a year, and Mother is still dead. That is unless you've found a way to resurrect her. In that case I'd like to buy shares in your company."

"I'm sorry, my skills don't stretch that far."

"Too bad. I miss her."

"But not your father?"

"I miss the way he used to be. Before Mother died."

"Your mother died when you were nine, right?"

"Old news."

"You were born here in Atlanta?"

"More old news. Check your black book. I'm sure you'll find that information under Born and Raised. Born in Atlanta, raised by my father."

"Don't you mean, raised by your father's house staff?"

"Always a stickler for details, aren't you Dr. Fielding? Okay, raised by the minions. Feel better?"

"My job is to make you feel better, not me. The staff was competent, yes?"

"Fork on the left, knife on the right. Manners are as important as a good education. Always tell the truth when you've been caught with your hand in the cookie jar. And no screwing the gardener's son no matter how cute he is, or how good his ass looks in his jeans. Yes, the minions saw to all of the important stuff."

"And did you have sex with the gardener's son?"

"Yes. I was desperate to feel something for someone. Tony came, and I didn't. I thought something was wrong with me so I did it with him again a few days later. The results were just as disappointing. A few years later I read a book about sexuality. It said with some men it's all about them and that was certainly true about Tony. He was a greedy little bastard."

"You mentioned you were desperate to feel."

"I was sixteen. I had no friends, and I was never allowed to leave the house without one of the minions. There were days I felt my father had wished that I had died in the fire with my mother. I thought, he's pretending I'm dead, that's why he never comes to see me. I thought that a lot."

"Where was your father during those desperate years? You've always avoided that question."

"I don't avoid that question. I don't know where he was. Away at work. Always away."

"Did you ever ask what kind of work kept him away?"

"Once, I did. He joked that if he told me, he would have to kill me afterward."

"Did he make jokes like that often?"

"My father never cracked a smile after Mother died."

"Was he kind to you when you saw him?"

"Yes. But then it's not hard to be kind to someone when you see them only one day out of every year."

"You felt deprived of love?"

"Of course. Doesn't every kid believe their childhood is cruel and unusual?"

"And in your case—"

"Mommy's dead and Daddy's too busy, and the Easter Bunny and Santa don't give a damn, you know."

"Yes, I believe I do. Define your relationship with the man you live with now."

"You want me to tell you about Simon?"

"Yes."

"You already know he's unique, has an IQ off the charts, and no soul. What more can I say?"

"Do you believe he loves you?"

"No."

"Does he tell you he loves you?"

"No."

"Do you love him?"

"That would make me a masochist, Dr. Fielding. I endure Simon. That doesn't mean I like living with him, or enjoy what he does to me."

"Love spins the cycle of life, Eva. To love and be loved, that's our heart's desire."

"Haven't you been listening to anything I've said this past year? Survival, Dr. Fielding, that is my heart's desire."

"I see bruises on your wrists today. How did that happen?"

"It could be worse, you know. Simon could have a fetish for knives instead of ropes and belts. Actually, if you look at it that way, I'm lucky, don't you think?"

"You make jokes to hide the pain."

"Do I?"

"You're making this complicated Eva. Unless you love him, it doesn't have to be."

"It's not complicated, Dr. Fielding. You're looking through your anal telescope again. You don't have to love someone to live with them and endure their quirks. The word *love* is overused and overrated. Overused by a society that is trying to rationalize and legitimize our existence on an emotional level. What we should be concentrating on is our physical needs. That's what will keep us alive. Like the air we breathe. We can't exist without it, Dr. Fielding, and yet we continue to pollute it like it's a dumping ground."

"Fascinating."

"Yes, isn't it? Air is the magic pill. Breathe in with me and exhale, Dr. Fielding. In with the new and out with the old. Yes, that's it. Again."

"Eva, please. Enough about the air. What I find fascinating is your analogy of love."

"*Love* is a word men use when they find it necessary to shackle a woman into believing her hell is worthwhile. It keeps her buying into the myth."

"Why are you whispering all of a sudden?"

"Because I feel like it. Because maybe these walls have ears."

"I assure you they do not. We are quite alone. Now then, tell me about this myth."

"It's an evil myth. And it's not going to save you, or me. Only mastering the game will do that. It's the air we should be having a love affair with. Shall we breathe again together?"

"Eva, please. No more about the air. Tell me how love shackles a woman."

"A woman's happiness should be exclusive unto herself. Not reliant on acceptance and approval by society's standards. By a man's standards. But that's not what we're taught, is it? We're taught that being loved by a man is the ultimate happiness. That offering love in return will set us free. It won't, you know. Only mastering the game will free us."

"Free us from what?"

"The shackles, Dr. Fielding. The goddamn shackles!"

"You seem especially agitated today, Eva. More than usual. Has something happened since our last session?"

"A lot has happened. A lot of the same, Dr. Fielding. Ten minutes of talking should be worth the prescription, with refills, don't you think? I really do have to run."

"I don't approve of giving my patients medication without supervision, Eva. You know I like to—"

"You created the headaches. I never had them before the hypnosis. Now you're going to have to help me get rid of them."

"But—"

"If I was going to kill myself with those pills, I would have done it months ago. The pills save me. You want to save me, don't you, Dr. Fielding? That's your job, right?"

"I thought that's what I was doing when I suggested the hypnosis. Maybe if we tried another session before you left for Greece. Maybe if we—"

"Breathe, Dr. Fielding. You look pale. Is it your love life? Feeling shackled by your husband?"

"We're discussing you, Eva, not me. I still believe you're suppressing something from your childhood. Something painful that wants to surface. But you're fighting it, and the headaches are a result."

"I'm not fighting it any longer."

"What do you mean by that?"

"There's no time to explain. I'm off to Greece."

"Will you see your father?"

"He'll be at Simon's birthday party. That's one of the reasons we go this time of year."

"You say that with a look of dread. Why? Is it the party, or seeing your father?"

"Simon's parties are memorable. Last year the party was in a reptile garden, and I wore a five-foot python around my neck like a fashion scarf. Do you have any idea what it's like to be draped in a live snake skin for an entire evening if you have a snake phobia?"

"Oh, dear God. Let's change the subject."

"Yes, let's."

"Let's talk more about Simon."

"Let's not."

"You were nineteen when you met him, right?"

"Yes, on Simon's twenty-first birthday."

"Here in Atlanta?"

"Yes."

"Tell me about that night."

"For the prescription?"

"Yes. For the prescription, plus refills."

"All right. My father took me with him to the party. It was at Boxwood Estate."

"You're frowning. Was it unusual for your father to take you with him?"

"Yes. Usually I was taken to meet him. But that day he came to the house to pick me up."

"And what happened at Simon's party?"

"If I told you what happened, you wouldn't believe me. And if you did, I would have to kill you. Can I get the prescriptions now? I really have to run."

Sly McEwen heard the tape recorder click off and he turned from the window. "Why did you shut off the tape, Bjorn?"

"Because that's it. The doc writes the prescriptions, and Eva Parish leaves. And she does run, by the way. Two blocks."

Sly moved back to the couch in his motel room and sat. It had been three weeks since he had turned down Merrick's offer and left Onyxx. Bjorn Odell, on the other hand, had agreed to be reassigned within the Agency as a profiler—a job that matched his skills.

The oldest of the rat fighters at thirty-eight, Bjorn was a close match in height, but where Sly's black hair was worn short, the man from Denmark looked like a long-haired blond Viking straight out of the history books.

"So what did you find out?" Sly prompted.

Bjorn hooked his ass on the motel desk and flipped open his log book. "If I go by the information you gave me, our Eva is the daughter of Muriel and Paavo Creon. The couple was married in Boston and moved to Atlanta a year later. Paavo Creon was a career military man. They had one daughter, Evka Amara Creon. The police reports state that the entire family died in a house fire fourteen years ago. No survivors, though we can't confirm that. The fire cremated the bodies."

"So what you're saying is the woman on the tape has been officially dead fourteen years."

"Yes, that's if your information and mine check out. Which I believe it will. She was tutored privately, and has no social security number. That's why she's still believed to be dead. Fingerprints would be the only way to verify that it's her for sure. Or dental records."

"Okay. What else?"

"She's twenty-three. That fits, as well as the description of the little red-haired Creon girl who supposedly died that night."

"The woman on the tape has red hair?"

"And green eyes." Bjorn checked his notes. "She is now five foot eight, weights one hundred ten pounds, and lives on Langdon Drive. Residence, Boxwood Estate. My records don't indicate she's married to Parish, though she uses his name."

"She have a routine? Any hobbies? Friends?"

"No friends. A boring routine. She swims early morning in the backyard pool. Likes to sit in the sun. Some days until noon. Parish takes her out to dinner on occasion. One day a week she goes into town escorted by Morris Gram, Simon's driver and overseer at the estate. From checking Dr. Fielding's appointment book it looks like the third Thursday of every month Eva plays her little game."

Sly rested his elbow on the arm of the couch and rubbed his clean shaven jaw. "Explain what you mean by that?"

"That's what I call her visits to her psychiatrist because she keeps them a secret from Simon Parish."

Sly stood, snagged his black V-neck T-shirt off the back of the couch and pulled it on over his head. He had arrived in Atlanta midmorning. After checking into the nondescript motel on the outskirts of the city, he'd called Bjorn, then headed for the shower. He'd barely gotten his pants back on when Bjorn knocked on his door.

"Game day goes like this," Bjorn continued. "Morris Gram and Eva leave Boxwood around one o'clock in Simon's black Bentley. At one-thirty she's dropped off in front of the Tastes of Paradise, a health food and pharmacy downtown. While Morris parks and waits, she enters the shop through the front door. She hands off the list to the clerk at the counter, exits out the back door, then runs two blocks to Dr. Nancy Fielding's office."

"Where they talk—" Sly interjected "—and she gets her prescription renewed, then runs back to Tastes of Paradise, entering through the back door."

"That's right. Eva hands the clerk her prescription, and gets a grocery-size bag in exchange, and a small white prescription bag. She removes the prescription bottle from the white bag and slips it into her cleavage, then exits out the front door. The minute Morris sees her, he pulls the Bentley to the curb and she climbs in. They're back at Boxwood within thirty minutes."

Sly hung a hand on his jean-clad hip. "Did you get a profile on Simon Parish, too?"

"Not as complete as I would have liked. I've been busy watching our Eva."

"I take it she's pretty?" Sly couldn't deny he was anxious to put a face with the smoky voice on the tape.

"I prefer blondes with boobs." Bjorn cupped his hand around an invisible grapefruit. "In Eva's case, one out of two ain't bad. If she dyed her hair, I'd be in love."

"So we've established she's got cleavage."

"A good two inches. There didn't seem to be a problem burying the bottle of pills."

"What did you find out about Parish?"

Bjorn flipped pages in his log book. "I couldn't find birth records on Simon Parish. But I did locate a medical report since he's been hospitalized on a number of occasions. He's an albino with a rare blood disorder. He's five-eleven, weighs 140. No wife or children."

"He's an albino?"

"That's right. White hair, white skin, red eyes, one hobby."

"One hobby?"

"Horticulture. He has a two-acre boxwood maze in his backyard. Guess that's why he renamed the estate after he purchased it from Langdon Hall. You'll have to see it to appreciate it."

Bjorn eased off the corner of the table and stood. Leaning heavily on his cane, he pulled a piece of paper out of the back pocket of his jeans and handed it to Sly. "That's what was in the grocery bag the clerk gave her yesterday."

Sly scanned the list. "I don't think I've ever known a vegetarian who takes barbiturates."

"Maybe Parish is the rabbit."

"What the hell are calimyrnas?"

"Figs."

"Mesclun?"

"Salad greens."

Sly read further, scowled, then gave Bjorn a puzzled look. "Edible flowers?"

"I questioned that one, too. The clerk told me pansies make a salad taste sweeter and look more colorful." Bjorn grinned, then closed his log book. "Isn't it about time you told me why I've been Eva Creon's shadow for two weeks? Why I broke into the shrink's office and stole that tape, and ten others like it?"

"Did you get photos?"

"Photos of our Eva and Simon Parish. I also made a copy of the doctor's appointment book for the past year."

"Did you get ahold of her black book?"

"No. The shrink must keep that on her. So what's this all about, Sly? Why are you interested in Eva Parish?"

"Because she's Paavo Creon's daughter. You just confirmed that."

"*Ja.* So?"

"Paavo Creon was an Onyxx agent. He was recruited for the first team twenty-one years ago."

It was obvious Bjorn hadn't expected to hear that. "An old Onyxx agent? Are you sure?"

"That's what my information tells me."

"The information you said arrived at your D.C. apartment with no return address?"

"That's right."

"Are you working undercover, Sly?"

"No."

"Then why did you get that information sent to you?"

"That's a good question." Sly rubbed his shoulder, paced back to the window and looked out. "What would you say if I told you I think Paavo Creon killed his wife, set that fire in his house, and walked away from it with his daughter?"

"I'd ask you for what purpose and how you came up with a crazy idea like that?"

"It sure would be a neat and tidy way to disappear and start a new life as someone else."

"True. But why would he do that?"

Sly turned from the window. "Because he needed to die in order to become the Chameleon."

There was a long minute of silence. Finally Bjorn said, "You should talk to Merrick about this."

Sly went back to looking out the window. "Not yet."

"Someone wants you involved in this. That someone obviously doesn't know you're no longer an Onyxx agent."

"Maybe. Or maybe someone inside Onyxx is trying to tell me something."

"That's scary. A mole inside the organization? You better talk to Merrick."

"Sully's dead. Jacy…" Sly stopped, rethought what he was going to say. "I've got time on my hands now. I think I'll play along and see what I can scratch up."

"Feeling guilty over Sully and Jacy isn't a good enough reason to get yourself killed, Sly. What if this is another set up? What if this is Onyxx's way of getting rid of you for turning your back on their reassignment offer? Why the hell did you have to quit anyway?"

"Would you have taken a job filing papers for Merrick?"

When Bjorn said nothing, Sly walked over to the desk and ejected the tape from the recorder and dropped it into the box with the others. "Is Boxwood Estate in Simon Parish's name?"

"It is, *ja*. This doesn't smell right, Sly. I don't like it."

"The copied documents look legit."

"Anything can look legit with the right equipment. I'll say it again. I don't like this."

"You never liked half the shit we did for Onyxx. That never stopped you." Sly located the documents that had been sent to him and dropped them on the table. "Take a look at these, then tell me you aren't just a little bit curious."

While Bjorn studied the documents, Sly confessed,

"I'm not going into this with my eyes closed. I know the risks."

"You just admitted you don't have a clue who is behind this, that means you're going in blind. You're too smart to be jumping into this, Sly."

"I owe them."

"The facts are, if Sully were alive he'd argue that point with you and win. He was as stubborn as you are. And Jacy would tell you things always look different after a week of hard drinking. Take a week, and if—"

"Sully shouldn't be dead."

"No, he shouldn't be, but that wasn't your fault."

Sly reached for a beer from the six-pack Bjorn had brought and tossed it to him, then took one for himself. "I was supposed to be watching Jacy's back, not using him for a goddamn shield to get my own ass out of there."

"That's not what you were doing and you know it. Jacy would have been dead for sure if you hadn't carried him out. The bottom line is because you did, he's going to make it. Hell, he didn't lose his leg. That's a damn miracle."

Sly couldn't get past the guilt that still shadowed that night at Castle Rock. The fact remained he was walking around on two strong legs and Jacy wasn't. And the doctors weren't sure yet if he would ever regain the use of his leg.

"So now what?" Bjorn asked. "What's next?"

Sly popped the tab on the can and took a swallow of warm beer. "You just confirmed Paavo Creon has a daughter still living here in Atlanta. That Eva Parish is really Eva Creon. That gives credence to my theory that Paavo may still be alive, living in Greece as the Chameleon."

"You really think they're the same person?"

"I think it's possible."

Bjorn tossed the documents on the desk and opened his beer. "You'll need someone helping you on the inside."

Sly smiled. "It would make things easier. Did you get pictures from the police station? Pictures of the Creon family?"

"There were no pictures. They were all destroyed in the fire. I did bring the surveillance pictures. If Paavo Creon worked for Onyxx there should be a file on record. Pictures."

"That's what I was thinking, too. You volunteering to break into Onyxx's archives and take a look?"

"If I can think of a reason to get inside."

"I no longer have authorization to get through Onyxx's front door," Sly reminded.

Bjorn downed half his can of beer. "I'll say it again. If you think the Chameleon and Paavo Creon are one and the same, I think you should talk to Merrick. After all he was a field agent in the early years. Maybe he knew Creon."

Sly finished his beer then pitched his empty can into the wastebasket across the room. "I'm going to see what I can uncover on my own first."

"You don't trust Merrick."

"Not at the moment."

"If Paavo's alive, why leave his daughter here in Atlanta?" Bjorn mused out loud. "Why not take her with him out of the country? Why chance someone discovering her?"

"I don't know. I'd like to talk to the people who raised her before she was given Parish's name and into his keeping. Can you do some checking on that, and see where they are?"

"I'll get on it as soon as I get back from Montana."

"All right. Jacy told me you volunteered to help him get settled in Montana. How long will that take?"

"A few days. He's got a cabin on a lake someplace high in the Rockies. I'm suppose to fly out with him day after tomorrow. I'll be back here inside of a week."

Sly asked, "How's Ash been since we got back?"

"No one's seen him since we filed our reports. He was feeling pretty low. My guess is he's blaming himself for Sully's death. Nursing a guilt sucker like you."

Sly scowled at his friend. "Give him some time. He'll come around."

"Is that what it'll take for you to get over kicking your own ass day and night over Jacy? Time?"

"There's only one thing that's going to make me feel better and that's finding out who the Chameleon is, and how to get close enough to him to send him to hell. And if in the process I find out Merrick's been jerking my chain…all our chains, and that he kept something from us that would have made a difference on that rock, I'm going to kill him, too. That's what I told Jacy, and now I'm telling you."

Sly took a deep breath and let it out slowly. It did no good to get worked up. Talk, as they say, was cheap. He knew what he had to do, and he would do it. He would get close to Eva Creon, and if Paavo was the Chameleon, he would eventually get close to him, too. He didn't believe she didn't know where her father was living.

"Merrick told me you saw Reznik at Castle Rock. Why didn't you mention it to me?"

Sly blinked out of his thoughts. "Because I know how you get when his name comes up."

Bjorn's upper lip curled. He raised his hand and rubbed his lower back. "Butcher Reznik. He's been on my kill list for four years. I still can't roll over in bed without feeling his bullet lodged in my spine. Why do you suppose he was there?"

"I don't know. You mentioned pictures of her." Sly stared down at the file Bjorn had compiled on Eva Creon. "Are they in here?"

Bjorn tossed the daily log down beside the file. "It's all there. Fifteen days of bloodhound surveillance."

Sly motioned to the cane his friend leaned on. "What's the prognosis?"

"The bullet missed the bone. I'll be filling my dance card before you will."

"No doubt. I don't dance. In fact, I didn't know you did."

"Not all of my years in Copenhagen were spent on the street."

Unable to contain his curiosity a minute longer, Sly flipped open the file. And there she was, Paavo Creon's daughter. Only she wasn't at all what he was expecting. Her smoky voice, and her mannerisms on the tape had led him to expect a face hardened by the games fate had forced her to play. But that's not what he saw when he looked at the woman in the picture. She had a pair of seductive, shy green eyes as sexy as her smoky voice, and a delicate pair of red lips. Her hair wasn't exactly red by his standards. It was the color of sun-lit cinnamon, and she wore it past her shoulders. Long sultry bangs hid her eyebrows and teased a pair of long eyelashes.

Sly picked up the stack of pictures and shuffled through them. Bjorn had taken one of her running out the back door of the Tastes of Paradise. She was wearing a backless white sundress, and she had hiked up the skirt to aid her as she ran. She had beautiful legs, long runner's legs with hard athletic calves. And like her arms, her legs were tanned a deep golden brown.

In another picture she wore jeans that hugged her show-stopper ass. In another her white blouse was open at the throat, and Bjorn had zeroed in on her breasts, showcasing the recorded two inches of sun-kissed cleavage.

"What do you think, Sly? Is our Eva your kind of woman? You've never talked about what flips your switch. Me…" Bjorn wiggled his eyebrows, and took up the accent he'd left behind years ago in Denmark. "I like my blondes *villin'*, and not too talkative. And I like pillows. *Vuns* nice and plump like pillows. As sweet as—" he pointed to the picture in Sly's hand "—Eva's *dere. Ja,* just like *dem.*"

Sly grinned. "I seem to remember you mentioning one blonde in particular a few years back. You wouldn't be thinking about that long-legged double agent you ran into in Vienna, would you? What was her name?"

"Nadja," Bjorn supplied without hesitation. "*Ja,* she was sure a fine-looking woman. She knew how to use her mouth for more than just talking, too. I'll never forget how sweet she smelled. Like Alpine heather, she did." Bjorn cleared his throat, losing his accent as he pointed to the pictures. "It's amazing she looks as good as she does considering who she lives with."

"Meaning?"

"Just that someone ought to give Simon Parish a ride on his own beast."

"His what?"

"It's an old Danish saying from my days in Copenhagen. It means get a taste of your own evil. Listen to the tapes. You'll understand what I'm talking about. Parish is a psycho." Bjorn flipped through the small box of tapes on the desk. "Here it is. Spend some time listening to this one. I've named it, 'S is for Snake.' Then this one, 'A is for Albino Asshole.' Once you listen to a few of these, you'll understand why I won't be mourning Parish's death once you get around to killing him."

Sly took the tape "S is for Snake" and dropped it back in the box with the others. "So Parish is a sadistic lunatic. And from what I've heard today his playmate could fall into the fruitcake category."

"I think Eva's playing her own game," Bjorn argued. "Listen to the tapes. A fruitcake wouldn't have survived what she's survived. If it was me, I would have been long gone, and she's had several opportunities. So why does she stay in hell?"

"If she's got a reason it must be damn good," Sly mused out load.

"I imagine you'll find out what it is once you talk to her."

"Who said I was going to talk to her?"

"That look on your face when you opened the file. I'll be back inside of a week. Call and give me an update."

Chapter 3

Eva had timed her entrance perfectly. She wore a rusty red-brown sweater dress dotted with shimmering sequins, the neckline so ridiculously low that her breasts resembled water-filled balloons a pinprick away from disaster.

The fox trim at her wrists and outlining her breasts added another level of warmth to an already too warm dress for October in Atlanta. But Eva didn't question Simon's choice. There was always a reason for everything he did. Before the evening was over, she would know why she was wearing fur and sequins.

Eva continued to eat her salad slowly while Simon watched from the end of a table that could easily seat thirty guests. They always took their evening meal in the formal dining room surrounded by silence.

Simon hadn't told her they would be playing a game tonight. She hoped...no, prayed, that she would be spared the event, but the dress she'd found on her bed when she'd stepped from the shower, and the tension that she'd felt the moment she'd walked into the room, suggested otherwise.

Simon loved to play games, and because of his fondness for the night, the games were often played after dark in the backyard.

A genius with peculiar tendencies, is how her father had described Simon the night he had escorted her to his party four years ago. She had arrived on her father's arm a starry-eyed nineteen-year-old, unaware that her boring restrictive life was about to take a drastic turn. Unaware that she would never again return to the house where she had lived for ten years with the minions. Unaware she was her father's birthday gift to the genius with peculiar tendencies.

Your stay with Simon will teach you things you wouldn't be able to learn anywhere else. Priceless lessons on how to live in harmony with a demon and survive his madness. I have no doubt you will survive. After all, you are your father's daughter. Living is not for the weak of body and mind. Those who master the game, master their own fate. Make your father proud.

A mad genius with a demon's heart. Or maybe a demon genius with an obsession for madness. Either way she had come to believe Simon was a pernicious package. An inventive sadist one minute, and a psychopathic child the next.

Eva sent her long lashes low over her eyes, discreetly studying him. His features were small, ultrafeminine, his short white hair and colorless skin a shocking contrast against the fluorescent blue silk shirt he wore tonight.

He owned a Bentley and a Porsche, three homes in the States, one in Venice and one on the island of Mykonos in the Greek Isles.

His amassed wealth was displayed everywhere in his homes. Here in Atlanta there were priceless paintings hanging in a temperature-controlled gallery, and elaborate marble statues guarding the pool and pavilion in the backyard. His other homes were just as lavish.

She had no idea how he made his money. They spent five months out of the year in Atlanta, and the other months divided between his homes in California, Florida and Venice, with a month spent in Greece.

She loved Greece. In Greece everything was different. In Greece, Simon gave her space to breathe.

Eva continued to study him beneath hooded lashes. Tonight he wore fitted black Gucci pants on his reed-thin hips, and black boots to his knees. His bright silk shirt was open to his waist, showcasing his hairless pale chest.

His blood disorder had forced him to become a vegetarian, which had been the reason she had been introduced to the Tastes of Paradise—and two blocks away, Dr. Fielding.

"We leave for Greece in a few days." His tone was low, one elbow braced on the table, his chin resting on his bony fist as he watched her eat. "Will you be ready?"

Careful not to let her excitement touch her eyes, she said, "I'll be ready. Will Melita be there?"

"Yes, my sister will be home when we arrive."

Eva smiled…not too much. "Will you let me go exploring the water caverns with Nemo again?"

"He tells me you're a natural in the water. He says you can hold your breath almost as long as he can."

Eva went back to eating her salad.

"I have a new toy and a new game. I can't wait to show you the gun and explain the rules."

Eva's fork stalled an inch from her mouth.

Slowly, Simon leaned back and stretched his long spiderlike arms out on the table, and that's when she saw his fingernails. They had been painted black. Black in celebration of tonight's game, and the madness she would soon be called upon to survive.

He smiled as if he had read her thoughts. Flashing his painted nails, his fingers danced theatrically upward to slide through his shocking white hair.

The display was well practiced. A show Eva had witnessed time and again. It was as much a warning as it was a promise. A prelude to the soon to come twisted game he'd thought up sometime during the afternoon.

I have a new toy. I can't wait to show you the gun.

She thought about her still-sore wrists from two days ago, and a renewed pain shot through them with the memory of how creative a madman could be with something as simple as a belt.

She had wanted to die in the narrow clothes chute. Then she had wanted to live. To endure the unendurable.

Living is not for the weak. Those who master the game, master their own fate.

"Say it. Say the words, sweet Eva."

She laid her fork down, the colorful pansies in her salad forgotten.

"Say the words," he coaxed. "Wet your lovely lips with your wine and speak."

Eva did as she was told and lifted the wineglass to her painted red lips. She drank deeply, then set the glass back on the table, while Simon's lizard eyes watched her in anticipation.

"I'm your game, Simon," she began. "Whatever game it is you wish to play. I'm yours. Mind. Body. Breath. Soul."

"And who will win the game tonight, sweet Eva?"

"You will win, Simon."

The rehearsed words delighted him further. Grinning openly, he stood. "Finish your salad. You're going to need your strength. Morris has pruned the boxwood. The maze is flawless. The sky is clear. The air…feverish. It's a perfect night for a fox hunt."

Chapter 4

Bjorn was right about the boxwood maze; it had to be seen to be appreciated. Sly stood perfectly still within the dense foliage labyrinth in Simon Parish's backyard dressed in camouflage, his face, hands and neck painted to match.

He had slipped past the electronic gate an hour ago, and like a ghost in a cemetery, he had made his way unnoticed into the backyard—drawn by the sound of a man's voice chanting taunts too peculiar to ignore.

Minutes later, hidden in a passageway of the maze, he'd gotten his first glimpse of Simon Parish. Dressed for a safari, he was outfitted with a headlamp strapped around the wide brim of his canvas hat. Thin as a blade of grass, he wore khaki shorts and a matching shirt. Add a silver holster cinched around his waist with an M26 Taser stun gun inside, and Sly was convinced Parish was further off his rocker than the tapes indicated.

Star Wars meets *Out Of Africa*.

Sly would have laughed if a hissing noise, followed by a woman's scream, hadn't stolen the humor out of the moment. Simon Parish might look like an idiot, but the games he played were very real.

The M26 Taser was effective up to twenty feet with a steady aim. It was as potent as a bolt of lightning, and just as painful. The one major difference was that it wouldn't kill you. It would however, knock you on your ass quick enough, paralyzing you in an instant.

Another scream went up, followed by a man's high-pitched laughter.

A lunatic's laughter.

"Like a fox, she runs looking for a place to hide. Run, little fox. Run and hide."

More lunatic laughter followed his lyrical taunts.

From what Sly could tell, Parish was herding his fox toward the center of the maze. There would be no escape if Eva became trapped at the heart of the boxwood. If she had played this game before—and Sly knew she had played similar versions from listening to the tapes—then she had to know her only chance was finding a hiding place, or an escape route altogether.

Sly maneuvered his way through another narrow passage, ignoring the heat, and the way it made his clothes cling to his body. He had just slipped into another hiding place when light illuminated the trail he'd just vacated. For a moment he thought the moon had come out. But then he saw her. She was running, her dress hiked high above her knees, and she was barefoot.

The dress was a beacon of light outlining every curve she owned. She wore an animal mask that concealed the upper half of her face. The mask had short erect ears and a long nose like a fox.

Like a fox, she runs looking for a place to hide. Run, little fox. Run and hide.

In an odd way the masked beauty did resemble a fox. Or maybe an exotic experiment that had stalled somewhere halfway between two worlds.

"Where are you, sweet Eva? Where-oh-where have you gone?" Parish singsonged.

She spun around releasing a desperate keening noise as she looked back the way she had come.

Like a dog on a fresh scent, Parish's laughter filled the maze warning her that he'd spotted the neon glow of her dress through the dense foliage.

"The game is, run until you drop, little fox. Don't stop. Run. Run fast. Run until you drop. Until I drop you."

Her chest was heaving, exhaustion becoming a factor in the game. Run, dammit. Run, Sly silently urged.

But she didn't run. She stood there while precious seconds ticked by.

Parish's laughter came again. Closer this time with another creative limerick.

"Run, dammit."

This time Sly's thoughts became audible words, and her head snapped a quarter-turn to the left. Shit! In the seven years he'd been an Onyxx agent, he'd done some reckless things, but never something as flat-out stupid as speaking his thoughts.

Sly held his breath as Eva searched the thick greenery that surrounded her. Instead of wasting her time looking for him, she should be hustling her ass out of there, he thought. Simon would be on her any minute.

More laughter.

Sly swore, then stepped out of his hiding place, grabbed Eva by the arm and pulled her into the hiding place with him. She tried to fight him, but he ignored her struggle, reached down and snagged the hem of her dress and pulled it over her head.

Turning the dress inside out was like turning a light switch off—the threat of discovery gone in an instant.

Simon's dulcet voice came again, telling them that he was close by. "Where are you, my little fox? Where-oh-where have you gone, sweet Eva? Answer me."

She stopped fighting him. Froze.

A bright beam of light appeared on the path, and Sly motioned for Eva to remain quiet. Parish soon walked past, stalking his prey in true hunter fashion.

After he had turned down another path, Eva whispered, "Is it you?"

Sly had listened to the tapes a dozen times, yet her smoke-filled husky voice gave him pause. It was like a slow-working sedative on his body.

"Who do you think I am?" he asked, countering her question with one of his own.

She studied his shadow in the dark. "You look too tall to be him," she whispered. "Who are you?"

"Would you believe a lost neighbor hunting for a way out of here?"

She angled her head as if considering the notion, then reached up and touched his face. Her fingers came away with paint on them, and she wiped them on his shirt. "He sent you, didn't he? Is there a message? Do you have the file?"

When Sly didn't answer, she tried to slip away from him, but he wrapped his arm around her waist and pulled her against him. "It's safer here than out there."

"I have only your word on that. The word of a stranger lost on private property." She brought her nose close to his chest, sniffed. "Bay rum. A stranger who spends money on soap and takes time to use it. Hmm…"

"Do you know the way out of here?" Sly asked.

"And will I be rewarded for my generosity if I show you the way? Do you have the Onyxx file? Do you?"

Her hands were suddenly on his hips, moving downward over his thighs. When she slipped them into his pockets to find them empty, she said, "Another game player, I see."

Sly had no idea what she was talking about, but she had used the word Onyxx, and that was good enough for him to play along.

He said, "I didn't bring the file with me, but let's get out of here so we can talk about it."

"And so the fox put her trust in the stranger and shared with him the secret passageway out of the labyrinth. And when they had finally escaped, the fox eager for her reward, did receive her recompense. She became the stranger's supper, and he gobbled her up in one fast bite."

When Sly, again, said nothing, she added, "Have you read them?"

"Read what?"

"*Aesop's Fables?* Have you read them?"

"No." Sly tried again. "Come on, let's go."

"Come, little fox. Come to me and I will take pity on thee."

The nearness of Parish's poetry confirmed that he was circling back.

Sly had been on his way out of the boxwood with Eva in tow. Now he stepped back, pulling her, once again, against him.

She laid a hand on his chest, whispered, "There is no escape for a fox in this maze. Here, there is only survival by surrender. I have no desire to escape."

Sly swore softly. "Do you have any idea what it feels like to be hit with an electrical current?"

"I imagine it's quite painful."

"If you enjoy playing games, I'll play with you, and I promise it won't be near as painful," he offered.

"Sorry, but tonight my game is with Simon. If you wish to play with me, when next we meet, bring the file."

With that, she scooped up her dress and stepped out onto the trail. Before Sly could stop her she was standing in the beam of light coming from Simon Parish's headlamp.

The minute Parish saw her, he began to laugh. He drew the Taser from his silver Star Wars holster. "You've run out of places to hide, little fox. Say it. Surrender to me."

"You've won the game, Simon. You've outwitted the fox. I ask you to take pity on me."

Laughing, Simon Parish aimed the Taser at Eva's stomach. "Request denied, little fox." Then he pulled the trigger.

Chapter 5

"I hear the voices, Dr. Fielding."

"What are they saying?"

"They're arguing. Yelling."

"Is your father there? Do you hear his voice?"

"Yes."

"What else? I've opened the door, Eva. Look inside. What do you see?"

"Mother is dead, and there are flames around her. Our house is burning."

"You said you hear two voices. Do you recognize the other voice?"

"No. He's no one I want to know. He's a monster. He's… No, no one!"

"Take it easy. I'm bringing you out now, Eva. Five, four, three, two—"

Sly watched from his seat on the airplane as Eva rubbed her temples. He was listening to tape number eight. Bjorn had titled it "H is for Hypnosis and Hell."

They were cruising at forty-two thousand feet. The sun was out, and the airplane had been in the air an hour. From his aisle seat in the sixth row, four behind Eva and across the aisle, he continued to observe her. They had left Atlanta at 1:30 p.m. Destination, Athens, Greece.

Eva hadn't recognized him in the terminal, but then why would she? He was in jeans and a gray shirt, not fatigues and face paint. Likewise, she was no longer wearing a fox mask and sequins, but a pale-blue shift and matching sandals.

Simon Parish sat beside her. He looked nothing like a safari hunter, either. He wore black pants, a lemon-yellow shirt, a black hat pulled low over his face, and tinted shades to conceal his unnatural eyes.

He looked sane. Sly knew different. The man was a lunatic.

Another hour in the air and Eva pressed the flight attendant button, then reached beneath the seat in front of her for her carry-on bag. The attendant arrived, Eva relayed a message, and a short time later the attendant returned with a bottle of water.

Eva popped a pill, maybe more than one, then sipped the water until the bottle was empty. She dozed after that while Parish read, and Sly listened to another tape. This one Bjorn had named "C is for Closet."

When Eva woke up an hour later, she stood and walked past him to use the rest room. She returned a little while later, and once she was seated, she went digging in her bag again. This time she produced a compact mirror and a gold tube of lipstick. She checked her reflection, pushed her shaggy bangs out of her eyes, then opened the lipstick and angled the compact.

Sly saw her mouth pucker up in the mirror's reflection. Watched as she painted her beautiful lips a shade of red. Her lipstick tube tucked away, she angled the mirror a little more to the right and puckered up again, this time blowing a kiss into the compact mirror. A second later, she turned her head and looked straight at him and mouthed the words, *bay rum.*

Sly changed tapes thirty minutes later. Flipping through the tapes once more, he spied one that he hadn't listened to yet and popped it into the cassette tape, then adjusted his headset.

This tape Bjorn had given the title "P is for Parish, Prick, Pecker, and Penance."

Eva stretched, then climbed out of bed to stare out the window. The sun was bright, the morning warm and the sight and smell of the sea elevated her mood.

They had landed in Athens two days ago, and immediately flown to Mykonos. She had fought a headache the entire way, and once they had reached Simon's estate, Lesvago, she had gone straight to bed. She had slept most of the next day, still battling the headache.

"Finally you're up. You look much better than yesterday. Do you feel better?"

She turned to see Simon standing in the open doorway to her bedroom. It took everything she had not to jump for joy when she saw him wearing a wide-brimmed hat and a long-sleeved shirt—he was going out.

"I feel better," she agreed. "The headache left me sometime during the night. Thank you for tending to me," she said respectfully, meaning it. Simon had ordered cool compresses for her head every half hour. It was rare for him to be gentle, but not unheard of. Last night he had offered her his human side, a rarity she was grateful for, considering she had felt so poorly.

"Good, then I'll be on my way. Nemo is taking me

to Naxos. I have business there. I've asked Melita to join me. She's agreed only if Nemo brings her back late tonight. She says you shouldn't be alone in case your headache returns. If you take a skiff out, I've instructed two of the men to follow for your protection."

"Enjoy your trip," she managed to say, trying not to sound too eager to see him go. "Not too much sun."

He smiled. "Like a wife, she worries about me. I think I like that. I'll be back the end of the week, in time to finalize the arrangements for my birthday party. I've decided to keep the location a secret to the end this time. It'll make it more of a mystery. Maybe even keep you up nights wondering, hmm?"

Worrying, he meant. Eva kept her voice mellow when she asked, "Have you spoken to my father? He's coming, isn't he?"

"Of course he's coming."

Simon stepped forward and took Eva's hand. "Now then," he said, examining the black-and-blue marks on her wrist, "I want you to do something for me while I'm gone." She was wearing a white chemise, and with his free hand, he peeled the narrow strap off her shoulder to expose a faint tan line.

"I want you to get rid of this while I'm gone. I want every inch of you brown. Hopefully your wrists will be back to normal, as well. Don't disappoint me."

"I won't, Simon. Every inch will be brown. And my wrists will be healed."

He brushed her cheek with the back of his bony hand. "I've got a spectacular costume in mind for you to wear to the party. No lines anywhere, understand?"

He slid his hand around her waist and over her hip to squeeze her butt cheek. The smile that followed turned wicked, warning Eva that his idea of spectacular and hers were entirely different.

He must have read her mind, or maybe she had allowed her concern to show in the depths of her eyes this time. In any case, his smile turned into an open laugh. A victory laugh.

"You're right. It's sinfully spectacular, and the party guests are going to love looking at every inch of you."

Simon hadn't been gone five minutes when Melita appeared at Eva's door. She slipped into her short white silk robe and greeted Simon's sister with a smile. Melita had long black hair, olive skin, and deep-set rich chocolate eyes that resembled those of an exotic cat. She was average in height, slight in weight, and definitely of Greek descent. She was a natural beauty, with a nonthreatening smile, and no ulterior motive that Eva could see.

There were no similarities between Simon and Melita, not in appearance, and not in mannerisms. She had often thought they couldn't possibly be brother and sister, but then she had no way to prove that they weren't. She knew nothing about their parents.

"Will you be all right if I go with Simon? He has an appointment to keep. I'll lunch with him on board the *Ventura* and catch up, then after I drop him off, Nemo will bring me straight back to Lesvago."

"There's no hurry. It's a beautiful day for a boat ride."

"You could join us."

"No. I'm still tired."

"But the headache is gone?"

"Yes."

"If you need anything while I'm —"

"I won't."

"If you get hungry there's fruit in the kitchen. If you want something more, cook will—"

"I'll be fine."

Melita touched Eva's arm. "It's so good to have you here again. I've missed you, and I love having another woman to talk to. We'll go out to dinner and go dancing one night soon. On my way out, I'll tell cook to bring you *ena kafe*."

"Thank you. Did Simon mention where his birthday party would be held?" she asked hoping he had shared the information with his sister.

"No, not yet. He says he's going to keep it a secret to the end this time. But I'll work on him. Some days he's like a child and can't keep a secret." Melita's smile faded. "The headache's aren't serious, are they? I don't remember you having them last year."

"They're not serious, just inconvenient." When Melita still looked worried, Eva added, "There's nothing to worry about, really."

From what Dr. Fielding had told her the migraines were caused by memory rejuvenation, which had occurred during the first hypnosis session. It was odd how the brain stored images and old data. How it protected you against certain painful memories you weren't strong enough to deal with.

But she was strong enough now. That's why she was remembering.

Maybe she should thank her father for that. Or Simon. She would never have searched out Dr. Fielding if she hadn't been strong enough to accept the truth. That's why she'd agreed to the hypnosis, and why she wasn't going to let the migraines stop her from remembering.

"I'm off, before Simon's mood turns sour. He's as fanatical about keeping on schedule as he is about the brim size on his hats."

They shared a laugh. Simon never ran late for anything, or left the house without a two-inch brim shielding his porcelain complexion. "Enjoy your day with your brother, Melita. If you return late, and my light's out, I'll see you tomorrow."

"Tomorrow then."

Eva walked Melita out, lingering on the terrace when the white pristine trideck yacht left the dock. Simon would expect that. She waved, and after he waved back from the upper deck, he wrapped his arm around Melita.

Eva sought out Nemo in the pilothouse. Before he turned the hundred-foot yacht out to sea, he blew her a kiss.

The guard's smile was oddly comforting. He was just one of many stocky, dark-haired guards in Simon's employment, but he had been there since her first trip to Greece three years ago.

When the yacht was out of sight, Eva turned back and disappeared inside the white stucco mansion. Lesvago was smooth in line and design like most of the Byzantine houses in Greece. But the estate's grounds were rich in colorful flowers, pebbled courtyards, statues and lookout balconies that showcased both the beautiful rocky landscape and the sparkling blue sea.

It was heavenly here, but the beauty wasn't the only reason Eva liked this place best of all Simon's homes. She liked it for the freedom he allowed her here.

Maybe it was the containment she'd lived with all her life that had fueled her vagabond spirit, but she longed to sail away with the wind in her hair. Sail the seas and live from port to port enjoying whatever whim caught her fancy.

The doors and shutters were almost always left open to welcome the balmy coastal breeze in from the sea. Eva walked barefoot down the hall to her suite of rooms. Entering the sitting room, she ran her hand over the back of the couch as she passed it on her way back to her bedroom, the white leather feeling cool to the touch.

Melita had picked flowers and several large vases of buttercups sweetened the air, welcoming her arrival. The mirror on the wall was long and narrow, gilded with gold. The closet was large enough to house a car, which only made her lean wardrobe look even more ridiculous in the expansive space.

She traveled light when she came to Greece. Mostly her wardrobe consisted of swimwear, shorts and sundresses. Not that there weren't times when she was required to dress up. But on those special occasions Simon would always buy her something for the evening.

He would be gone four days. Eva gave in to a smile, but it left quickly as she recalled last year's birthday party in the reptile gardens. A shiver attacked her and she shook off the unpleasant memory. She didn't want to think about that night. She wished she could forget it, but the only way that would happen was if she replaced the memory with another. Only she was sure Simon's future party would hold its own nightmares when it was over.

She pushed the upcoming party out of her head for the time being. Maybe by then Merrick's man would hand over the file, and maybe she'd get lucky and something in the file would spark her memory. If that happened there would truly be cause to celebrate.

She retrieved her skimpiest bikini from the closet and headed to the bathroom to take a shower. She shrugged out of her robe, then peeled her chemise off her shoulders. The pale tan line was barely noticeable in the mirror. From there she searched out the others along the swell of her breasts, and the line low on her hips.

I want every inch of you brown, sweet Eva. I have something spectacular in mind for you to wear to my birthday party. Sinfully spectacular.

Chapter 6

On another small island south of Mykonos, the Chameleon stood at the window of the renovated monastery feeling more alive than he had in years. Merrick had actually surprised him this time. His unexpected siege on Castle Rock had killed six of his men, but the attempt had been a refreshing change. It meant Merrick was still sulking and nursing his wound—still interested in playing their game.

From the window he had a perfect view of his private lagoon. That is, if he was inclined to use the highpowered telescope that stood within reach as he often liked to do. Today he wasn't taking pleasure in the azure water lapping at his billion-dollar motor yacht he'd appropriately named, the *Pearl*. No, today his pleasure was a bit more carnal. Today he was focused on the entertainment going on below the window in the private garden where two of his men were taking turns throwing punches at his latest prisoner.

A sturdy wooden post stood in the middle of the garden specifically for such amusing activities. The man had been tied to it to keep him upright. A lot of blood had been spilled so far, but the prisoner no longer objected to the force of the punches. He had long since stopped groaning, though he hadn't done much pleading for mercy to begin with.

This prisoner was a tough son of a bitch. He would be hard to crack, but there were few men he hadn't been able to break open...eventually. And those who had held out soon realized that there was no escape once the Chameleon had decided you were worth his trouble and patience.

Patience was a talent. There was something to be said for a man who had learned how to master the game of life to its fullest potential through patience.

He watched as his men continued to take turns flogging the hell out of his newest prisoner. He didn't believe that the man had lost his memory, though his head wound had been extensive and it had required surgery to keep him alive.

The Chameleon checked his watch to find that time had gotten away from him—he was always fascinated with the human body's ability to withstand pain, and he'd completely lost track of time. It was nearly dinner hour and his wife would be expecting him soon. He'd promised Callia that he would take her on a boat ride tonight, and he always kept his promises to his angel-faced wife.

He called down from the window, "He's had enough. Take him back to his cell and clean him up. See to his injuries and feed him."

"Yes, sir," the senior guard answered.

"If he dies, so will you," the Chameleon warned. He turned to gather up the papers at his desk when the phone rang. Recognizing the number, he picked it up quickly. "Are you here in Greece?"

"Yes. We're here."

"Are you well, Simon?"

"Well enough."

"And Evka, is she also well?"

"She is."

The Chameleon smiled pridefully. "Tell me, how does she look? Is she even more beautiful than last year?"

"More beautiful, yes. She has a changed look about her. I think you will be surprised."

"You know I don't like surprises, Simon. But I do like to hear good news. I'm anxious to see her, and I know that I told you I would meet you in Naxos early tomorrow, but there's been a change in plans and I will be delayed until afternoon. I'll see you then."

"Is there a problem? Some unpleasant business?"

"There is often unpleasantness in our line of work. Tomorrow we will discuss it."

Once he hung up the phone, the Chameleon reached for a cigar, ran it slowly beneath his nose and inhaled the rich expensive tobacco. Cutting off the end and discarding it, he lit the cigar with his silver lighter, then pocketed the shiny rectangle deep into his white linen trousers. He drew deeply on the cigar, holding it a bit awkwardly since the index finger on his right hand had been severed years ago.

A false wall moved at the touch of a button on his ornate watch and he followed the stairs to the passageway. Reaching the bottom, he walked past a number of cells.

Knowing the men behind the bars hated him and ached to kill him, he smiled at each one of them as he passed by, saying, "You can wish me dead, but it is you who are dead. None of you will see the light of day ever again. You breathe, yet you are dead to the world and your families."

He noticed that his newest prisoner, the one who had been beaten in the courtyard was sitting up watching him. He'd taken a helluva beating, and yet he was far stronger than the others. That wouldn't last long, he thought.

As he passed the guard, he said, "Beat that one every other day until he is ready to tell me his name."

The guard nodded, and the Chameleon followed a second stairway, stepping out into the warm sunny afternoon. As he puffed on his cigar and walked along the path, his thoughts returned to Evka. Simon said there had been a change in her, and he wondered about that. Maybe it meant she was ready, ready to fulfill his plan for her.

He walked along the flower-lined footpath, past the bloodstained terrace, not giving it a second's notice. He continued to puff on his cigar, letting the balmy breeze lift his white hair.

He looked older than his fifty-eight years, but he was as healthy and horny as a prized stallion, and with that his thoughts shifted to Callia. She would be dressing for dinner soon, and he wanted to be there to watch her as she left the bathroom. He wanted to be sprawled on the bed, relaxed with his hands behind his head, awaiting the sight of her magnificent naked body.

His own body hummed with the anticipation of seeing her curvy tanned flesh so flawless in the lamplight. He wet his lips, eager to taste her. She would lie down on the bed at his command and then he would stretch out beside her. Her scent would fill his head, and when she looked at him, he would smile knowing she could not resist him.

He would cover her slowly. Enter her completely. Then the reckless hunger he felt for her would rise up and she would speak his name as he filled her. And with his claiming, she would know he loved her like no other.

He boarded the *Pearl* in a state of readiness—stone hard and anxious to put his hands on his wife. He motioned to his captain, and when they were underway, he went to stand at the railing.

His wife was forty-five, past her prime, but no other woman could match Callia's beauty. She was exquisite perfection. As flawless as the day he had met her. And she would remain that way. He would see to it. He'd spent millions to preserve her angel-like face, and he would spend millions more in the years to come to keep her exactly the way she had looked the first day he'd laid eyes on her.

The Chameleon spoke his feelings to the blue sea. "Yes, my longtime friend and eternal enemy, I am here, and you are still wondering where that is. It tortures you, and I rejoice in the knowledge that the wound I inflicted on you so long ago still pains you. But have no fear, we will meet again. We will come face-to-face when the time is right, and still, I will not kill you.

"Death will not be your escape, Adolf Merrick. Those who betray me can never escape me. They breathe, exist, yet they are dead."

Her bedroom had been ransacked. Eva stood in the doorway between her bedroom and private bathroom, the evidence staring her in the face. Her closet door stood open, and her vanity drawers were left in disarray. The intruder had even drunk her *kafe*.

Wearing a brown crocheted bikini that left nothing to the imagination, she glanced around, then sniffed the air. She had an uncanny sense of smell and she picked up the scent of bay rum without half trying.

It was obvious he wanted her to know he'd been there. That he'd followed her, and knew where she was staying. Had he left her a note? Did he have the file and want to meet?

She checked the room, but there was no note. She was annoyed by his brashness, and yet she smiled. Once again he had successfully broken into another of Simon's heavily guarded homes without any trouble. He had slipped into Boxwood Estate after dark, wearing camouflage clothing and face paint. Here he'd chosen a sunny morning. Both estates were guarded by close to a dozen men.

After their encounter in the maze she had been curious which one of his men Merrick had sent to her. It had again prompted her to hack into Simon's computer and read the profiles on Merrick's current list of agents. With no pictures to aid her, she'd tried to pick *her* man from the list, wanting to put a name with the man whose smell lingered in her mind.

She'd formed a picture of him in the dark that night. Wanted a name to go along with that picture.

And then she'd seen him on the plane.

No, first she'd smelled him. She'd been already seated on the airplane when he'd walked past and the bay rum scent had alerted her that he was there. She had wanted to turn immediately, but she'd waited. Waited for over an hour.

The idea of using her mirror came to her by accident, but she'd immediately liked the concept. It was a way she could look without Simon getting suspicious, and guard herself at the same time. She was glad that she had. The picture she'd envisioned didn't do the man justice. Over six feet, he appeared to be in his midthirties, had bad-boy blue eyes, and nice ears.

She'd noticed his ears because he wore his black hair short, with a pair of sideburns that followed his square jawline in a neatly trimmed chin strap. Though his hair was shorter than she liked on any man, she had to admit it looked good on him.

His nose was sleek, his mouth attractive enough to distract her. No, there was nothing that had matched the picture she'd formed in her mind.

She blinked out of her muse and glanced at her image in the small mirror, then touched the faint line on her shoulder. "It's all going to work out," she whispered. "It has to. I've been at this too long. There has to be an end soon."

She had to believe that, but for now the order of the day was getting rid of her tan line and making sure everything was brown before Simon returned.

With that, she left the house and followed a footpath to the dock where a number of skiffs were tied. Lesvago had been built against a massive rock. It was rather like having a giant watching your back, Simon had once told her.

She glanced up at the rocky giant before stepping onto the dock. There were two ways to reach the house: either by rappelling down the peak, or slipping past the guards posted seaside. Both would require more than a little talent. Merrick's man was either an excellent swimmer, or part mountain goat.

She headed for a small skiff, nodding to the guard posted on the dock. "I'm going to the caverns," she told him.

"*Endaxi*, Miss Eva," the guard replied. "I'll send four eyes to keep you safe."

With another nod, she tossed her small pack into the skiff. The guard quickly untied the rope and she climbed in. He shoved the boat away from the dock, then she started the motor with a push of a button and headed up the shoreline toward the caverns, while two guards scrambled for another skiff to follow her.

The Cyclade Islands were some of the most beautiful in Greece, and Eva marveled at the sight as she sailed toward the caverns. The clear blue water, and the warm air had her tossing her head to catch the balmy breeze on her face. It felt good to be back, even though Simon's upcoming party hung over her head like a dark cloud. But today she wasn't going to think about what would happen by week's end. For now she would indulge her vagabond heart, and pray that Merrick's man would deliver her the file soon.

A stretch of sugar-sand beach and a number of colorful outcroppings later, Eva cut the motor and tossed out the anchor. Beyond the caverns, high into the side of a cliff, stood an abandoned monastery, stark white against the rocks that surrounded it on three sides.

Nemo had told her a story about the monk who had been exiled there to live out his life after he'd fallen in love with a beautiful village girl half his age. Nemo said after the monk's death his ghost still wandered the tower. He said, to this day, fishermen returning home spoke tales of seeing the monk's image high in the window of the tower.

Nemo swore he had seen the monk's likeness, too. He claimed it was truly the ghost of Father Talamoss in prayer at the window asking the Almighty for absolution for his cardinal sin.

Eva tied her hair back from her face, then slipped into a BC vest. Strapping on a diving mask and snorkel, she flipped backward out of the boat like a water nymph, eager to return to the sea. Her first dive was exhilarating, the second rekindling her love for the underworld and the amazing marine life that lived in their own private world.

She would sun herself on a rock and work on the tan lines soon, but first she would take a quick look around.

It was while Eva was enjoying the curious fish and the coral formations along the entrance into a narrow sump that she saw the light, then *him*. It was such a surprise that for several seconds she didn't move.

When she realized that he was swimming toward her, she quickly turned and began to swim back to the boat. She wanted to speak to him, but suddenly she was afraid.   She kicked hard, hoping to surface before he caught up to her, but her attempt fell short a few feet from the surface.

A hand gripped her ankle and gave it a hard jerk. Eva tried to shake him off, but it was no use. His grip was as solid as an iron shackle. He gave her leg another jerk, then let go. Suddenly he was beside her, his arm sliding around her waist, carrying her along with him.

She expected him to surface then since he had no tank, only a vest and mask like her. But instead he headed back down into the depths, kicking his powerful legs and moving so swiftly along that he appeared to be more fish than human.

Her lungs started to burn as her air supply began to wane. When she saw that they were heading into a sump she renewed her efforts to free herself. Whether he understood why she started to fight anew or not, he swam faster—if that was possible—swiftly taking her through the passageway.

He let go of her a minute later and once she was free, Eva kicked hard to reach the surface, desperate for air. When she surfaced, she pulled up her mask and concentrated on breathing deeply through her nose to fill her lungs. Feeling marginally better, she took inventory of her surroundings.

The sea cavern was familiar—she had explored it

with Nemo. She should have felt relief with the knowledge, but she didn't.

This particular cave had only one exit. No wonder he'd let her go so easily. She was trapped.

Sly surfaced ten feet from Eva. He treaded water while she pulled herself onto an outcropping. The cave was small, no more than a twelve-foot hole inside a giant rock formation.

Mykonos was full of caverns for tourists to explore. He had familiarized himself with them as well as the main island since he had arrived, waiting for the appropriate time to meet with Eva alone.

In the past two days he'd explored the island extensively, except Lesvago—that is until this morning when he'd rappelled the rock wall and dropped behind the guarded perimeter without being spotted.

Simon's estate was ten minutes from Mykonos city, and the estate was secured by nine guards which had made his job a little more difficult, but not impossible.

He would have spoken to Eva that morning when he'd slipped into her room, but once inside the house he'd located a number of sophisticated security alarms, and he had changed his mind. It occurred to him if the house was full of surveillance devices, there might also be hidden microphones as well.

Sly took his time leaving the water and taking a seat on the rock not far from where Eva had exited the water. He removed his goggles, and as he made himself comfortable he watched her fit her back against a solid rock wall.

His eyes traveled the length of her body, the sight of her returning his thoughts to the maze. Revisiting that night in the boxwood wasn't smart. He realized he enjoyed looking at her too much, and why not? She was a beautiful distraction, but that was the point. She was a distraction he didn't need or want. Still, he mentally measured the length of her legs, sized her tempting breasts, and envisioned his hands on her narrow waist, his fingers stroking the rise of her ass.

She raised her chin, and then her husky voice filled the cave. "What the hell were you trying to do down there, drown me?"

"If I wanted you dead you would be."

"Is that supposed to make me feel better?"

"It should."

"My lungs hurt like hell. Did you bring the file?"

Sly rested his arms on his knees and leaned forward. He wore black water pants, a BC vest and nothing else; his usual underwater attire.

Comfortable with his form-fitting second skin below the waist, he said, "It's not that simple."

"It's simple to me. You get access to the database at Onyxx's headquarters and you copy the file. If Merrick thinks I'm going to lead you to the Chameleon without the file, he's been watching too many James Bond movies. This is the real deal. You get only if you give. In this case, that would be the file." She angled her head. Studied him a minute. "Which one are you?"

Sly arched his black eyebrows. "Which one?"

"Are you Bjorn or Pierce? Or maybe Sully? No, you don't look like a Sully. And Bjorn was blond. I think the one they called Jacy had black hair. Are you him?"

She took another few seconds to study him further. Suddenly she raised her chin a little higher, made a face. "You're him, aren't you? You're that badass ex-con. You're Sly McEwen."

It was true he'd spent a healthy stretch behind bars before becoming an Onyxx agent. Living with LeRoy, his psychotic criminal stepfather, it was bound to happen. He supposed LeRoy was responsible for the ornery attitude that had kept him alive on the streets, then later in prison. The same attitude that had landed him a spot in the lineup as one of Merrick's rat fighters.

The position suited him. By the time Sly was ten, LeRoy had taught him how to swear in three languages, piss on the run and pick a door lock in two minutes flat. Hot-wiring cars came easy, and driving them at breakneck speeds had earned him the honorary position as LeRoy's getaway driver as early as age thirteen.

LeRoy's other specialty besides being a professional criminal had been being an abusive son of a bitch. Which had taught Sly how to dodge and duck with lightning speed. Only his mother hadn't learned that maneuver and one night LeRoy's fists had found her vulnerable. That's the reason Sly had been sent to prison at age sixteen—he'd drilled his stepfather between the eyes with a .38 after LeRoy had beaten his mother unconscious.

He'd been convicted of murder. Had beaten Life, and gotten twelve years in a maximum security prison. If he had it to do all over again, he wouldn't do anything any different. After all, he'd learned that being a badass was better than being dead.

The way she was looking at him, Sly wondered just how much dirt she knew. Obviously enough. She had wrapped her arms around herself, and if he wasn't mistaken, she had tucked herself a little tighter against the rock wall.

If she knew he was an ex-con, and worked for Onyxx, the question was, how had she gotten the information? None of that was public knowledge.

"Simon takes a lot of medication for his allergies. It makes him sleepy," she said, as if she'd read his mind. "I discovered the password for his computer one morn-

ing a few months ago. I had been working on breaking
the code for over a year. I must have tried every word
combination twice. All but the right one, of course. I
should have realized it would be something too simple
to take seriously."

"What was it?"

"My name."

"Eva Parish, or Creon?"

"Creon. When I found the file labeled Onyxx it was
like a flash of lightning opened up my memory. You see
when I was young I was trapped in a house fire. While
trying to escape, I fell down a flight of stairs. I must
have been knocked out for a while, because some of my
memory is foggy about that night. Over the past two
years, however, things have been coming back to me.
Seeing the word Onyxx on the computer file triggered
some things."

"Like what?"

"I'll keep them to myself for now. All except Adolf
Merrick and the strawberry suckers."

"What's important about that?"

"Adolf Merrick used to bring me strawberry suckers when he came to visit my father."

Testing her, Sly asked, "How long ago was that?"

"I think it started when I was seven."

"Did your father work with Merrick at Onyxx?"

"Yes."

Sly was determined to keep her talking. "So Simon
Parish has a file on Onyxx. Why?"

"I don't know. But it's quite impressive. It details
Onyxx's most successful missions, and its most
embarrassing failures. And it lists the agents alphabet-
ically, with a profile on each. No pictures."

"Explain the other night in the maze."

"What do you want to know? How to get a ticket to

an upcoming performance? Or do you want to audition for a part so you can play, too?"

There it was again. She either had a bizarre sense of humor, or she was touched in the head. On the tapes he'd noticed that she'd answered a number of Dr. Fielding's questions with some eccentric logic. It was either part of her game, or she was as loony as Parish.

She didn't look loony. She looked intelligent and beautiful. Too beautiful for everything on her body to be real.

"Did you volunteer for this job, or did Merrick pick you hoping to scare the pants off me?"

Her words sent Sly's gaze on another slow appraisal of her too beautiful body. The little brown bikini bottoms barely covered her gender.

He rubbed his jaw. "As you said, I'm the ex-con. I'm the scary one."

"You can go back and tell Merrick if he thinks sending me his badass is going to frighten me, he's mistaken."

"If that's the case, why don't you come on over here and have a seat." Sly patted the rock next to him, knowing he was expecting a lot.

She was definitely scared of him. Her breathing was still erratic and her pretty green eyes had been checking him out since he'd pulled himself out of the water.

The question of the hour was, how unlucky could she get? Of all the men working for Merrick, how could she have gotten stuck with Sly McEwen? This man had sent chills down her spine just reading his profile on Simon's computer.

Granted, none of the men who worked for Onyxx at present had shining resumes, but this man was definitely the black sheep of the outfit. And all male—every hump, bump and lump accounted for.

His chest was corded, his torso densely muscled, and his legs looked like they could run a three-minute mile. He also carried a nasty-looking knife strapped to his bulky thigh.

It was obvious he'd been sent to intimidate her. Was she suppose to shake and tremble, then give in to whatever he asked for? If that's what they were expecting, they were going to be disappointed. She'd survived Simon's worst and she would survive Sly McEwen's worst, too.

Eva held his gaze. He was built with a machinelike efficient body that he balanced with a quietness that was almost spooky. It was obvious that his survival record hadn't involved luck. Not in prison, or as an Onyxx agent.

Simon's file on the man listed him as impossibly tough, and dangerously efficient. The words *rebel-ready* came to mind.

Determined to hold her ground against the baddest of the bad, she forced herself to move away from the rock. She stripped off her mask and shook out her wet hair, aware that he still continued to dissect her.

Her bikini was one of her skimpiest, but she'd worn it with the intention of getting rid of tan lines. In fact at one point she'd been planning to strip it off completely.

"Okay, McEwen. In good faith I'll give you a brief history lesson. It'll prove I'm not blowing smoke, and convince you that handing over the file will be worth it. That is if you want back on the scent of the Chameleon."

"I'm all ears."

Eva glanced at his attractive ears. No, he wasn't all ears. They were flat to his head, and suited him and his haircut.

Pushing the crazy thought out of her head, she said, "The data in Simon's computer outlined the past twenty years of Onyxx. It listed agent requirements, and even went through the early years when only recruited military men qualified for the elite force. It profiled over fifty agents. At the present, as you know, things are different than they were in the early years. Agents no longer need to come from military backgrounds. The only requirement is that they are single. The rat fighters are civilian rebels who possess extraordinary survival skills. How am I doing?"

"Keep going."

Eva chose her next words carefully. "There was a section dedicated to the Chameleon, with a list of his triumphs over Onyxx. It seems he has become the ambassador for international criminals looking for full-time employment."

"Does the file confirm who he is?"

"I'm coming to that. When I hacked into Simon's computer and found the file things started coming back to me. Things I'd forgotten."

"Important things?"

"Only time will tell. The memory of the suckers put me on Adolf Merrick's trail and then one day a few weeks ago, after learning how to contact him, I gave him a call. And the rest, as they say, is history."

"Not quite. What happened when you called him? Relay the conversation so I know you're telling me the truth."

Eva frowned. "All right. I explained to him who I was."

"And?"

"And he didn't believe me."

"Why would he?"

"Exactly. He said Eva Creon was dead. It was the

first I'd heard that. I thought about it, considered all that had happened, how I was living. Had been living before I went to live with Simon. The world believed I had died with my mother."

"But you were able to convince Merrick otherwise."

"The suckers could hardly be refuted. Only three people knew about them. Merrick, my father and me. Well, my mother, too, but she's truly dead. I saw the flames take her. After I reminded Merrick of the suckers, I told him why I was calling. That I wanted to read my father's file."

"And did you tell him why?"

"You know I didn't."

"He told you the file was confidential, right?"

"It was understandable for him to be wary of Paavo Creon's daughter, I suppose."

"You'd risen from the dead."

"Yes, I suppose it looked that way. And how could he trust a woman rumored to be the Chameleon's daughter?"

"Exactly."

"The data Simon had on Onyxx suggested that my father and the Chameleon were one and the same. I got the feeling that none of what I told Merrick on the phone was news, except my resurrection from the grave."

Eva waited for a reaction from Sly McEwen, but his stoic good looks never cracked, and his blue eyes never blinked. She supposed he hadn't survived his tour as one of Merrick's elite by giving away what he was thinking, or what his next move would be.

But then she hadn't survived four years playing games with Simon for amusement's sake, either.

She said, "He's mastered the game, you know."

"Who has?"

"The Chameleon."

"What game is that?"

"Survival, of course. Can you imagine what kind of scandal the news media could create if the world learned that a government agent had gone rogue and was now the richest criminal in the country? It's been fourteen years, and Onyxx can't stop him."

"Should he be stopped, do you think?"

Eva didn't answer.

"Is your father, Paavo, the Chameleon?"

She shrugged. "What do you think?"

"I think, yes. What changed Merrick's mind about giving you the file?"

"I gave him the location of one of the Chameleon's compounds."

This time Eva got a reaction. Sly McEwen's blue eyes narrowed, the muscles in his arms bunched, and his big hands formed fists.

"You're Merrick's informant?"

"Is that what he's calling me?" For some unexplained reason Eva was pleased, and she smiled.

"You're the reason we were sent to Castle Rock?"

"Yes."

"You're the one who fed Merrick the bullshit story?"

"It wasn't bullshit."

"The Chameleon wasn't there."

"I never said he was going to be there. I said the compound was his. And it is. And I imagine that's what you reported back to Merrick, and when he called me afterward, besides being angry, he was also ready to take me more seriously than he had days earlier."

He came to his feet, his height and shoulder breadth doubling his intimidation. "Serious enough to strike a bargain?"

"Yes,"

"The file for more bullshit?"

"The file for the Chameleon's location on a certain date."

"And he fell for that? He believed that you would hand over your own father?"

"Offering the location is no guarantee that you'll be able to catch the Chameleon."

"Not too loyal of you, either way."

"This coming from a man who shot and killed his father, then spent twelve years in prison paying for it."

"Stepfather."

"Give me the file, and in return, I'll give you a date and location. You'll get an opportunity to identify the Chameleon, and maybe even get close enough to catch him."

Suddenly Eva didn't like the way he was looking at her. As if she were some worthless barnacle clinging to a cave rock.

"What's wrong?"

"You set Merrick up to set me and my team up."

"I suppose that's one way of looking at it. But everything worked out. Adolf Merrick now believes me, and you have a chance to become a hero. And I get…" Eva paused. "I get to remember what I've forgotten. The last missing puzzle pieces," she whispered to herself.

She didn't intend to detail what those puzzle pieces were. This man would never understand, or believe her if she tried to explain it. She could hardly believe what she'd begun to remember herself. Maybe Simon's madness had finally rubbed off on her. Either way she was in too deep to turn back now.

Her words didn't seem to appease him. In fact they seemed to add fuel to a smoldering fire that had started to burn in his eyes from the moment she had mentioned she was Merrick's informant. She saw his fists open, then close again. Saw his jaw clench tight.

"Why are you looking at me like that?"

"Because your bullshit game killed Sully Paxton, you little bitch. He never made it back to D.C. And Jacy Madox may never walk again."

Eva blinked. She didn't know. Adolf Merrick hadn't mentioned any casualties. In defense of her actions, she said, "You're supposed to be the best special ops fighters at Onyxx. You're the rat fighters."

"So it's our fault we got set up and shot to shit."

Eva winced at his tone. She felt awful. No, she felt worse than that. She also felt cornered. "Yes. I mean, no. But…"

He curled his hand around the handle of the knife sheathed high on his thigh and started to advance on her.

Eva backed up. "What are you going to do, kill me?"

"Something like that."

"I have a deal with Merrick. You need me alive."

"The game of the hour, Eva Creon, is run like hell." He motioned to the water. "Get going."

She inched toward the edge of the rocks. Another few steps and she'd be forced into the water. "Wait!"

"I'm giving you at least a chance. You've got a minute head start. Move!"

Chapter 7

Until now Sly had been sympathetic to Eva's situation. How could he help it, after listening to the tapes? She'd been living in hell. Still, this minute he wanted to strangle her. Sully was dead and Jacy's future would likely consist of him viewing the Montana mountains from a wheelchair off the front porch of his cabin.

That one very poignant fact leaped to the forefront of everything else as Sly watched Eva dive into the water. He waited a full minute, breathing fire, and keeping his eyes on his watch. When the minute ran out, he pulled his goggles over his eyes and dived off the rock.

Like a shark on the hunt, he headed straight for the passage that led to the open sea. She had exited the sump and was trying her damnedest to reach the surface when he saw her. He pulled harder with his arms, kicked faster with his legs, and easily gained on her. A few more kicks and he reached out, locked his hand around her ankle, and gave a hard jerk backward like he'd done before. Her momentum lagged, and with one quick calculated move, he was beside her, encircling her waist.

She tried to twist free as he headed in another direction, thrashing and clawing at his arm. Her fight was impressive, but futile. Sly had no intention of letting her go. His entire reason for giving her a head start out of the cave was simply to prove to her that he was superior in strength and speed.

He knew approximately how long she could stay underwater. He'd observed her earlier while she'd explored the shoals surrounding the skerry.

He'd enjoyed watching her. She was as graceful as a mermaid. A competent diver. She could actually hold her breath for a long three minutes below the surface. But he could do better—another gift LeRoy had given him back in the day when his stepfather's psychotic boredom had extended to playing a game LeRoy liked to call, "How bad do you want to live, you little shit?"

The game required a bathtub full of water, Sly scared speechless, and LeRoy's black disposition magnified by several empty bottles of whiskey.

Sly scissor-kicked his powerful legs as he swam toward another cave passage. When she saw where they were headed, that he intended to enter another sump, she renewed her efforts to free herself.

Her lungs couldn't be stinging already, he thought. They would eventually, then the stinging would become a slow burn, before they turned hot like someone had lit them on fire with a match. That's when you knew you were in trouble.

No, Eva wasn't there, yet.

Eva stopped fighting halfway through the cave passage. What was the point? It was too late now. Sly

McEwen had proven to be stronger than she was, and unless he had a tank of air stashed somewhere around the next turn she wasn't going to last another minute.

She had been in a number of sea caves in the past four years, but it hadn't been until last year that she had attempted any of them on her own, and never this one. Nemo had labeled this sump the death channel for a reason. He had explained that it was twice as long as any of the others and required air tanks to successfully reach the cave on the other end.

She forced herself to relax, trying to conserve the last of her air. Why, she didn't know. She was going to die either way. She felt a wave of dizziness take her, then a burning sensation in her lungs.

Death by drowning…

She had never imagined that was how she would die. There were times when she had thought Simon would kill her by mistake. That he would take one of his games too far. Once she'd imagined being forgotten in the clothes chute. But never had she imagined that she would die surrounded by so much beauty.

She closed her eyes, let her body go limp. In that second she felt Sly McEwen's arm loosen around her waist. Their momentum slowed, then stop completely. She blinked open her eyes, tried to focus on the small lights surrounding his water mask. His hand palmed the back of her head. Then he brought her close, covered her mouth with his and began sharing his air.

The reality of what he was doing didn't register at first, but when she realized what he was offering, she greedily accepted the air and chose life over death. Within seconds she was lucid again, the burning in her lungs subsiding enough to allow her mobility.

When she was in command of her senses, he was

moving again, taking her with him once more as his legs propelled them farther into the deep.

His power underwater was incredible, and unbelievable. He swam through the channel with the speed of an eel now. With renewed hope, Eva began to kick her legs and become a helpmate instead of a burden.

Several seconds later the passage opened up and Sly McEwen started kicking his way to the surface, powering them upward until they broke out of the water like they'd been shot out of a cannon.

Eva gasped and began to cough as he swam with her in tow until her feet touched bottom. He quickly picked her up then and carried her to a narrow strip of sandy shore, depositing her there without saying a word.

Too exhausted to move, she lay there as he walked away from her. His breathing was a little irregular, but that was all. She studied his broad muscular back, then his sculptured ass and long legs in his water tights. She had known he was strong, but the word somehow seemed inadequate at the moment. After giving her his air, he should be as weak as she was. Shouldn't he be?

He shook his head and shed the water that clung to him. Staring out over the water, he said, "Sully was a good agent. More than that—" he turned to face her, his jaw set, and his blue eyes drilling her with disgust "—he was a good man and my friend."

Eva looked away, sick inside, and angry that he could so easily shame her into feeling guilty. He didn't know her. Didn't know how she'd been living. What she'd endured. He had no right to judge her.

She'd never given any thought to anyone dying when she'd offered Adolf Merrick the location of Castle Rock. She only wanted him to reconsider giving her a copy of her father's file.

Her lungs still hurting from the long swim through the sump, she said, "I'm sorry about your friend."

"It falls short. If you were a man, I would have killed you down there."

Unable to stand the contempt in his eyes, she glanced past him, noting that this cave was larger than the others, less rocky, and not as dark. The sandy beach was spare but comforting in a way she hadn't imagined it would be. She supposed coming so close to dying was affecting her thinking. How could she feel any amount of comfort here with a man who wanted her dead?

Across from where she lay were outcroppings of vertical rocks. She looked up and found the source of light—a fissure in the rock some thirty feet up allowed a slice of sky to peer through.

"Simon's guards will be looking for me if I don't surface soon."

"Let them look. They won't find you here."

"They might."

"Only if they're carrying air tanks on board. They're not."

The comment was spoken with confidence. He must have found a way to inventory the guard's boat before they had left Lesvago to follow her. The thought reminded her of how he'd left her room in disarray.

"Did you find anything of interest in my room this morning?"

"I found the coffee too sweet, and the bed too soft." He glanced around, then up to the fissure. "If you're thinking of running, there's your escape route." He brought his eyes back to her. "Unless you were faking it down there and you really can hold your breath four and a half minutes."

Four and a half minutes...

Was that how long they had been underwater?

The memory of what had transpired between them down there had her searching out his lips. He'd shared his air with her and it was the only reason she was alive. His lips parted, the smile that followed cold and smug, telling her he had locked into her thoughts.

"So is the Chameleon's daughter a chip off the old block, Eva? Are you a player in his world, or do you have your own agenda? What are you looking for in that file?"

She definitely had her own agenda. But she was done sharing information with him for the moment. She studied the man Merrick had sent to her. He had squatted down to lean his back against a sizable rock. There was a raw-looking scar on his shoulder. It was fairly recent. Had he gotten the injury while at Castle Rock?

She looked past him to the water, contemplating what it would take to escape.

"Four and a half minutes," he reminded, answering her silent question. "You don't have it in you."

"So now what?"

"Now you convince me that bringing you out of here alive is worth my trouble."

There would be no convincing this man of anything if he didn't want to be convinced. Eva shook off the thought, as well as the first signs of a nasty migraine knocking at the base of her skull. Not now, she thought. She couldn't think clearly when her head was splitting in two. Correction, she couldn't think at all. Her migraines were of the debilitating kind. She would be at his mercy, and it was obvious Sly McEwen didn't know the meaning of the word.

Before she lost her faculties and became a slug in the sand, she said, "I'm worth keeping alive. I'm your link to the Chameleon. I know where he's going to be in a few days," she lied. "I get the file and you get the location. It's a simple deal."

"How do I know this isn't another trick? That you're not going to double-cross me like you did Merrick?"

"Castle Rock is owned by the Chameleon. I told you why I gave Merrick that information."

"Maybe this entire game has been orchestrated by you and your father. In the past he's targeted Onyxx agents. Maybe this is his way of weeding out the rat fighters."

Her headache was on the move. Eva pressed her fingers to her temples as if that would, or could, delay the inevitable.

"Another one of your famous headaches?"

The ache inside her head was making her feel nauseated. Making it hard to speak.

"Need a pill?"

If only she had one, she thought.

She rolled to her side and drew up her legs as she watched him shove to his feet and stalk toward her. She felt dizzy and she knew the color had left her cheeks. She closed her eyes, wanting to cry, refusing to give in to the weakness.

He crouched beside her and studied her face.

"Where are they?"

She blinked open her eyes. "Where are what?"

"The pills?"

"In a waterproof pack onboard the skiff."

"Poor place for them to be, don't you think?"

She tried to sit up, but he shoved her back down and pulled his knife from his sheath. For a moment she thought he intended to kill her. Instead he drove the blade into the sand beside her and took her hand and curled it around the handle. "I spied some sea snakes down there. That's in case one decides to pay you a visit. I'll be back as soon as I can."

He started to get up. Eva let go of the knife and grabbed his arm. "You can't leave me. What if—"

"What if I don't come back? Then I guess you'll become a bone pile, won't you? Or you could use the knife."

"Closer," she whispered, afraid of him, yet so very desperate.

He leaned over her so his face was mere inches from hers. She could feel his breath on her cheek. Still smell the distinct scent of bay rum.

"Merrick's men are supposed to be loyal. Are you?"

"I extend my loyalty to a damn short list of people, Evy. Your name isn't on that list."

Evy... An odd sensation came over her and she smiled feeling close to the name for some odd reason. "You have a nice face."

"You have nice legs, and a memorable ass."

"You're going to leave me here, aren't you?"

"Tell me something to make me want to come back."

Her head was pounding fiercely. She closed her eyes and tried to think of something that would ensure his return. She could tell him about the party. She could tell him that the Chameleon would be there. The location wasn't an option because she still didn't know where it was going to be held, but...

She forced her eyes open, parted her lips to speak, but nothing came out. Sly McEwen was no longer there. He'd left her without making a sound.

Sly made it through the sump in under four minutes. When he surfaced behind a sizable rock, he saw that the short stocky guard, the one with the hairy face, had boarded Eva's skiff. He dived for the anchor attached to the skiff and moved it closer to the outcropping of rocks, carrying the boat with him on the tide.

When he surfaced, he heard the other guard yelling.

"Hey, Gino, what are you doing with the boat? Why did you pull the anchor?"

"I did nothing with the anchor, Ennis. A fish musta bitten the rope. You think?"

"It would have to be a big fish."

Sly saw Gino stand up and peer into the water searching for the reason the boat had gone adrift. Sly swam behind the rock again to listen to the exchange. "Where is she, Ennis?" Gino asked. "If we lose her we are dead."

"She likes the caves. She's just down there lying on a rock," Ennis assured his friend.

"Naked, you think? She has nice tits."

"I like her legs. You can dream about your hands on her tits. Mine are on her legs wrapped around my waist."

The men chuckled and exchanged more talk about what they would like to do to Eva Creon on an isolated sandy beach.

Sly grew anxious. He glanced at his watch, and knew that for someone in pain, minutes seemed like hours. He didn't want Eva alone too long in the cave. Leaving the knife with her had been a stupid idea. So was that crack about her using it on herself if he didn't come back. He didn't think she would be stupid enough to try to swim the sump, but if she thought he'd left her, would she slit her wrists?

He was angry with her, with good reason, but he wanted her alive.

Aware he would have to create a diversion to speed things up, he slipped away from the rock and swam beneath the boat. Nudging the boat with his shoulder—like a big fish—he heard Gino cry out in surprise.

"What was that, Ennis? Ennis, did you see it? Something hit the boat."

"I saw nothing."

Sly made another pass under the boat, rocking the skiff harder. On the third pass, he pitched the boat out of the water and forced Gino to lose his balance. As the man plunged headfirst into the water, Sly rocked the boat on its side, snagged Eva's bag and disappeared into the depths.

Four minutes later he found Eva where he'd left her. Her eyes were closed, and her hand was curled around his knife.

He left the water, opening her pack as he came to his knees beside her. He stripped off his vest and goggles, located the pills, then scooped her up and pulled her into his lap.

"Come on, Evy," he muttered, "open your eyes."

She blinked, stared up at him. "You came back," she whispered, her head cradled against his shoulder.

"Open your mouth."

She did, and he fed her the pills. She swallowed them, then took a swig of the juice he also found in her pack. She closed her emerald eyes seconds later and sank into him with a little shiver.

Sly leaned against a rock and curled his arms around her body. "Sleep it off," he said. "I'll be here when you wake up."

She snuggled closer and whispered, "I believe you."

Chapter 8

Two days later Sly stood on the deck of the *Hector*, an eighty-foot motor yacht, and looked out on the harbor of Mykonos at sunset. He was still waiting for Bjorn to return his phone call. The message he'd left two days ago had been short and to the point.

Call me.

It was possible that Bjorn wasn't back from Montana yet, but patience wasn't one of Sly's strong suits. Oh, he could be patient if he had his enemy in sight, waiting for him to make the wrong move, but the Chameleon's whereabouts was still anyone's guess, and he hadn't figured out how Simon Parish fit in yet. He'd looked into Parish's finances, and so far all his investments looked legit. Of course, that wasn't unusual. Even lunatics could be geniuses.

When his cell phone rang, Sly pulled it from his pocket and looked at the number. Receiver to his ear, he said, "It's about time."

"I just walked in. What's up?"

"I need something."

"Ask and you shall receive," Bjorn said. "At least that's the way it's supposed to work."

"I need the file on Paavo Creon right away."

"Last time we spoke you wanted just a picture. Now you want me to steal his entire file?"

"Make two copies. Stash one, then bring me the other one."

"Bring you a copy? You mean fly to Greece?"

"Do we have a bad connection, or are you just trying to piss me off?"

"Since the Castle Rock mission, security at headquarters has been beefed up. It's as tight as Fort Knox."

"It's always been tight. Besides, you like tight spots."

"Cute. I take it the investigation is paying off."

"Maybe."

"Just maybe?"

"Make up some excuse why you need to get into the archives. I want everything you can get on Creon."

"I'll see what I can do. How's the weather there?"

"Hot."

"And our little Eva? Is she hot, too? What's your take on the long-legged redhead now that you've gotten a closer look? You talk to her yet?"

"We've talked."

"And is she everything you expected?"

"Women are never what you expect. You know that. This one isn't even close." Sly watched as Parish's yacht, the *Ventura*, docked a short distance away. Scanning the upper deck he saw Eva and Melita Parish standing along the railing.

He said, "Bring me that file as soon as you can."

"Anything else? Maybe some perfume for Eva, or

some lingerie to impress her into thinking you're a generous guy?"

"She doesn't wear either."

"No shit?"

"No shit. See what you can find out about Merrick. Where he goes after work. Who he sees. What he does on his days off."

"What's that all about?"

"Pull his file, too."

"You want me to spy on Merrick. He's a damn legend at Onyxx, and you want me to—"

"Don't get caught. Gotta go."

After Sly hung up, he left the *Hector* to follow Eva. She wouldn't be hard to spot in a crowd. She was dressed in a white, off-the-shoulder blouse and a colorful skirt in shades of green, red and gold. Her hair was twisted and clipped off her neck, and as she walked the night breeze played with the hem of her skirt.

He studied her legs, recalled how satin smooth and shapely they were. He'd held her for over an hour in the cave while the pills worked on her migraine. After she'd been lucid enough to sit up on her own power, he'd insisted they stay another hour to make sure she was strong enough to make the trip through the sump. He'd worried about her the entire way out, holding on to her like before, he'd shared his air. Only this time, it had been different. His anger had cooled, allowing him to notice things, feel things. Things he was now having a hard time forgetting.

Dressed in jeans and a blue shirt, he left the yacht and began weaving his way through the islanders and tourists who had come to party in the streets after dark. Keeping his distance, he dissected the guard that trailed Eva and Melita. He was all business, staying close. He carried a gun inside his shirt at the small of his back, and a knife on his hip.

Neither would do him any good when the time came—Sly was determined to talk to Eva before the evening was over one way or another.

At Eva's suggestion Melita had jumped at the chance to spend the evening at a local taverna. It was no secret Simon's sister loved to dance.

It wasn't unusual to enjoy the weather and Greece's famous cuisine at the same time in an open-courtyard setting. But that wasn't the reason Eva had suggested Popeo's Taverna. It had been two days since she'd seen Sly McEwen, and she had no idea if he was still on the island.

If he'd left, her chance of getting the file before Simon's party was poor, and without the file, her hands were tied.

She glanced around, wanting desperately to catch a glimpse of him somewhere in the open. The taverna was busy, but not so busy that he wouldn't be able to spot her, and likewise, she, him.

She had dressed to be noticed, hoping that would draw him in. She would settle for just the sight of him, she decided—no words—just a glimpse to assure her he was still in the game.

She had mixed feelings about this man Merrick had sent her. She was wary of him, she would be stupid not to be. But in the cave he'd surprised her. She never would have believed a man who looked as he did could be gentle; not with what she'd read about him on Simon's computer. But she was wrong. The man was definitely not what he appeared to be, which warned her that he was even more dangerous than she'd first thought.

The idea that he might be watching her at that very minute sent a flutter into the pit of Eva's stomach. She had been with him half naked in the cave, and when she had awakened she had found herself cradled in his arms. She'd kept her eyes closed as she's listened to the rhythm of his heartbeat next to her ear. One of his big hands rested along her thigh, while the other had been drawing imaginary patterns along her cheek.

She'd lain so still, trying to keep her breathing even so he wouldn't know she was awake, but he had known. Finally he had said in his deep rusty voice, "You feelin' better? Headache gone?"

Eva followed Melita to an outside table. Popeo's was known for its grilled octopus and *souvlakia*—skewered meat and tomatoes served on pita bread. It was also famous for its music, and she knew before long Melita would be tapping her foot and swaying in time to the lively Mediterranean beat.

The table was sheltered from the seaside wind, yet visible enough to be seen if someone was looking for her.

"*Ouzo?*" Nemo asked, smiling at Eva, then Melita. "Or something stronger?"

"*Ne,*" Melita answered, "*ouzo* is fine."

The flavored aniseed drink was famous in Greece. Eva nodded. "Yes, *ouzo* is fine."

"I'll be right back," Nemo said.

Eva sent her eyes around the courtyard again and when she looked back Melita was watching her.

"Are you looking for someone?" she asked.

"Looking for someone? No."

"You seem anxious, and you look especially beautiful tonight." Melita reached out and touched a wisp of hair that had come loose from the clip. "You're not expecting someone, are you?"

Eva forced a laugh. "And who would I be expecting? Simon is away, and I know no one in Mykonos except for you and Nemo."

"I suppose you're right." Simon's sister sat back in her chair. She had the darkest eyes and hair of anyone Eva knew. Her hair was almost blue it was so black and her eyes so intense that there was no separation between color and pupil. Her skin was an almond brown, a gift given freely by the Mediterranean sun and her Greek heritage, Eva thought.

They were so very different and yet Eva felt a kinship with the young woman. They were close to the same age—Melita a little younger, she suspected. But that's not what seemed to bind them. It was their situation. They were both prisoners of circumstance. Though Melita never spoke of it, Eva knew she was not living at Lesvago of her own free will. It was true she wasn't guarded as closely as Eva was, but she was a prisoner nonetheless. Nemo watched her like a hawk.

Melita asked, "Where were you a few days ago when Ennis and Gino couldn't find you? I don't think I ever heard your side of the story."

"I went exploring the caves near the monastery."

"Yes, that's what they said. They also said your skiff went adrift, and yet the anchor was still attached to the rope. That's not possible."

"I agree. Do you believe that a big fish capsized my boat?" Eva asked. "That's the story Ennis is telling."

"Gino swears it is true. It would have to be a very big fish."

Eva played along, knowing it had been Sly who had upended the boat when he'd gone to get her pills. He'd offered the information to her while she'd been regaining her strength in the cave.

She said, "I saw no fish big enough to capsize the skiff."

"Then they were likely drinking again. I'll tell Simon."

"Don't, Melita. Please," Eva begged. "I would hate to see them punished for something so silly. No harm was done."

"All right, I won't tell Simon, but I'm going to ask Nemo to warn them about their drinking, and next time you go exploring, I'll go with you. The caves are too dangerous to go alone."

Melita had no idea how dangerous, Eva thought, envisioning Sly McEwen in her mind.

"Eva? Did you hear?"

She blinked. "Yes. I heard. I didn't spend all my time underwater. I also spent time on the beach." She glanced at one of her exposed shoulders. "I think the tan lines are almost gone."

"Tan lines?"

"Before Simon left he told me to make sure that there were no tan lines visible by the time he got back. I'm trying to make sure that, as Simon put it, everything is brown."

Her confession had Melita swearing softly, before her eyes drifted to the harbor. "That's why you've been in the sun so much the past two days."

"Yes."

Quietly, Melita said, "I'm sorry. I know it isn't easy for you. And though we've never discussed it—" her head turned back to level Eva a direct look "—I sympathize with you. Life with Simon must be a nightmare." She leaned forward and lowered her voice. "I tried to find out where the party was going to be held, but Simon wouldn't tell me. Nemo says there was some mention of it being held on Milos or Santorini. Simon referred to it as the island of paradise."

The island of paradise... Eva could only imagine what that could mean to a man like Simon. How it could feed his colorful imagination.

Her thoughts were interrupted when Nemo appeared with the *ouzo*. Minutes later they placed their order with a waiter, Eva settling for a delicate fish soup, and Melita ordering a feather-light phyllo pastry of feta cheese and stuffed spinach.

Nemo sat at a table a short distance away watching over them, his knee bouncing to the lively music coming from inside the taverna. When the sun set, the courtyard lights came on, filling the intimate space with amber lights.

Their food arrived, and Eva's soup was delicious, as she had expected it to be. They ate in silence enjoying the balmy island breeze and the music. When their plates were nearly empty, Eva noticed Melita's eyes were wandering.

Suddenly she asked Eva, "Do you mind if I ask Nemo to dance with me?"

"No. Go ahead." Eva glanced at Nemo and saw he was staring at them. No, he was staring at Melita. It was then that she understood something that had eluded her over the past three years. Nemo watched over Melita like a hawk because he wanted to. There was something between them. Something they had successfully kept a secret from everyone.

"I'm going to freshen up and order an after-dinner brandy at the bar," Eva announced. "I'll meet you back here in a little while. Enjoy the music."

Eva lingered out of sight to watch Melita and Nemo as they joined the dancers, then she disappeared into the crowd. She visited the rest room, then steered herself in the direction of the bar and ordered a brandy. She was about to pay for the drink when a body wrapped around her and leaned in.

"I've got it."

Eva's heart skipped a beat. She didn't need to look

to know who it was. His voice was deep and distinct, as powerful as the arm that stretched forward and slid the money to the bartender.

It was noisy, and the party atmosphere was perfect for two strangers to meet at the bar, Eva thought. She took a sip of her brandy to fortify her courage, then turned slightly and looked up into Sly McEwen's sober face.

He looked good. That's what immediately came to mind. It was a crazy thought. He'd shaved off the chin strap, but kept the sideburns. He wore faded jeans and a blue cotton shirt, a pair of sunglasses tucked into the pocket made him look like a tourist. A rich, badboy tourist.

"I was hoping you'd be close by."

He leaned in a little closer, his thigh making direct contact with her hip. "Where's the guard?"

"Dancing with Melita. Is Sly your real name?"

"Will that be a problem?"

"No. I was just curious."

"It's short for Slayton. I'm told my father came straight from Kilkenny, Ireland."

It was awkward, standing there having what appeared to be a normal conversation with a man who was in the business of killing people. A man who wanted to kill her father. A stranger who had held her for over an hour while she slept off her migraine.

He glanced at her exposed shoulders, then lowered his gaze to her chest where her breasts rose and fell with each labored breath she took. "And you, Evka Amara Creon—is that a Slovakian name?"

"Yes, I suppose it is."

He knew her middle name. Knew about the migraines, and the pills. Knew she lived with Simon and how they spent their evenings in the backyard. What else did he know? Was there a profile on her somewhere like the one she'd found in Simon's computer on him?

"I've never done any research on the name, though I'm sure there would be something in my father's file at Onyxx," she prompted.

An anxious customer knocked into Eva at the bar, shoving her forward into Sly's chest. He reached out and pulled her more tightly against him, then gave the rude man a threatening look.

The man quickly apologized. "*Me sing-horite,* miss."

"*Ne. Endaxi,*" she answered then looked back up at Sly. "He meant nothing by it." She followed his eyes and saw that he was staring at her hand flattened against his chest, her fingertips pressed to his warm skin and a smattering of hair in the open vee of his shirt.

She removed her hand and said, "There are balconies above the taverna. I'll meet you on the third level. It is more private than the others. Not many people go there."

She slipped out of his protective circle and started weaving her way through the crowd. She found the stairs, started up them as she scanned the dance floor. Nemo was wearing a bright-red shirt and she spied him easily as he twirled Melita in her full yellow dress. The timing was perfect, she decided. They were laughing and enjoying the music. Enjoying each other. They wouldn't miss her for a while.

To her disappointment two couples were already on the balcony when she arrived. They were both in passionate embraces, paying her no mind. Still, the situation made her feel awkward and she started back down the stairs, only to meet Sly on the way up.

"We can't be here," she told him.

He glanced over her head, assessed the couples and

what had brought them to the private spot. Then he grasped hold of her hand and led her back up the stairs.

On the opposite side of the balcony was a small alcove. He took her there, and backed her into it.

Because she was at a loss for words, she raised her glass to her lips and sipped the brandy. As she was lowering the glass, he took it from her, finished it and set the empty glass on a ledge. He stepped into the alcove and backed her up, making it look like they had come to the balcony for the same reason as the other couples.

Eva opened her mouth to protest, but he spoke first. "Since you've had so much experience playing games, you should have no trouble putting your arms around my neck and pretending you can't wait for me to touch you."

She hesitated, and Sly wondered what she was thinking. Then she raised her arms and laced her hands around his neck. The action was stiff and unnatural. Wary.

"How's this?" she asked, looking up at him through her long wispy bangs.

"It'll do," he said, then slid his arm around her waist and brought her lower body against him. "How's the head?"

"All right. The migraines come and go. I might not have one now for a week if I'm lucky."

She avoided his eyes, stared at his chest.

"What's wrong? This doesn't bother you, does it? We've been this close before."

"It was dark in the maze."

"Then close your eyes."

She scowled at him.

"In the cave you slept in my lap."

"That was not my idea."

Sly decided not to examine what had happened, or hadn't happened in the cave. Or examine what had gone through his mind yesterday when he'd followed her to a private beach where she'd stripped off her bikini to lie naked in the sun.

"Where's the Chameleon?" he asked.

"The file first?"

He slid one hand over her hip and rested it there. Her skirt was lightweight and he could feel her through the fabric. Knew she could feel him, too.

She said a little breathlessly, "I thought you didn't like me."

"What makes you think I do?"

He saw her cheeks flush with color. Knew she wasn't going to answer him.

"Oh, that. Don't read too much into it," Sly lied.

"You're just doing your job, is that it? Like me, you know how to play the game."

"That's right."

"A painful job, by the feel of it."

He was in the middle of smiling down at her when he heard voices coming up the stone steps. He sobered, and said, "We're going to have to look a little more convincing in a few minutes. The game has moved to a new level. Kiss me."

He dipped his head and chased her lips as she wrenched back and tried to avoid his mouth. When she ran out of room, his lips slowly descended.

Her whispered protest left her mouth opened and Sly took full advantage, thrusting his tongue inside as he covered her mouth. She squirmed momentarily, then gave in to him with a little moan. He continued to kiss her as he gyrated his hips until the firestorm in his gut was an open blaze.

When he backed off, she opened her mouth to speak,

but Sly laid a finger to her lips, then lowered his head and started kissing his way down her neck.

"Please..." she whispered, her hand now on his chest trying to push him away. "Please, stop."

Her voice sounded desperate. Sly slid both hands over her hips to palm her backside and bring her closer against him. "We're just pretending," he whispered, knowing he was full of shit.

For days he had been telling himself that she was the means to an end, just part of the job. But no woman had ever been able to get him this hard and bloodhound ready so damn quick.

She'd been burning a hole inside him since he'd heard her voice on the tape back in Atlanta. Seeing her pictures had only doubled his interest. In the maze she'd bewitched him, and yesterday watching her on the beach had sent him to bed with an ache so big he'd been *up* all night. And now, tasting her lips had put the final nail in his coffin.

He wanted to hate her for Sully's sake. In fact, he'd managed it for about ten minutes after she'd confessed that she was Merrick's informant. But then the truth of her situation settled around the hate, and he couldn't deny that Eva was simply trying to survive in a world that someone else had created for her.

He knew about survival. Growing up with LeRoy had forced him to do all kinds of things he had known were wrong. Still he had done them anyway just to survive. And that's why he couldn't condemn her.

The voices on the stairs brought him out of his muse and he wedged his leg between her open thighs, then pulled her blouse lower off her shoulder. Angling his head, he kissed his way down to the exposed swell of one lovely breast.

"Come on, Eva," he coaxed, "pretend you like it. Pretend you like me."

She arched her back when Sly brushed his lips over the rise of her breast.

"That's it." He gathered up the soft fabric of her skirt and slid his hands underneath. When his palms cupped her satin-smooth ass, she shuddered violently.

"Please…" she breathed, trying to wiggle free.

He could have easily moved his fingers past the slight barrier of her panties, but he didn't.

He said, "Listen to the voices on the stairs. Sound familiar to you? Do you recognize them?"

For a moment she said nothing. Then, "Oh, God, it's Melita and Nemo."

The voices had become more discernable now, the couple had reached the balcony.

"Put your hands on me. Somewhere. Anywhere," he told her.

She did what he said, slid them down his chest and around his waist. She snuggled closer, lowered her head to his chest and brushed her lips over the skin in the open vee of his shirt.

"Where do you think Eva went, Nemo? She's not in the rest room or at the bar."

"She's probably back at the table by now. Don't worry, sweet. Come here. As long as we're alone…"

"Nemo, no. We're not alone."

"Just a quick kiss, Melita. It's been days. No one will see us up here. This is a place for lovers, and they are all too busy to notice us. Come on, Lita. Let me hold you."

Eva listened for Melita to say something in answer to Nemo's plea. She couldn't see them, but by the silence that hung heavy in the night air, she knew Nemo had won and Melita was now kissing him.

As the minutes lagged, she listened to Sly's heart

beating strong against her ear, and the scent of him filling her senses. She was aware of his hands on her backside, holding her firmly against him in a way she had never been held by a man before. She reminded herself that they were pretending to be lovers, and it seemed Sly McEwen was as good at this as he was breaching iron gates and swimming like a shark.

Several more minutes ticked by, and then Nemo and Melita were talking again, their soft voices gentle with each other as they left the balcony.

The second it was safe, Eva wiggled out of Sly's arms and pushed his hands away from her. As her skirt drifted back into place, she said, "Don't ever touch me like that again."

He took a step back and relaxed his shoulder against the wall as if what they'd just been doing was all in a day's work and pulled a pack of cigarettes from his shirt pocket. Shaking one out, he curled his lips around it, returned the pack to his shirt, then lit up. "Did you know?" he asked around a puff of smoke.

"Did I know what?"

He arched an eyebrow.

"A kiss on a balcony doesn't mean that they're… doing it."

"Doing it?" He chuckled. "You surprise me, Evy. I never expected you to be so naive."

Evy… She liked the name, liked the way it made her feel. "I'm not naive."

"That's debatable. You kiss like you haven't had much practice." He took another drag off his cigarette. "You were sucking on my lips like—"

"Don't you wish."

"Doesn't Parish kiss you?"

"As a matter of fact, no, he doesn't. The human mouth is a germ trap. Simon's immune system is delicate."

She tried to walk past him, but he pulled her back.
"What else doesn't he do to you?"

"That's none of your business."

"That's where you're wrong, Evy. I bled at Castle Rock, along with five other men because of you. Sully's dead. The minute you called Merrick, you put yourself in my world, and I'm not leaving yours without satisfaction."

"I need the file. Once I have it, you'll get what you want, and then we can both be rid of each other. Don't ever put your hands on me again." She touched her bruised lips. "Or your mouth. Now I have to go."

She tried to shake off his hand because he still hadn't let her go. He pulled a pen from his pocket, opened her hand and wrote a sequence of numbers in her palm, then curled her fingers inward.

"So you can reach me day or night."

Chapter 9

Dressed in a black sweater and gray pants, Adolf Merrick stood beside his wife's grave. It was misting out and the air was chilly. He used to like autumn with all its fall colors. But since Johanna's death, he had changed his favorite season to summer for the sake of the roses.

Johanna loved roses. Peach-colored roses were her favorite, and for the past fourteen years he had a standing order at the corner flower shop for two dozen peach roses every Saturday to be picked up at four o'clock.

He'd gotten to know the owner of the flower shop by name. Harry was a good man, and he knew roses. Today he had hired Harry's daughter to deliver Johanna's flowers to her for the next several weeks while he was out of the country. It wouldn't be the same. Johanna would miss his company, and their conversations, but he knew she would understand. He'd had to make similar arrangements in the past when he'd had to leave D.C. on business.

Adolf squatted next to Johanna's grave and placed the roses in the brass cone-shaped vase to the left of her headstone. The roses smelled sweet in the damp humid air, and he inhaled the scent as he arranged them like he remembered Johanna doing on the dining room table in their country home during those blissful first years of their marriage.

"I'm taking another trip," he told her, letting his hand slowly move over the headstone to outline the letters of her engraved name and the inscription that read: Johanna Merrick, beloved wife.

A wave of dizziness stalled his hand and he concentrated on breathing through it. When it passed, he said, "I'm not sure how long I'll be gone this time. I've arranged to have Harry's daughter visit you. You remember Sarah. She's decided to take over the flower shop. Harry told me he's going to retire. He's almost seventy. I guess it's time. She'll do a good job. Sarah's like Harry. Dedicated to the roses."

He stood, waited as another dizzy spell threatened his balance.

"Your maple tree in the backyard is turning red. It's a little late this year. I think it's grown another foot since last year. You wouldn't recognize it if you saw it."

The mist had turned into a heavy drizzle, but Adolf ignored it and sat down on the stone bench a few feet away. After a time the dizzy spell let up. He'd been having them more often. His doctor said it was a warning sign that he needed the surgery soon.

He would have had the surgery by now if it hadn't required a long week in the hospital. That hadn't fit into his plans. And now that he was off to Greece, it was going to have to wait a little longer.

Eva had mentioned the island of Mykonos, and a place called Lesvago. She said that's where Parish would be taking her. He would start there. He didn't doubt for a minute that the information he'd sent Sly McEwen had piqued his interest and put him on Eva's trail. Maybe, with any luck, McEwen would pick up the phone and contact him. That's why he'd given him his number.

"I had an offer to sell the house, Johanna. I figure you'd want someone to enjoy the place. The couple seem nice. They're young, and have a little boy. Remember how we always talked about having children? A son. That's why we bought a place in the country, so there would be plenty of room for the kids to play."

Adolf shivered, looked at his watch, reluctant to leave. Five minutes, he thought, just five minutes more.

"The day has come, Simon. It's time for Evka to spread her wings and fly," the Chameleon said.

"Fly? But she's mine. You gave her to me."

"To teach her patience and survival. I never meant for you to keep her indefinitely."

Simon and the Chameleon were seated on the upper deck of the *Pearl*, sipping wine. The afternoon was full of sunshine, the water a mirror of azure glass.

"But I thought after so many years you had decided to let her stay with me."

"There was no hurry for her to leave. I needed a safe place for her to grow and develop. If you remember, when I brought her to you she was not yet a swan."

"A swan?"

"She needed time, Simon. Time to learn things that her private tutor couldn't teach her. Things only you could. You have a rare talent for the eccentric. It's a gift, really. When I brought her to you, she was a delicate flower. Untested. She knew nothing about the world as we do. I knew you could teach her how to endure, and at the same time, she would be safe."

"So I was her baby-sitter. She would learn how to play my games, and survive them, and remain untouched in the process because I'm only half a man."

If that, the Chameleon thought, but he didn't say it. He suspected that Simon had never really come to grips with what had been necessary years ago.

"You are alive, Simon."

"And I should be grateful for the privilege. Yes, I've heard you say that more than once."

"Yes, you should."

"Spoken by someone who has no idea what it is like to have an erection in your mind when your body fails to make the connection on a physical level. I'm a freak. I look like one, and live like one. Tortured by both."

The Chameleon kept his voice level when he said, "Your castration was necessary, Simon. It wasn't done on a whim. The doctor's or mine. It saved your life."

"So save it once more. Don't take Eva from me," Simon said.

"I have no choice. I'll get you another beautiful toy to amuse you."

"Eva doesn't amuse me, she completes me. I don't want another. I want Eva."

"You sound like a five-year-old, Simon. In a few days you will be twenty-five. Grow up."

"Grow up, and do what? Become what?"

"I've given you houses, cars and enough money to have anything you want. I know you enjoy your freakish life."

"Now I do. I hated my life before Eva came, and I shall hate it again if you take her away. I love her."

The Chameleon refused to argue further. "I have

many enemies, Simon. You know this. They need to be dealt with."

"What does that have to do with Eva?"

"I've made an offer to someone who is in the business of dealing with enemies. He's countered my offer, as I knew he would."

"What is he asking for? It can't be what I think it is. You wouldn't—"

"Eva caught his eye a few years ago. He wants her, and ten million."

The Chameleon watched as Simon set his wineglass down and stood. He seemed thinner than usual, as emaciated as a scarecrow. He asked, "Are you taking your vitamins?"

"Yes. All thirty-two of them." With that, he turned to face the sea. "How can you give her to a stranger?"

"You were a stranger to her once."

"That was different. You knew I would follow the rules. How can you be sure he will follow your rules?"

"If I agree to this there will be no rules. Eva will be his. But he has assured me that she will be treated well. I've given this a lot of thought, Simon. This is the perfect alliance."

"No rules? He'll take her to his bed. Have all of her. She'll experience a man physically."

"Yes. I think it's time."

Simon turned. "I could have touched her. Given her pleasure in my own way if you would have agreed to it."

"It would have only frustrated you more. And what of Evka? It's time to reward her for her dedication to the games, don't you think?"

"How soon do you plan to take her from me? Not before my party."

"No, not before your party. Sit, and finish your wine."

Simon sat, yet his gaze roamed the sea instead of looking at the Chameleon.

"Pouting will not change my mind. Look at me."

He obeyed, said, "She will not want to go. She cares about me."

"Don't be a fool. She doesn't care for you as a woman cares for a man. I have instructed her to obey you and endure your games, that is all. Still, it hardly matters. I have made my decision. Eva will be given to Holic Reznik."

"The assassin? You're giving her to a married man rumored to have a dozen mistresses?"

"He assures me that she will want for nothing."

Simon left his chair once again to pace the sunny deck.

"I brought you an early birthday present."

Simon stopped pacing. "A present for me?"

"More than one. They are beautiful, germ free, and willing to play any game you wish. No rules."

"No rules?"

"None."

"They're waiting for you below."

A smile back on his face, Simon started toward the stairs no longer pouting.

"Did you miss me?"

Eva turned around to see Simon leaning against the stone wall in the private courtyard outside her bedroom. It was late, after dark, and he must have just gotten home because he was still wearing his hat. Slowly he removed it and that's when she saw the blisters on his face.

"You know the sun is brutal on your skin. How could you have forgotten that? If you get an infection again—"

He looked her up and down, his eyes lingering on her breasts and the way her pale nightgown clung to her.

"Come to my room."

As he turned to walk away, Eva noticed Simon lower his head. That wasn't normal, and neither were his dull, lifeless eyes. They lacked the usual deviant sparkle.

Maybe an infection was already attacking his delicate system.

She stopped in her room for her robe, then followed the long corridor to the master bedroom at the end of the hall. He'd left the door cracked a few inches and she slipped inside, closing it behind her.

He was already undressed and she paid his bony back and skinny pale butt no mind as she went into the bathroom to retrieve a medicated ointment his doctor had prescribed for his skin.

She set the ointment on the table near the bed, and while he slipped into a pair of plain white cotton boxers, she stripped the bed down to the white cotton sheet, then retrieved a bottle of gin and a glass from the liquor cabinet.

Life with Simon was like riding an emotional roller coaster. Most days he was in his devil mode, angry at the world for the cruel joke he faced daily in the mirror. But there were just as many days when his body would play devil's advocate and he would be forced into a childlike subservient role. At those times, like tonight, she was required to play nurse. But by tomorrow the demon might be back, and she could find herself tied on a chair, listening to the rules for some new bizarre game that had come to him during the night.

In the beginning the hardest part had been not knowing what to expect. She understood that Simon's radical behavior was due to a combination of things. His appearance was atypical, he suffered from dozens of allergies, and was prone to infections that required his house staff to sterilize everything that came in contact with him. She was even required to bath with a special soap, and forbidden to wear cologne.

Several months after she had come to live with him, he had contracted an infection. Quarantined, he had sent for her on the third day. When she had entered his bedroom, she'd found him lying naked on a white cotton sheet. It was then that she'd understood the full extent of Simon Parish's perpetual torment—he'd been castrated.

At that moment, she had felt sorry for him, as well as a willingness to understand what drove him to his eccentricities. More importantly, she knew why the twisted games he played had never involved sex.

Simon stretched out on the bed and closed his eyes. "Forget the ointment and come lie down beside me."

Surprised by the request, Eva hesitated.

He patted the mattress beside him. "An odd request, I know, sweet Eva. Do it anyway."

His firm tone was back, warning her he would have his way. She stretched out beside him, unsure if this might be the prelude to some strange game she had no wish to play.

"Simon…"

"Lift your head."

She obeyed him, and he slid his arm behind her and curled his hand around her shoulder. "Simon…"

"Quiet. I'm tired. I want to sleep now, and I want you to sleep with me."

"But…"

"Quiet, I said. Sleep."

It was midnight when Eva last glanced at the clock, still expecting the demon within Simon to surface. But the demon slept along with the child; and sometime during the night, she relaxed against Simon and slept, too.

At midnight Sly stood at the railing on the *Hector* and watched the last light go out at Lesvago. The night was a carbon copy of the past four—a balmy breeze and a starlit night. Parish had returned, and with his return, Sly's mood suddenly turned black.

Eva was once again at Simon's mercy.

He wasn't used to having to analyze his emotions because normally he didn't allow himself to feel. But like it or not, he was feeling all sorts of emotions since he'd let Eva walk away from him on the balcony at the taverna.

He swore, and refocused his thoughts.

We always go this time of year. Simon likes to celebrate his birthday in Greece.

Why that came to him all of a sudden, he didn't know, but in response, he raised his wrist and pushed a button on his watch causing a calendar to replace the time. He ran several ideas through his head, then turned from the railing and went below deck.

He had converted a small storage room under the stairway into his office. He went inside and turned on his computer. Pulling up all the information he and Bjorn had compiled thus far—knowing there was no birth certificate for Simon Parish—he used Parish's extensive medical records to learn his date of birth. Two days from now, on November 2, Simon would turn twenty-five.

Sly shut down his computer and went into his stateroom where he kept the tapes of Eva's sessions with Dr. Fielding. He retrieved one from the cupboard titled, "S is for Survival and Shackles." In the cassette player, he hit Fast Forward, then Stop, then Play.

"Only mastering the game will free us."

"Free us from what?"

Again he hit Stop, then Fast Forward. Play.

"I'm not fighting it any longer."

"What do you mean by that?"

"There's no time to explain. I'm off to Greece."

"Will you see your father?"

"He'll be at Simon's birthday party. That's one of the reasons we go this time of year."

Sly hit Stop again. The Chameleon would be at Simon Parish's birthday party in two days. A smile parted his lips. He didn't need to play Eva's game any longer. If he stuck close, she would lead him straight to the Chameleon.

Eva… Without warning his thoughts returned to her, and he soon found himself back on deck scanning Lesvago with a pair of high-powered night-vision binoculars. Knowing where her bedroom was located, he watched the dark window for several minutes. He didn't know what he expected to see, movement maybe, some sign that she was all right.

He never did see any movement, and after an hour he sailed the *Hector* back to the caverns where he had been successfully hiding out since he'd arrived. He went to bed in a sour mood, and fell asleep with Eva's husky voice teasing his subconscious. Soon he was dreaming she was in his bed, her lips pressed against his.

But instead of him kissing her, she was the one doing the kissing. She was astride him, caressing him with her hands and telling him how much she needed him.

She stayed with him all night feeding the dream and fueling his need. Before dawn, he blinked awake drenched in sweat, with his hand wrapped around his cock.

He let out a labored groan, slid his hand to the base of his hard shaft. Groaned again. Determined to rid himself of Eva and the solid ache that had awakened him, he began to move his hand in an age-old rhythm.

The next morning during breakfast, Sly received a message from Bjorn that read "Athens 4:30, gate C. It's raining in D.C. and I'm cold." Translation, Athens 3:30, gate B. The rest was just Bjorn being Bjorn. He hated cold weather, and complained about it every time the temperature dropped below fifty when all his aches and pains surfaced, reminding him how close to forty he was.

Sly flew from Mykonos to Athens, anxious to learn what was in the file Eva wanted so badly. His flight was a jackrabbit flight and he was in Athens in twenty-five minutes. As he made his way to gate B, he kept a watch-ful eye out for anyone who might be following him, but he was fairly confident that his cover as a tourist was still intact. But underestimating the Chameleon, or Parish, would be a mistake. One he didn't intend to make.

Bjorn was the second passenger off the plane. He was no longer using his cane, but he still had a slight limp.

"Here, I'll get that." Sly took Bjorn's bag.

"Jesus, I hate flying," his friend grumbled.

Sly slung the duffle on his shoulder. "I've rented a boat to take us to Mykonos. That way we'll be able to talk without any ears listening."

"And there is much to talk about, Sly."

Bjorn's comment, and the look on his face, kept Sly on edge the entire cab ride to the harbor. They set sail quickly, and were en route back to Mykonos within thirty minutes of leaving the airport. Miles from nowhere, Sly cut the engine and asked, "Do you have the file?"

"No."

"No?"

"I'll explain in a minute. First of all, I followed up on the house staff that took care of Eva when she was a kid. She did have a private tutor. The woman was a live-in." Bjorn checked his notes. "Carolyn Hunter. She's dead. Some kind of freak accident once she was let go, after she moved into a small apartment. The police report stated she fell in her kitchen and hit her head. Then there's the cook and housekeeper, Helen and Lida. They're also dead. A car accident. And the gardener and his son Tony, they're dead, too. Boat accident. Drowned while fishing on the Chattahoochee River. Looks like our Eva has a deadly effect on people she comes in contact with."

"What else?"

"That's not the only *dead* end."

Sly grunted his acknowledgement of Bjorn's pun.

"Sorry. I couldn't resist. Okay, when I got into the database, Paavo Creon's file was already gone. I checked the date log. Three weeks ago someone tapped in and pulled up Creon's file. Everything's gone."

"Was there an access number used to get in?"

"Yes. On that day six people accessed records."

"Who was it?" Sly asked, already knowing the answer.

"Merrick's access number is on record that day. He signed in the afternoon of the third of September."

"That was two days before we left for Castle Rock." Sly looked out to sea trying to make sense of it all.

"You get anything out of our little Eva?"

"She gave Merrick the information that sent us to Castle Rock."

"She was the informant?"

"That's right."

"The little bitch. She set us up."

"In a way, but not really."

"Sully's dead. We got our asses nearly shot off. What do you call that?"

"Don't look at me like that. This is complicated. She claims Merrick refused to give her the files after she called him and told him who she was. She says he didn't believe she was Eva Creon, so she offered him the compound location as a way to convince him."

"Which means he believed she was dead like the reports claimed."

"That's right. After we got back from the mission and reported our findings, Merrick knew she was telling the truth, and agreed to give her Paavo's file in exchange for the Chameleon's location."

"And to think I liked her."

Sly could hear the same disgust in Bjorn's voice that he had felt when she'd told him she was Merrick's informant. He said, "You're a good profiler. You liked her in the beginning for a reason. She's likable, and I don't think she thought we would see action at Castle Rock."

Bjorn was about to light his cigarette. He stopped and locked eyes with Sly. "Did I hear you right? You like her?"

"She's lived with a lunatic for four years. Her own father put her in that situation. I don't know why, but you can't hate someone for trying to survive hell, can you?"

"Low blow, Sly."

"Just the truth."

"Have you considered she's playing you, Sly? What do we really know about her? Before you take this any further you better find out what she's after. Where her loyalty is. Get in her face, make her talk."

"And if she won't talk, do I put her in a dark closet with a mouse for ten hours, or hang her in a clothes chute with a belt around her wrists?"

"You've been listening to the tapes. If not by force how about using your charisma? Why not seduce her?"

"I can't do that."

"Sure you can. I've seen you disarm a woman before, Sly. You've got a look in your eyes when you're on the hunt. Women like that. They like the strong, mysterious type. Your charm got us out of Vienna in '98, remember? And into Bangkok in '99. Use that charm on our little Eva. Draw her in, set her up, and use her. By the look on your face, you find that distasteful. And that, my friend, can only mean one thing. You've allowed your feelings into this. Am I right?"

"There's something about her," Sly agreed. "She's a victim. I have a hard time victimizing a victim."

"Here's what I know. I know a man can't fight his feelings. He might not be able to act on all of them, but denying they exist is pointless. Sometimes these things don't make sense, and over the years I've decided they don't have to. Using her is the only way, Sly. And if you do it right, she'll enjoy it. And in the process, you'll get what we need to catch the Chameleon, and you'll both have a memory."

Sly swore, then asked, "What did you find out about Merrick?"

"I did get into his file. Made a copy."

"And?"

Bjorn bent over and pulled up the Velcro strap on his duffel bag and retrieved a disk. "Merrick's carrying around a lot of baggage. He has been for a long time."

He handed the disk over to Sly. "This is for you. I'll give you the five-minute version if you want."

"Go ahead."

Bjorn reached into his pocket and pulled out a small notebook. "I did tail him for a few days. He lives a pretty boring life outside the office. He's got an apartment in Somerset, and a country home north of Rockville where he spends his weekends. Saturdays seem to be his special day."

"Meaning?"

"He leaves his house about three and goes to a flower shop, buys two dozen roses, then drives to Pleasant View Cemetery." Bjorn paused, then added, "He goes there to visit his wife."

"Wife? I didn't know he was married."

"Neither did I. Johanna Merrick has been dead fourteen years."

"That's a long time."

"...to be delivering roses," Bjorn finished. He took another cigarette from his shirt pocket and lit it. "He talks to her."

"Talks to his dead wife?"

"*Ja.* He sits on a bench and talks to her. He spent over two hours with her Saturday."

Sly frowned, not sure what to make of the information. He had always felt that Merrick was living with some black monster eating away at his insides. Was this it? "How did she die?"

"This is where it gets sticky and a little gray. It seems someone kidnapped her."

"For ransom?"

"No, not exactly. It was more like someone wanted to play a little game."

The word *game* had Sly raising his eyebrow and sitting a little straighter.

"It came as a riddle sent to him on e-mail. A riddle with pictures of his wife tied up on a bed. She had C4 wrapped around her."

Sly reached out, stole Bjorn's smokes and lit up. "So she was wired to blow. Keep going."

"The e-mail showed her crying and begging Merrick to save her. There were two clues sent to solve the riddle as to who had kidnapped her. If Merrick managed to type in the correct answer it would cancel the detonation. If not…" Bjorn rubbed his jaw, sucked the life out of his cigarette, then tossed the filter overboard. "I'm sure you know how this story turns out. Merrick ran out of time and his wife died while he watched it all on the computer screen."

"God!"

"There's more. The riddle was signed, 'the Chameleon.'"

Sly cut the engine on the boat. Finally, he said, "I need to talk to Merrick."

"That makes sense," Bjorn agreed. "There's something else that I want to run by you. Aren't you curious who the messenger was who sent you that information about Eva?"

"You think it was Merrick?"

"Yes, I do. After we got back from Castle Rock we were all reassigned. Our tours were up and each of us was offered a new job according to our expertise. All except you. Merrick offered you a desk job shuffling papers, which you rejected. Everyone knows you should have been offered a job as a marine cartographer. He knew you were upset about losing Sully, and Jacy almost ending up the same. He knew with a little push you'd be off and running, looking for answers because you're so goddamn loyal and bullheaded."

Sly considered what Bjorn was saying. He picked it

apart, ran a number of cross thoughts into the mix. He said, "He wanted me out of Onyxx to do his leg work for him. He's been leading me every step of the way since I walked away. It makes sense."

"You bet your ass it does. He's still at the Agency after fourteen years. Why, because he can't let go. And every time the Chameleon slips through Onyxx's fingers, it reopens the old wound. He wants him and he wants him bad. More now than ever because medically he's a mess."

"Meaning?"

"Merrick's got a brain tumor."

"A tumor?"

"*Ja.* He needs an operation, but he's been putting it off."

Sly got out of his seat and stared across the water. "He's feeling frustrated. The Chameleon's still on the loose, and he might die before he gets his revenge. Then one day out of the blue Eva calls and says she's Paavo Creon's daughter."

"And Merrick believes he's been blessed with a gift from God," Bjorn added.

"She offers him information that he can't ignore and we're off to Greece to check out Castle Rock."

Bjorn supplied, "He sent you that envelope of info knowing you'd end up on Eva's tail."

Suddenly Sly was back in the seat turning the engine over and spinning the boat around.

"What the hell are you doing?" Bjorn asked.

"You're going back to D.C."

"I'm what? What for?"

"To tell Merrick I want a meeting with him, here. And make sure he brings the file on Paavo Creon."

"I just got here, Sly."

Sly ignored the sick look on Bjorn's face. "I could

call him. He gave me a private number, but that's what he's expecting and I'm not going to do this his way. He's going to have to play it my way from here on out."

"He gave you a number where you can reach him?"

"I should have picked up on that as suspicious. I admit, I didn't."

"So I show up in his office and tell him what exactly?"

"You don't show up there. You're going to stake out his apartment and kidnap the son of a bitch."

"I am?"

"At gunpoint."

"That should strengthen our relationship."

Sly shrugged. "I wasn't aware you cared a damn about relationships. Aren't you the guy who just told me to use Eva Creon?"

"I hate flying," Bjorn grumbled. "You know I hate flying. It took me ten hours to get here."

"And it'll take another—" Sly calculated the time back and forth, figuring in the kidnapping "—twenty-five hours to get back here. Give or take an hour."

"I can't sleep for shit on an airplane. That means thirty hours without sleep."

"Eat a pill. You'll sleep."

"I took this profiling job to keep my feet on the ground, and normal working hours. I—"

Sly cut him off. "The quicker you get going the quicker you'll get back with Merrick. After that you can keep your feet on the ground. I don't think you'll need to force Merrick to board a plane, but if he gives you any trouble at that point, tell him I'm so close to the Chameleon that I can smell him. That should bring him here on the run."

Chapter 10

Simon kept the location of his birthday party a secret until they docked on the island of Santorini. From the upper deck of the *Ventura*, Eva surveyed the volcanic city of Fira. It was after dark, and the island was lit up as bright as an evening star. The petrified lava varied from fire red to purple, and it gave the city a magical glow.

So this was where Simon's party was going to take place, where her father would join them in a rare appearance that happened only once a year.

She had hoped to have read the file by now. But time had run out. She wasn't sure what to do now. Her options were to do nothing and go back to Atlanta with Simon when the time came, or tell her father what she'd been up to this past year and see what kind of a response she got.

She felt like a pawn in a chess set. If she didn't make a move she would never get out of the box. She couldn't imagine living with Simon one more year.

"What are you thinking?"

Simon's arm slipped around her shoulder and Eva willed herself to relax. Last night he had held her while he slept. He had never done that before. There was a reason behind it. She didn't know what, but experience told her she had only to wait to find out.

"I love this island," he said. "It's always been one of my favorites."

He usually didn't like people to look at him, but he suddenly gripped her chin and forced her to meet his red eyes. "I want you to stay here, on board the *Ventura*, tonight," he said. "I'm going ashore to see how tomorrow evening's party plans are coming along. I'll be back in the morning. You'll join me for breakfast at eight sharp. Be waiting for me…here. Wear the strapless dress, and the white sandals to match. Hair up. No jewelry. Not too much makeup. Red lipstick."

Eva kept her eyes locked with his. "All right. I'll be here in the morning waiting for you wearing white, and looking exactly as you wish."

He suddenly pulled her into his arms. "I don't know how I could have resisted kissing you all these years, but I no longer have the willpower. Germs or not, I'll have your lips on mine, sweet Eva. I'll have them now."

The request was so unexpected that Eva froze. Last night he had held her while he slept, something that had never happened in four years, and now today he was telling her to kiss him. What was going on?

"Eva…"

She came to her senses quickly. Knowing Simon never asked twice for anything she leaned in, angled her head and pressed her mouth to his cold, thin lips. His response was delayed and horribly awkward, as if it had been years since anyone had kissed him, if ever.

He stepped back from her after the flat kiss was over. He smiled, kept the smile with him as he walked away. He even looked back before taking the gangplank to see if she had moved.

She hadn't, she was still trying to make sense out of the changes in Simon that had virtually taken place overnight.

Sly boarded the *Ventura* with the knowledge that at any moment one of the guards patrolling the yacht might spot him and put a bullet through his skull. Slipping past them as stealthily as a pirate, and just as surefooted, he found the stairway that led below deck and disappeared.

The passageway was empty, lit by small clear lights. He moved quickly, his jaw set and his mood black, as black as the drysuit he wore.

Within minutes he located Eva's stateroom and disappeared inside. She wasn't there, but then he knew that. She was up top with Melita.

He removed his diving attire, then ransacked her room waiting for her to show up. When she didn't come after he'd gone through the entire room, he stretched out on her bed. Sucking on his sour mood, he dozed with one eye open and an ear to the door.

At eighteen minutes after midnight, she stepped into her stateroom wearing the same lavender skirt and white blouse she'd had on earlier when she'd kissed Parish before he'd left for the evening.

The stateroom was dark, save for a small amount of moonlight that shone through two windows. Sly left the bed, and without making a sound, slipped into the hall that led to the bathroom.

He heard her sigh, watched as she stretched. Her fingers found the zipper at the back of her skirt and she slid it down. The skirt fell from her hips with ease, and she stepped out of it. The buttons on her blouse, she worked at slowly. She walked to a small table and turned on a mood light, offering him a better view of her sweet ass, half-hidden by the bottom edge of her blouse.

She kicked off her sandals as she shed her blouse, leaving her in a white lacy camisole and matching panties. She tossed the blouse on a chair, then suddenly sniffed the air. Slowly she reached for the blouse and clutched it to the front of her as she turned around.

"You should have smelled me sooner," Sly said, stepping out from the shadows. "If I had been out to kill you it would have been over for you minutes ago."

"But we both know that's not what you want from me, is it?"

"Why didn't you call me and tell me you were leaving Mykonos?"

"Do you have the file?"

"No."

"Then we don't have any business to discuss, and you need to leave."

Sly tried to stay calm. All day he'd been chasing her in the *Hector*, trying to keep from losing sight of the *Ventura*, and at the same time trying to stay far enough away so he wouldn't draw attention to himself. If she had left a day earlier when he'd been in Athens picking up Bjorn, he would have come back to Mykonos to find her gone.

Still pissed about that, that she had almost slipped through his fingers, he started toward her, stalking her until he had backed her up against the bed.

"What game are you playing now?" he asked.

"A game that requires only one player since you have no file for me."

Sly's nostrils flared. Bjorn had said he should use his charisma, but right now all he wanted to do was shake her and scare her into giving him a straight answer.

"I'm not afraid of you. As you said before, if you wanted me dead, I would be. So don't bother thinking you can intimidate me by glaring a hole through me. Do your worst, Sly McEwen, it won't be enough. I visit hell regularly."

He knew what kind of hell she had visited. Knew what had been required to survive. "Why didn't you tell me about the party?"

"What party?"

"Simon's birthday party."

"How do you know about that?"

Sly didn't answer. Instead, he said, "He's coming, isn't he? The Chameleon is coming to the party."

Her green eyes widened. "How do you know that?"

"You're not the only one with secrets, Evy. Should we share?"

She tried to step sideways and move past him, but Sly blocked her. "I was wrong. He does kiss you."

"It's not what you think."

"What do you care what I think?"

"I don't. You had to be close to see that."

"Close enough to know he doesn't do it often. He didn't know what to do with his hands."

Sly moved his arms around her and palmed her ass, showing her he was experienced enough to know what to do with his. Slowly he brought her against him.

"I told you never to touch me again."

"Or kiss you." He lowered his head, and, while she stood there unflinching—unflinching and unresponsive—he kissed her lips in a tender, seductive manner no one would expect from a rat fighter.

A long minute later he released her and stepped back. "You're trying too hard, Evy."

She wiped his kiss from her lips. "What is that supposed to mean?"

"Say it. Say it started out as a game on the balcony the other night, but somewhere in between the kissing and the touching, things changed."

She said nothing. Just stood there clutching her shirt to her breasts.

"Okay, have it your way, I'll say it for you. The game we played on the balcony was an excuse for both of us to put our hands and mouths on each other."

She shook her head. "Nice try, Agent McEwen, but you would say anything right now to get me to give you what you want. Even pretend you have feelings for me."

"I already know the Chameleon will be here tomorrow. Bottom line, Evy, I have no reason to be here except one. You."

She gave him a hard shove, then turned and tried to escape by diving across the bed. Sly easily grabbed one of her shapely legs and flipped her onto her back. She fought him for only a minute, then went limp.

"Sly, please don't do anything you'll regret."

He came down on the bed, straddled her body. "No regrets, no remorse. That's the motto at Onyxx. I never look back. Men like me can't afford to."

"Let me up."

"If you're going to scream, I suggest you get to it. That way the guards will be able to save you before this thing between us gets any hotter."

"You want me to scream?"

"No. But if I'm wrong, that's the only way you're going to stop what's going to happen next."

"You would be caught."

"I would be out that window before they got in here. You don't strike me as a coward. Afraid you might like me if you let yourself, Evy?"

"You flatter yourself."

Sly waited another minute, then leaned forward and brushed a lazy kiss across her parted lips. She let out a strangled cry, then closed her eyes.

"Come on," he whispered, kissing the corner of her mouth. "What's it going to be?"

"I can't want this...you."

Sly raised himself up to stare down at her. "Then you should have screamed because you're out of time."

She blinked open her eyes, must have heard the resolve in his voice. She shook her head. "No, you're out of time. Nemo, help me! Help! Someone, help!"

"Shit." Sly rolled off her and headed for one of the windows. Shoving it open, he glanced back and found she had shoved herself against the headboard, her long legs drawn up to help cover herself.

"You better go. Simon's men are instructed to shoot first and ask questions later." Then, she tipped her head back and screamed again. "Help, Nemo! He's getting away!"

The door flew open just as Sly dived out the window. When he hit the water, he went deep, kicking hard, gunfire following him all the way. He made a sharp right and swam beneath the *Ventura*, searching out the rope he'd anchored there earlier. When he found it, he followed the rope knowing it would lead him to the *Hector* three hundred yards away without having to surface.

Four minutes later he climbed aboard the *Hector*. On hearing sirens blaring, he quickly disappeared below deck. The blood on his side told him he'd been shot. It was just a flesh wound along his rib cage, but he was leaking enough to guarantee he would be stiff and sore in the morning.

Son of a bitch.

In the bathroom, he cleaned himself up, then used a wide piece of tape to stop the bleeding. That accomplished, he searched out a bottle of whiskey. Thirty minutes later he heard footsteps overhead. When he went up on deck to investigate, he was greeted by two harbor policeman.

Wearing jeans and a black T-shirt, faking a yawn, Sly said, "Is there something I can do for you?"

They explained the nature of their business.

Sly shook his head. "Sorry I can't help you. I haven't been off the boat all night. And I haven't seen a man in his twenties with a long brown ponytail and a tattoo of a raven on his left shoulder."

The fact that Eva had given the police a false description of her attacker did nothing to ease Sly's anger. He would thank her for that small favor after he strangled her.

Back in his stateroom, sprawled on his bed, he drank more whiskey, and nursed his wounded pride. Another hour passed and then the phone rang. His mood black as the sand beaches the island was known for, he let the answering machine take the call. But when he heard *her* voice, he turned slowly and stared at the machine.

"Are you there? I...I just wanted to make sure you were—"

Sly hit the speakerphone switch. "Dead or alive?"

"Where are you?"

He took a long pull off the whiskey bottle and emptied it.

"Are you all right?"

"A little late to care about that, isn't it?"

"You sound strange. Have you been drinking?"

"It's an effective painkiller. I'm about ready to start on bottle number two."

"Why do you need— You're in pain? Oh, God, were you shot?"

"Gotta go."

"Sly, wait! What can I do?"

"You've already done it."

"Where are you?"

"Like I'm as crazy as you. Not a chance."

"Where? I never meant for you to get hurt."

"Forget it."

"Sly...please tell me where you are. I need to see for myself that you're all right."

"With Simon's watchdogs following you. I don't think so."

"I need to explain. I'll come alone, or I won't come. Please."

She had given the police the wrong description. It was the only reason Sly considered giving up his location. And even then, he needed his head examined. "If you sell me out, I'll kill you."

"Where?"

"The *Hector.* A yacht three hundred yards east of you. Listen, Eva...Eva?"

What the hell was she thinking? She'd almost gotten him killed.

The obvious answer was she hadn't been thinking at all. But then whose fault was that? He shouldn't have said those things to her. He shouldn't have touched her. Kissed her.

"That's what you get," Eva chastised herself as she passed by the mirror in a flurry to get dressed, "when you allow your emotions into the game."

She knew better than that. Knew it, and still she was

going to go to him. But only to make sure he was all right. She had to. He'd been shot, and he was drinking to dull the pain.

The man was made out of steel girders. If he was drinking that meant it was serious. He could die.

She slipped into the hall wearing a black wraparound dress and flat sandals. If she was stopped, she would say that tonight's ordeal had set her nerves on edge and she was unable to sleep.

To her relief no one stopped her, and once she was off the *Ventura* and out of sight, she finally let herself believe that she'd made a clean getaway.

She was accustomed to sneaking around. She'd had years of practice. Years to perfect a number of survival techniques. Even before she'd gone to live with Simon, she'd learned at the age of twelve how to flip the switch on the electrical box so that the house alarms wouldn't go off. Then she would escape out a window to explore the neighborhood where she had lived.

Yes, she was good at sneaking around, and that's why she'd been able to meet with Dr. Fielding for a year without Simon knowing about it.

When she spotted the *Hector*, it was all she could do not to run to it. But that might draw attention to her, and so she kept the same strolling pace, as if she were truly out for a walk to enjoy the moonlight harbor after midnight.

The yacht was bigger than she thought it would be. Long and sleek, built for speed and endurance. A modern seagoing vessel, with a touch of vintage craftsmanship that guaranteed it would last and last.

She boarded without any fanfare and slipped down the stairs before someone caught sight of her. Worried about Sly, she barely noticed the clean galley or plush sitting room where a large green velvet couch curved along the wall. Her eyes drifted to the end of the hall. A door stood ajar, and she hastened her steps and pushed it open.

She scanned the room, her eyes settling on the built-in wooden berth that took up an entire wall and half of another. Sly McEwen was there, his broad back propped up against a carved headboard. There were lantern sconces on either side, above his head. He wore a nasty scowl, and held an even nastier-looking gun, leveled straight at her head.

If you sell me out, I'll kill you.

Eva leaned against the doorjamb and tried to look confident. She dismissed the gun, and sent her gaze down his bare chest to a gash that stretched along his side. It was awful-looking, a strip of wide tape across it holding it together. Moving down his body, she saw that the rest of him was intact, and she sighed in relief.

The question *how do you feel?* seemed redundant. The empty whiskey bottles beside the bed guaranteed he was in a degree of pain, but not enough to have drunk himself unconscious. His eyes appeared clear, the gun in his hand steady.

There was a bloody towel in the middle of the floor. Eva took another step into the room, said, "Did you get the bleeding stopped?"

"For now."

"I just came to make sure you were all right."

"We both know why you came, and there's more to it than that."

"That's true. I said I wanted to explain why I..."

He came off the bed smooth and easy, stalked toward her without faltering a step. She was right, he was made of steel. The wound had slowed him down only slightly.

She backed up through the door. The most important thing was to stay out of his reach. "If you need something, I can get it for you."

"I need something all right. But I'll get it myself."

She didn't like the look in his eyes. "Don't touch me," she warned, backing farther down the hall. He ignored her plea and when she reached the sitting room, she turned and headed into the galley. There she spun around, no longer willing to run.

She was up against the counter, not a good place to be, she realized. He wasn't touching her yet, but it looked like it wouldn't be long before he did.

She shivered with the thought of his hands touching her. Just one touch and it would start again. That strange bone-melting desire she couldn't explain.

On paper Sly McEwen was the too tough dangerous agent with a record for never giving up. He'd said that earlier—no regrets, no remorse. And the way he was looking at her, she was afraid he wasn't going to give up tonight, either.

She remembered how warm his lips were, and she sought them out. Stared.

He closed the distance, brought his body in alignment with hers. Eva's stomach did a slow flip in anticipation. And then she realized as his head lowered, that she had been doomed from the minute she'd stepped onto the *Hector*'s deck.

He was right. There was something between them, something that had been born that night in Atlanta.

Eva sagged against him as he took her mouth in an explosive kiss. She struggled not to lose her head, but he seemed to know what she wanted, what she needed, even if she didn't.

She felt his hand glide over her hips, his fingers pulling up the hem of her dress.

"No," she whimpered when she felt his warm fingers move slowly over her thighs. Her stomach.

His fingers were inside her underwear and slipping between her legs before she could stop him. She squirmed nonetheless, tried to dodge his fingers, but it was impossible. His thumb moved along her slit, stroking her sensitive flesh. She moaned, tried to push him away, making one last weak attempt to save herself. It didn't faze him. In one smooth maneuver, his free hand lifted her off her feet, while his fingers pushed into her.

Her cry was stifled by another scorching kiss, and then he was carrying her back into the sitting room to the couch that wrapped the wall. He sat down, cradling her on his lap.

"Sly, please," she pleaded, burying her head against his bare chest.

He sent his fingers deeper, pumped then quickly in and out. Then again in a way that told her he knew what he was doing, what would render her helpless.

Her dress was bunched at her waist, his hand deep in her panties. She was squirming on his fingers, dying of shame, dying from the desire she could no longer deny.

He was rubbing her everywhere. Rubbing everything. Touching her in ways she'd never even touched herself.

"So wet. So hot."

Eva felt a rush of sensations, the beginning of something wonderful. She bit her lip to stifle a moan. Her hips arched on their own, and then the beginning of a spasm sent her clinging to him.

"That's it." He brushed her hair away from her face, kissed her parted lips, thrusting his tongue into her in the same manner as his fingers. "It's mine," he whispered against her mouth. "Give it to me."

As if he were dragging it from her, the spasm pitched her over the edge and she rode his fingers, wanting him to stop, wanting him never to stop.

"Come for me," he coaxed, sending his skilled fingers over her sensitive nub.

Emotions rushed her senses and ignited her body, and the orgasm that followed came in waves so raw and potent that they demanded Eva cry out. And so she did.

Chapter 11

Sly slipped his fingers out of Eva's body and pulled her close, shifting her so she had no choice but to let him kiss her. He used his tongue again, possessively taking and giving at the same time, in the same manner his fingers had taken her body, and given her pleasure in return.

It was like in the dream he'd had, and he let the scent of her climax fill his head and fuel his blood.

He felt her resurfacing, felt her shoving her dress down. He ended the kiss and she sat up, avoiding his eyes. He let her go when she slid off his lap and stood, sensing she needed time to accept what had just happened.

She had told Dr. Fielding she'd had sex twice with the gardener's son. He had listened to that tape a dozen times, and all those times he had heard something in her voice, a regret and at the same time a lingering question.

I thought something was wrong with me so I did it with him again a few days later. The results were just as disappointing...with some men it's all about them. Tony was a greedy little bastard.

Knowing what he knew about Parish, it was safe to assume that she hadn't been touched the way he had touched her. And from what just happened, as hard as she'd climaxed, he'd venture a guess that she hadn't soloed much, either. If ever.

"There's a bathroom in my stateroom."

"Thank you."

She still hadn't looked at him, but he was looking at her as she left the room and disappeared down the companionway.

If she thought that was it, she was wrong. They weren't finished. Hell, they had barely gotten started. But from here on out things would slow down.

He let a few minutes tick off the clock, then followed her. Inside his room, he closed the door and leaned against it. He heard the water running, a few more minutes lagged, and then the door opened and she stepped out brushing the hair away from her face. She looked pale.

"I didn't hurt you?"

"No." She wet her lips, raised her chin. "I'd like to leave now."

"You're sure I didn't hurt you?"

"Yes. I mean, no. You didn't."

"Then what's your hurry? You said you came to explain something. We haven't gotten around to talking yet."

"It doesn't matter anymore. I was going to give you all the reasons why we couldn't..." She shrugged. "It seems my explanation comes too little, too late. It's over."

Sly shook his head. "It's not over, Evy. Not nearly over."

"You move fast, Sly McEwen. Too fast for a woman like me."

He shoved away from the door and started across the room, watching her with every step he took. "I can move slow if you like that better."

She hadn't cracked a smile since she'd arrived, but she did now. But when her eyes lowered to his crotch, the smile faded.

"You said you're not afraid of me."

"It's not fear that I'm feeling."

"Then what is it?"

"You want something from me and you think by seducing me you're going to get it. But—"

"I told you I don't need the Chameleon's location from you any longer. I already have it. He'll be here tomorrow."

"Continuing this would be a mistake."

"I think the only mistake so far was letting you off my lap." With that, Sly took three steps and pulled her against him. This time, however, when he kissed her, he didn't take. He teased her lips into joining him, into sharing the moment.

He felt her shiver, and on her breathless sigh, he slid his tongue inside, while she wrapped her arms around his waist. When she grazed the bandage, she stopped suddenly and tried to pull away.

"Easy."

"You've been shot. You need to be in bed."

"I agree. In bed with you."

"Sly, please. This is real, not some crazy dream."

The word *dream* caught him by surprise. "Explain that."

"Explain what?"

"What you just said. Have you been dreaming about me?"

"No, of course not."

"Spoken too fast, with guilty eyes. Have I been visiting you while you sleep, Evy, like you've been visiting me?"

His confession seemed to surprise her. "On the balcony at the taverna you kissed me like you had kissed me before. Like I had already given you permission. Did I give you permission in your dream?"

"Yes."

"Was it over there?" Her eyes focused on the bed in the corner.

"Yes."

"In my dream there was music playing."

"Mine, too."

"Do you have it? The music in your dream?"

"Yes."

"Put it on."

Her body had relaxed, and she was no longer looking at the door like she could bolt any second. Sly stepped away from her and walked to the built-in entertainment center and opened the cupboard. He put the music on that he used at night to relax. A favorite was an instrumental CD that was a mix of guitar and ocean waves rushing a lonely shoreline. When he turned around Eva was taking the clip from her hair and shaking it out to fall around her shoulders.

"This is a mistake. I'll tell you that up front. But I want more than the dream to remember you by. And I'm prepared to live with the consequences. But you have to promise me something first."

"What's that?"

"Simon is somewhere in the city tonight, but he'll be back in the morning to take me to breakfast. He'll be back to pick me up on the *Ventura's* deck at eight o'clock. Do you promise to wake me if I fall asleep?"

"I promise. You'll be there." Sly held out his hand.

"And so the stranger seduces the fox and she willingly lets him devour her in a single bite. Did you get yourself a copy?"

"As a matter a fact, I did."

She looked as if she didn't believe him. He pointed to the bookshelf within arm's reach of the berth. "Red spine."

She glanced at the book, her expression a little puzzled.

"Come here."

She looked at his hand stretched out to her, then walked to him slowly and clasped it, the other hand sliding up his chest. She leaned in, swayed to the music.

"Did we dance before you put me on the bed?"

"No," Sly admitted. "I don't dance."

She rubbed herself against him, then turned her back into him and brushed her sexy ass against his crotch. "When we were on the balcony I liked the way your arms felt around me. Put your arms around me, Sly McEwen, like you want to protect me from everything bad and ugly."

Her words reminded him of how she'd been forced to live, and he vowed that before this was over, he would find a way to protect her.

He wrapped his arms around her, and she countered his move by sliding her hands along his thighs. She angled her head and he lowered his to cover her open mouth. Still holding on to the kiss, she turned in his arms and pressed herself to him.

"What's next, Sly? How did the dream start?"

He scooped her up into his arms and strode to the bed. "My dream starts and ends here. You came to me while I slept."

She smiled. "So I pursued you? And I suppose I was naked."

"No. You were wearing white satin. You looked like an angel come to rescue me."

"And did I rescue you?"

"Yes, you did."

"Did we do it more than once?"

Sly smiled, laid her down on the bed. "Do it?"

"Or were we animals all night long?"

His smile spread. "Something like that."

"I like your smile."

He gave the bed his weight and rested his hands on either side of her slender waist. "Are you through talking?"

"When I'm nervous I talk."

"Nervous, not afraid?"

"No, but by the size of that stick you carry around in your jeans, maybe I should be?"

Sly laughed out loud. He hadn't done that with a woman in a long while. He stretched out beside her and pulled her close. "In my dream you liked my stick."

"Mine, too," she said, softly searching his eyes.

He kissed her nose, then her mouth again, his need for her driving him forward to the next level. She responded by caressing his bare chest, then curling her finger around his neck to pull him closer.

He deepened the kiss, his hand slipping underneath her dress to touch her satin-smooth thigh. The room turned hot as passion smoldered between them. Sly was breathing heavily and Eva was clinging to him when he pulled away and climbed off the bed. When he came back to her, he made a point of letting her see the condom he'd pulled from the dresser beside the bed. Tucking it in the bookshelf, he lay down beside her again and gathered her close once more.

She shoved him to his back, her mouth moving over his chest with featherlight kisses. When her hand again brushed over his crude bandage along his ribs, she whispered, "I'm sorry. I didn't mean for you to get hurt. I—"

"Shh…"

She sat up and untied the wrap belt and slowly slid the dress off her shoulders leaving her in a black camisole cut low enough to expose a generous amount of cleavage. She stretched out on his bed again beside him and said, "Show me how we made love, Sly. Make the dream real."

He rolled to his side, her request sending him on a mission. He lowered his head, kissed her pretty mouth, then began to touch her in all the ways he had touched her in the first dream.

Caressing her breasts, he said, "You liked me touching you."

"I do like you touching me," she confessed, arching up when he pulled her camisole aside and tasted one ripe perfect breast. Gathering the nipple into his mouth, he sucked and licked, stroked and nipped until she was shivering and moaning.

He slid lower, shoved the camisole high and kissed his way past her sexy navel. Anxious to put his mouth on her where his fingers had been, he shoved her panties past her hips. She sucked in her breath as he worked the elastic past her knees.

"In all my dreams you like it when I taste you here." With his words, he sent his thumb over her slit encouraging her to open her legs for him. He slid the thick pad of his thumb over her clit and as he did, he looked up at her.

She hadn't closed her eyes, and he liked the way she was watching him.

Sly lowered his head, ran his tongue over her. She gasped. Moaned. He urged her to open for him wider, sliding his hands beneath her ass. "This is about you, Evy. This is for you."

Then he was there, stroking and licking, and bringing her quickly to another explosive climax. She arched her back, dug her fingers into the mattress. Her body convulsing, his name on her lips as she reached for that perfect pleasure.

She was spiraling back to earth when Sly felt something wet along his side. He eased back from loving her and saw that he'd reopened his wound.

"Shit," he muttered.

"Sly?"

He pressed his hand along his side, shifted forward. "I'm sorry, baby, but my side's bleeding. Don't move. I'll be right back. Don't go anywhere."

It was perhaps the most delicious feeling Eva had ever experienced in her life—Sly McEwen's mouth adoring her flesh.

If she lived to be an old woman with a cane, she would never forget this moment in time. Sly had just shattered her reality, and doomed her for all eternity. As the saying went, you can't miss what you've never had.

But now she'd experienced the fantasy, knew it was possible to feel cherished outside of the dream. Knew why women gambled, and were willing to play life's unfair games.

This is about you. This is for you.

His words fed her like none other could. He wasn't even aware of it, but he had reached down inside her and touched her deepest secret, arresting her darkest fears. It was like he'd always known her. Had tapped into her most private desires.

Who would have thought this man could be so gentle and unselfish. A man who had spent years in prison. A man reported to be the most vicious rat fighter in the business.

Eva stretched like a cat and sat up slowly. She looked around the room, saw her dress on the floor not far from her sandals. The room was quiet. The music had stopped.

Sly was in the bathroom with the door closed.

She slid off the bed and walked to where she'd seen him retrieve the CD from the cabinet. She opened it and stared at his collection. It wasn't much of a CD collection, but he seem to have a large variety of cassette tapes.

Curious, she began to sift through the cassettes. They were labeled and dated. "C is for Closet," she read.

Suddenly her heart rate picked up and then her throat closed off making it hard to breathe.

She picked up two more, read the titles. The cassettes she realized, were copies of her sessions with Dr. Fielding.

This is about you. This is for you.

No wonder he was so in tune to what she needed. What she feared. Every secret. Every private thought.

Eva felt sick. So used and violated that it made her nauseous.

She flipped through the tapes, selected "S is for Survival and Shackles," and popped it into the recorder.

"When the game is over and the predator has caught his prey, what are you thinking about, Eva?"

She hit Stop, then Fast Forward. Stop. Play.

"I'm off to Greece again."

"Will you see your father?"

"He'll be at Simon's party."

Her knees buckled and she sank to the floor. Sly had

copies of all her private sessions with Fielding. Knew everything.

Everything…

She suddenly felt cold. Cold and so sick she covered her mouth to keep from retching.

She crawled to her dress and scooped it up along with her shoes. Slipping it on, she dismissed her underwear and slid on her shoes.

She had to get out of there before he came out of the bathroom. She scrambled to her feet and bolted for the door. Before she reached the companionway tears were stinging her eyes, making the stairs a blur. She stumbled up them, bile filling her throat.

It was all a game. Everything in her life was a game. Nothing was real. Nothing.

Not even Sly McEwen.

Chapter 12

"I've waited a long time for this day. Of course we have a deal," Holic said. "Evka has been in my thoughts since the day I laid eyes on her. She is worth any price. A few worthless lives? Certainly."

"It will be more than a few," the Chameleon assured.

"Ten, twenty. A hundred. The number is insignificant for someone who enjoys his work as much as I do."

Holic Reznik was a man who had made his mark early in life. By age twenty-five every government agency in the country had put him on their most-wanted list. Now at age forty, with hundreds of kills to his credit, he was not only a legend in his own right, but the most feared international assassin across the country.

The Chameleon smiled. "Simon assures me that Evka is more beautiful than last year."

Holic's dark eyes danced with lust. "It is hard to imagine that she could be more magnificent than the last time I saw her."

An Important Message from the Editors

Dear Reader,

Because you've chosen to read one of our fine romance novels, we'd like to say "thank you!" And, as a **special** way to thank you, we've selected <u>two more</u> of the books you love so well **plus** an exciting Mystery Gift to send you — absolutely <u>FREE</u>!

Please enjoy them with our compliments...

Pam Powers

Lift here

Peel off seal and place inside...

How to validate your Editor's
"Thank You"
FREE GIFT

1. Peel off gift seal from front cover. Place it in space provided at right. This automatically entitles you to receive 2 FREE BOOKS and a fabulous mystery gift.

2. Send back this card and you'll get 2 brand-new *Romance* novels. These books have a cover price of $5.99 or more each in the U.S. and $6.99 or more each in Canada, but they are yours to keep absolutely free.

3. There's no catch. You're under no obligation to buy anything. We charge nothing—ZERO—for your first shipment. And you don't have to make any minimum number of purchases— not even one!

4. The fact is, thousands of readers enjoy receiving their books by mail from The Reader Service. They enjoy the convenience of home delivery...they like getting the best new novels at discount prices BEFORE they're available in stores... and they love their Heart to Heart subscriber newsletter featuring author news, horoscopes, recipes, book reviews and much more!

5. We hope that after receiving your free books you'll want to remain a subscriber. But the choice is yours— to continue or cancel, any time at all! So why not take us up on our invitation, with no risk of any kind. You'll be glad you did!

GET A *Free* MYSTERY GIFT...

SURPRISE MYSTERY GIFT COULD BE YOURS **FREE** AS A SPECIAL "THANK YOU" FROM THE EDITORS

▼ DETACH AND MAIL CARD TODAY! ▼

Yes! I have placed my
Editor's "Thank You" seal in the
space provided above. Please
send me 2 free books and a
fabulous mystery gift. I
understand I am under no
obligation to purchase any
books, as explained on the
back and on the opposite page.

PLACE
FREE GIFT
SEAL
HERE

393 MDL DVFG   193 MDL DVFF

FIRST NAME	LAST NAME

ADDRESS

APT.#	CITY

STATE/PROV.	ZIP/POSTAL CODE

(PR-R-04)

Thank You!

© 2003 HARLEQUIN ENTERPRISES LTD.
® and ™ are trademarks owned by Harlequin Enterprises Ltd.

The Reader Service — Here's How It Works:

BUSINESS REPLY MAIL
FIRST-CLASS MAIL   PERMIT NO. 717-003   BUFFALO, NY

POSTAGE WILL BE PAID BY ADDRESSEE

THE READER SERVICE
3010 WALDEN AVE
PO BOX 1341
BUFFALO NY 14240-8571

NO POSTAGE
NECESSARY
IF MAILED
IN THE
UNITED STATES

If offer card is missing, write to: The Reader Service, 3010 Walden Ave., P.O. Box 1867, Buffalo, NY 14240-1867

The Chameleon handed Holic a glass of his best brandy, then raised his own glass. When Holic followed suit, he toasted, "To our alliance, and to my Evka."

"Prost!" Holic cheered in his Austrian accent. "To our mutual business, and to the most beautiful woman I have seen in years."

"I have registered you at Cupata under the name Edwin Casta, as you instructed. After midnight I will bring Evka to your unlocked room. At twelve-thirty you will enter and find her there waiting for you."

"Naked in my bed."

The Chameleon thought about arguing, but he didn't. Once their deal was made she would be Holic's property. "As you wish. Evka will be in your bed."

"Excellent." Holic set his glass on the table. "Do you have the list?"

The Chameleon reached into his pocket for the small canister. "The names are in order, with a date and location behind each one. Several months' work."

He handed over the microfilm—marked men and women who had found their way on to his kill list. All powerful people on both sides of the spectrum from government agents to underworld associates who could become potential threats to the Chameleon's self-proclaimed destiny.

Holic pocketed the canister. "Is your old enemy, Adolf Merrick, on the list?"

"I killed Merrick years ago, and though he still breathes, he is a walking corpse. I rejoice in that. It is the ultimate victory to know that your most hated enemy's suffering will never end."

"I've heard he is dying. Maybe Fate will end it for him."

The Chameleon's lip curled. He knew Merrick had been diagnosed with a brain tumor. But Adolf wouldn't die. He wouldn't dare.

His curiosity piqued, he asked, "Is there a reason you're watching him?"

"I watch everyone. Even you, my friend." Holic rarely smiled, but he did now. "That is, when I can find you. Your name is appropriate. You can vanish with the wind in a blink of an eye."

"Invisible men live long fruitful lives," the Chameleon acknowledged. "I will see you tonight at Cupata."

"Tonight," Holic agreed. Raising his glass from the table, he swallowed the brandy then left the compound balcony and headed down the trail to the hidden lagoon where he'd docked his boat. His stride was long and as confident as a panther's, his flowing black hair as shiny as a raven's wing.

The Chameleon watched Holic leave. It was done, then. Evka would soon have a new home, and he would soon be able to sleep better knowing that his enemies were about to be thinned down to a comfortable number that would be more manageable.

Again he acknowledged that patience was the key to success. In this case, patience had allowed him to exploit Holic's weakness. Smiling, his thoughts returned to the night three years ago when he had invited the assassin to one of Simon's birthday parties for one very specific reason—to introduce him to Evka. The man known to be a connoisseur of beautiful women had not been able to take his eyes off her the entire night. That's when he had known it was within his power to buy Holic Reznik, and his talent. And today he had done just that.

The Chameleon poured himself another glass of brandy, then relaxed in a chair on the balcony to enjoy the morning sunrise. He would never leave the Greek Isles, he vowed, slowly sipping the expensive brandy as his gray hair caught the morning breeze.

Yes, he thought, he was truly invisible here. Invisible and invincible for as long as he wished. And he wished it forever.

Not even God dared alter his plans. Not even God, or Fate.

Eva stood on the deck of the *Ventura* wearing a white strapless dress, matching sandals and red lipstick. It was 8:00 a.m., and she had taken great pains with her appearance to please Simon. By the look on his face she had succeeded, and she pasted a smile on her own as he came toward her.

"Happy birthday," she said.

He tipped his wide-brimmed white hat and offered her a childish grin. Then without warning, he pulled her into his arms, and again, for the second time in four years, he kissed her. Only this time he moved his lips with a concentrated effort to make the kiss more enjoyable—it appeared as if he'd been practicing since yesterday.

As he stepped back, his smile disappeared. "Nemo said there was an intruder on board last night. That he was in your room."

"Yes, but I wasn't hurt."

"I can see that you weren't. What did this man say to you? Did he tell you what he wanted?"

"He didn't say anything. I surprised him when I went below to go to bed. I think he was a thief."

"What makes you think that? Was something taken?"

"No."

"But you still think he was there to steal something?"

Eva shrugged, not wanting to be reminded of what Sly had come to steal. *I have no other reason to be here but one. You.*

"I don't know what he was there for."

"Nemo should have called me after it happened."

"He wanted to, but I told him not to disturb you. I knew you would be busy getting things ready for the party."

"That was considerate of you, but your safety means more to me than a party."

"I'm sorry."

"Next time, Nemo calls, understood?"

"All right."

"Now then—" his smile was back "—the party begins in eight hours. I thought I'd take you to breakfast, then give you a tour of our hotel before the guests start arriving and the games begin."

The word *games* sent a chill up Eva's spine. What would the evening hold? she wondered, dread seeping into her bones, as well as an anxious need to see her father.

Simon took her arm and led her off the *Ventura*. "I have rented the Hotel Cupata for my party. In the thirties and forties it was a private pleasure palace. Like so many of the buildings here on Santorini, the Cupata was partially destroyed by a volcanic eruption. Restored, it is now listed as one of the island's most beautiful tourist attractions. Some say in all of Greece. Many of the rooms have been returned to their original grandeur, but others have been left uniquely primitive as a memorial to what Cupata survived when hot lava nearly smothered the entire city of Fira. Cupata's grand ballroom is spectacular. It has cavelike petrified walls and is open to expose all four balconies on each level. Come. Breakfast awaits us at a lovely little bistro overlooking the harbor. We'll walk. It isn't far."

They left the blue bay, brimming with yachts in all shapes and sizes. The *Hector* was one of them. Eva kept her eyes averted. She would not think about Sly McEwen. For if she did, she would be forced to remember the way he had touched her, how intimately he had come to know her body, and how she had responded.

They followed the cobbled streets, and twice more, Simon kissed her.

After breakfast Simon gave Eva a grand tour of Cupata. The hotel was truly a work of art, part mansion, part mausoleum.

Simon had ended the tour by escorting her to her room after walking her through his connecting plush suite with mosaic floors and lace curtains. The room he'd chosen for her was cavelike with dome lighting and polished rust-and-purple lava floors.

Her bed was built into a stone wall, or maybe *carved* was a better word. It looked as if a master craftsman had molded the hot lava into a grotto. It looked primitive, until you lay down on the plush mattress. There was recessed lighting overhead, a pedestal-like table within reach and animal furs scattered on the floors.

Eva found the bathroom by following a lit tunnel. When she emerged from it, she was relieved to see that the bathroom was spacious and more importantly, conventional.

It was while she was still acquainting herself with her room that she heard a rap at the door, followed by Melita's voice. "I have your costume for this evening."

Eva answered the door, and Melita walked into the room wearing a short white skirt and a blue halter top. She carried a garment bag over her arm, and a small box in her hand.

"I have no idea what's inside either of these, and Simon told me I couldn't peek. He says he wants me to be as surprised as the rest of the guests when they see you descend the stairs."

For all of Simon's recent affectionate behavior over the past two days, Eva didn't hold out much hope that it would influence his plans for the evening, or what form of humiliation was inside the garment bag.

"I've got to go. I've been trying to find Nemo all day, but I haven't seen him since I had to leave the yacht early this morning. You haven't seen him, have you?"

"No, but then I left early, too."

"Maybe they found the thief from last night and he's been called down to the police station. Oh, well, I'll find him. The caterers have been delivering food all day. You should see the desserts. They're almost too pretty to eat. This is much better than last year. It actually looks like it might turn out to be a real party."

"Think so?" Eva tried not to sound too skeptical, but by the look of pity that touched Melita's eyes, she knew she had failed.

"I absolutely flipped out when all those snakes came out of that cake last year," Melita confessed. "And I'm sorry for not speaking to you the entire night, but I couldn't force myself to come near that snake. I swear Simon chose the ugliest one for you to…"

"Wear around my neck," Eva supplied.

"God, let's not talk about it. It still makes my skin crawl." She gave Eva a little hug. "Let's hope Simon's games this year are a little less hair-raising. I'll see you downstairs after five." Melita started for the door then stopped. "Don't forget to look inside the box. Simon said it was important that you wear it."

The Chameleon stood on the fourth-story balcony sipping brandy as he observed the crowded ballroom below. He was dressed all in black except for the red leather mask that covered his face depicting a long-beaked bird.

The grand ballroom was decorated with linen-covered tables and glowing candles. All the guests wore costumes, everything from depictions of animals, to fairy-tale characters, and beyond.

He checked his watch, anxious for five o'clock. He'd come early to the balcony in anticipation of seeing her before she saw him. It was a game he played with himself, seeing Evka first. She was a pleasure to watch, and he enjoyed trying to define the changes in her from year to year. She'd transformed slowly but steadily, and with each year, had become more beautiful than he had ever imagined possible. And to think, that beauty had almost been lost in the fire along with her mother.

Fate, he decided. He had never given way to letting Fate rule the day, but on that night so long ago, he was willing to concede that Fate had spared Evka.

He heard footsteps and turned quickly.

"What do you think?"

"I think you shouldn't paint your face. You know how prone to infections you are. It can take only the slightest thing," he said studying Simon's face, then his costume as a court jester, minus the hat.

The leotard emphasized his frail stick-shaped body. Half of the costume was white, the other half black. Along with half of his face being painted black, he'd colored half of his hair black as well.

"The paint is made from natural products. And see, it won't rub off." He rubbed his neck. "Not until I want it to, anyway."

The Chameleon wasn't amused. Simon looked like an idiot. He nodded just the same, willing to play along tonight because it was Simon's special day. "Where is Evka?"

The smile on Simon's face left him. "You're not taking her away before the party begins are you?"

"No. She's yours until midnight. But I am anxious to see her." The Chameleon turned his attention to the crowd gathering below, then to the ten-foot-high pedestal that rose out of the middle of the ballroom like a giant mushroom. Two men in shackles, with black hoods over their heads, stood on the stone pedestal. They wore wide belts around their waists, and there was a long relief-cable that hung from the ceiling attached to each. "I see you have a game planned for the evening."

"What is a party without entertainment? I have circus performers, too. But that—" Simon gestured to the pedestal "—will be the grand finale. A little blood sport for the wolf that lurks in all of us. What do you think?"

"I think you have again outdone yourself."

The Chameleon heard a door open and close across the balcony and he turned to see a lovely creature standing in an alcove. He knew it was her. Knew it was Evka.

"Magnificent," he muttered, totally captivated.

"Yes, isn't she?" Simon agreed.

"What is she wearing?"

"When you told me it was time for Eva to spread her wings and fly, I knew just what she needed. A pair of butterfly wings."

The Chameleon watched her come to him and felt an overwhelming rush of pride. She was his creation, and he would let no other take credit for what she had become.

He rubbed the scar on his chin and thought back to that night so long ago. The night of the fire when she had proven herself worthy of life.

"Leave us, Simon. You know the rules."

"Yes, I do. Send her down when you are finished talking to her."

As Simon walked away, the Chameleon set his glass of brandy on the railing. Sliding the red bird mask up to rest on his forehead, he waited for her to stop before him.

She wore a sheer black body stocking. Her long legs were beautiful, her breasts full, with black star-shaped pasties covering her nipples. A black thong concealed her sex, and a black leather harness curved her ribs and wrapped her shoulders to support a colorful pair of four-foot Monarch butterfly wings.

The mask covering her eyes was a smaller version of the wings. It outlined her emerald-green eyes and curved over her delicate nose, leaving her mouth exposed.

She had her mother's lips. Lush and full. Red and wet, like dew on a piece of fruit.

"You look well, daughter. Stunning, in fact. The year has served you well."

"And you, Father," she answered in her smoky voice. A voice he had come to look forward to hearing.

When she stepped forward and dutifully kissed his cheek, he made no attempt to touch her. Hands clasped behind his back he said, "Simon has outdone himself this year on your costume."

"Yes, I would have to agree. But then it's not my place to agree or disagree, is it?"

Her answer was sweet music to his ears. Four years ago she had accepted Simon as her keeper because he had wished it and demanded she comply. Tonight she would acquire a new keeper because he wished it, and he didn't doubt that she would again respect his wishes and surrender once more to his demands. Yes, Simon had taught her well.

He said, "You are the perfect daughter, Evka. No father could ask for more. Discipline will serve you well in your next life."

Eva willed her body to relax, telling herself that all her private parts were covered. When she had opened the garment bag an hour ago and looked inside at the sheer body stocking, she had wanted to cry. But she hadn't, not until she'd found the thong and black stars. Then she had wept with relief that she wouldn't be completely naked among two hundred strangers.

She studied her father, again aware of why she had loved him so much. He was a prodigious force like no other, and it was that supreme energy surrounding him that had made the little girl in her so proud to be his daughter. Seeing him again…it validated all the reasons why she had wanted so desperately to please him—for him to love her.

It was why she had offered him unconditional love, in hopes that one day she would understand why he had surrendered her to Simon and a life of pain and suffering. But she was no longer a little girl anymore. Fourteen years later, the little girl was now a woman, a woman no longer wanting to understand, but needing to.

"Is something wrong?"

Eva blinked, looked down at the crowd wondering if Sly McEwen was one of the cloaked figures. Would he be wearing a mask? Was he one of the beasts, or the knight with the sword?

"Eva?"

"No. Nothing's wrong."

"But you have something on your mind."

"Yes."

"Can I help?"

"Why didn't you want me with you?"

"Excuse me?"

"Why didn't you want me with you after Mother died? The fire was traumatic, and—"

"You needed a safe place to heal. I did what was best for you. Safest. Why ask me about this now? You've never brought it up before."

"Then it was for my safety that you left me behind?"

"I left you with a competent staff that was paid well to care for you."

"And when I was given to Simon, what purpose did that serve?"

"You were nineteen. Old enough to be on your own, and yet too naive to survive. I realized that you needed further instructions."

"So you gave me to Simon."

"Life is about survival, Evka. I instructed Simon on what was permissible, and what wasn't. He was to teach you patience and strengthen your will to survive any situation you were faced with. You have learned patience, have you not?"

"Yes, I suppose."

"And survival. Do you feel more confident this year over last?"

"Yes."

"Then Simon has done his job."

"I would have liked a friend over an eccentric teacher."

"Friends are a luxury few of us can afford. An expensive luxury if they turn on you. The fire that killed your mother was an attempt on my life by a friend."

His admission silenced her and she glanced over the railing to the white pedestal high above the crowd. "Those men, are they—"

"Part of Simon's entertainment for this evening. You know how he enjoys a good game."

She brought her eyes back to him. "Yes, I know well his love of a good game."

"Do I detect anger in your tone?"

"I admit to tiring of Simon's games."

"Then the surprise I have for you comes at an appropriate time."

"Surprise? What kind of surprise?"

He pointed to the room behind him. "Meet me there at midnight. The door will be unlocked."

"All right. Father?"

"Yes."

"Thank you for the ring."

She held her hand up to show him that she'd opened the box.

"Your mother would have wanted you to have it. Her wedding ring was important to her."

"I've been remembering things," Eva confessed.

"What kind of things?"

"How happy we used to be. You used to laugh when I was little."

"The loss of your mother killed my spirit. I find it hard to laugh. What else have you remembered?"

"Your friend coming to visit."

"What friend?"

"Adolf Merrick from the agency."

"You remember Merrick?"

"Yes. And those silly suckers, too."

"What?"

"The suckers he used to pull out of his pocket and give me."

The music had started and both Eva and the Chameleon turned to study the crowd. He said, "It sounds like the party is underway. Simon requests that you meet him downstairs."

"Aren't you coming?"

He pointed to the intimate portico overlooking the ballroom. "I've elected to watch from the crow's nest. A fitting place for a bird of prey, don't you think?"

Eva reached out and slid her father's mask back into place. "I'll meet you back here at midnight."

"Yes, midnight. Your surprise will be waiting."

The crowd quieted, and Eva knew what that meant. She'd been spotted. She started down the stairs, searching the crowd for Simon. She told herself that she only looked naked, that everything vital to her gender was covered.

She spotted Melita, and as she descended the last staircase, Simon's sister greeted her wearing a red gypsy costume covered with a dozen colorful scarves attached to her skirt, and one tied in her hair. She wore large gold hoop earrings and a belt around her waist that jingled when she walked.

She said, "You've never lacked guts, but I have to tell you, I'm more impressed than ever. You're amazing."

"And you're fully clothed," Eva replied. "I'm jealous."

She surveyed the crowd still looking for Simon. When she didn't see him, her eyes drifted to the pedestal twelve feet in the air, deciding that things could be worse—she could be on display wearing chains.

She studied the two men. Their chests had been oiled to make their muscles gleam. One wore skintight striped pants that reminded her of a zebra, while the other wore leopard print.

It was while she was comparing the two that Simon appeared and took her arm. His black-and-white bodysuit fit him like a glove, making his legs and arms look like twigs. One half of his face was black.

He leaned forward and whispered, "You make a

beautiful butterfly, sweet Eva." His red eyes glowed as he started at the top of her head and slowly examined every inch of her. Seemingly pleased with her appearance, he turned to Melita. "You are a wild vision, sister. We must dance together later."

"I accept," Melita promised. "Happy birthday, Simon."

"Thank you. Our table is over there." He motioned to a table on a platform two steps above the ballroom. "I want to introduce Eva to someone, then we'll join you."

As Melita headed for the table, Simon took Eva's hand and led her through the crowd of masked guests. He motioned to the pedestal. "I thought a little game of muscle versus muscle might excite the crowd," he said by way of explanation. "What do you think?"

"I think this is your party and you should enjoy yourself in whatever way pleases you."

He stopped and turned her to face him beneath the pedestal and that's when she saw that his fingernails were painted black. He smiled, and he flashed them as he had done so often in the past right before he announced something terrible.

"Look up, Eva."

He gestured toward the pedestal, and she looked up, her heart beginning to race as she locked eyes with the man dressed in the zebra pants. She suddenly wanted to run when she lowered her eyes to the white bandage along the man's rib cage.

Oh, God. Sly McEwen was one of the men in chains on the pedestal.

She felt her heart slam into her chest, felt a wave of dizziness threaten her knees.

"Easy, sweet Eva." Simon grasped her arm to hold her upright. "Don't be frightened. He can't hurt you.

Though I imagine he would like to slit your throat. I told him it was your idea to trap him on board the *Hector*."

Eva couldn't speak. She shook off Simon, but it didn't last long. He gripped her wrist. Squeezed.

"Simon, please…"

With a deviant smile, he said, "Underestimating me was a mistake. I must say, you've been entertaining this past year. You're wrong, however. I am capable of love. Just because I can't show you physically, doesn't mean I don't love you."

"Simon, let go, you're going to break my wrist."

"I'm smarter than you gave me credit for. Smarter than all of you."

"Simon, please. My wrist…"

He let go. "I know everything. All your secrets. Dr. Fielding shared them with me."

If Eva thought seeing Sly on the pedestal was the worst thing that could happen, Simon's next admission drained every ounce of color from her face.

Eva stared into his demon eyes, and she could see he was telling the truth. He knew about Dr. Fielding.

"I believe it was on your third visit that I discovered your deception," he said. "Did you hear the recent news? The dear doctor is no longer seeing patients. So sad to hear that she overdosed on her own medication. A troubled woman in the business of psychiatry. Hmm…an irony, don't you think?"

Eva shook her head as tears clouded her vision.

"Not to worry, sweet Eva. I did the appropriate thing. You sent flowers to her distraught husband. I thought roses were fitting. Bloodred. Two dozen. That's how many pills I made her swallow."

He'd killed Dr. Fielding. Oh, God!

"I must tell you that I have barely slept a wink this past year. What with your running off to your shrink by day, and hacking into my computer at night, I've had to increase my vitamins."

He knew about the computer, too.

"As I have heard you say often enough, you are your father's daughter, determined to endure and survive. Well, sweet Eva, I am my father's son. And what that means is that a crazy genius should never be taken for a fool. Tonight all will see that Simon Parish may look like a freak of nature, but he knows how to play the game and win."

"Simon, please."

"Shh… You know begging disgusts me. Pull yourself together. The night is young and there are more surprises to come."

Sly watched Simon Parish lead Eva toward the table on the platform where Melita sat. He glared at her bare backside, hoping she could feel his eyes on her, feel his raging anger. But if she felt anything, she never acknowledged it, or him.

This wasn't exactly how he had planned to attend the party—as part of the festivities—but he certainly had the best view in the place.

Or did he? He shot a glance to the man high in the crow's nest, suspecting that the man wearing the red bird mask was most likely the elusive Chameleon.

He surveyed the ballroom, located the exits, counted the number of guards, where they were stationed, how fast he would have to scale the stairs to reach the Chameleon to avoid being shot in the back—that is if he could get free of the chains that kept him a prisoner.

A few minutes later, he was back watching Eva wondering if she had really set him up last night. He didn't want to believe it, but it was the most logical explanation for Simon boarding the *Hector* minutes after she had run out on him.

It had been a stretch from the beginning to believe she would turn over her father for a measly file. It made more sense that she had been working with the Chameleon from day one. He didn't know what that meant exactly. Had he been the target all along then? Or was he the bait?

As the music played out, the guests took their seats at the tables surrounding the pedestal. Then the lights dimmed.

Until now, Sly had pretty much ignored the man who stood across from him. He took a moment to study him now. Taking his measure in much the same way he had dissected the ballroom. The guy must be some poor cretin who had been in the wrong place at the wrong time, he decided. The cretin's body was in shape, but not nearly as muscular as his. He wasn't nearly as broad, or as tall, and likely not as tough. Sly was determined to prove the latter the minute he got the chance.

After all, Eva was watching him and he wanted her to know just who she had betrayed. He wanted her to know what she would have to face later once he escaped the chains that kept him center stage like a trained animal waiting to perform for the crowd.

To confirm the irony of his thoughts, circus music filled the ballroom. Then a spotlight appeared overhead to showcase a man and a woman seated on a trapeze swing.

Chapter 13

The trapeze artists performed overhead while Eva fidgeted in her chair. She couldn't have thought up a worse scenario than this one. She would gladly wear a snake scarf for a week if she could bring Dr. Fielding back to life. But that wasn't possible.

Her father had been wrong about Simon. He was far more dangerous than anyone imagined.

She glanced at Sly where he stood like an oak on the pedestal. At first she had thought that Simon had kidnapped him off the *Hector*, but she didn't believe that any longer. Sly had Dr. Fielding's tapes. Simon knew about her sessions with the doctor. Did that mean Sly McEwen was working for Simon?

As hard as she tried, she couldn't envision it. But she couldn't dismiss the possibility, either.

She glanced up to the crow's nest to where her father sat. To her surprise she saw that someone had joined him. The man was broad-shouldered like her father, and wore street clothing and a mask—a sleek black panther mask that hid his entire face, but not his long black hair.

When the trapeze act was over and the pair slid down a cable to land deftly on their feet in the middle of the ballroom, the crowd applauded. Bowing at Simon, then to the crowd, they skipped off toward an exit.

The evening progressed slowly. There was an act with a lion, a juggler and a ventriloquist, and then suddenly a circle of lights surrounding the pedestal in the center of the room flashed, signaling the grand finale. The circus music ended and a drumroll announced the fun was over and something a bit more eventful was about to take place.

The crowd immediately responded with a hush.

Simon stood. "For your entertainment tonight," he said, "I give you a test of strength versus experience. The object of this game is simple. The first beast to knock the other off the pedestal wins the round. Ten rounds win the game. At that time the winner will remove his opponent's hood, then his own. There are no rules. I champion the zebra, he wears my colors."

If Eva doubted that Sly was working for Simon, she doubted no more. She sat silent now, resigned, while the guests each selected a champion to cheer for.

The pedestal lowered and two men dressed as pirates entered the ballroom. One of the pirates carried two eight-foot-long poles, the other a simple ring of keys. The one with the keys leaped onto the pedestal and stripped the shackles off Sly's wrists and ankles, then off the other man's. The second pirate then tossed each man a pole. As the pedestal began to rise, the pirate with the keys leaped off.

Once the pedestal stopped high above the crowd, colorful disco lights built into the lava walls began to flash; at the same time, music started up again. Only this time the music was loud, with a wild techno beat.

Eva had no idea what the poles would be used for until Sly immediately used his to support his weight as he kicked out and sent the man in the leopard pants flying off the pedestal.

The relief-cable attached to the wide belt around the man's waist sent him sailing out over the crowd. The crowd went wild. The man spun and flipped, then swung back to the pedestal.

A blonde dressed in purple stood on a smaller pedestal in the distance. She held a large score card which she raised. The zebra had won round one.

Sly stalked the man, his stick poised. But this time the leopard was prepared, and when Sly swung his pole, the leopard spun away, then struck with his stick, cracking it across Sly's back, knocking him off the pedestal.

As he flew over the cheering crowd, the blonde in purple held up the score card. Round two had gone to the leopard.

The guests who championed Sly shouted at him to tear the leopard's head off. The woman in purple put another win on his side when he ducked a blow, and used his fist to send his opponent into the air.

Eva watched while Sly won the next round, and the next. It looked like he would continue to win until the leopard jabbed his pole into Sly's injured side, and sent him swinging out over the crowd, passing her where she sat frozen in her chair.

When he returned to the pedestal, the bandage at his side was stained red—evidence that his gunshot wound from the night before had been ripped open.

Like an animal who had picked up the scent of blood, the leopard stalked Sly with more confidence. Using the pole, he tormented the wound twice more, both times successfully knocking Sly off the pedestal and into the air. Blood was flowing freely now, and the sight of it seeping into his waistband and down his muscular thigh seemed to fuel the crowd's need for more of the same. They began to call out for more, and the very idea made Eva look away.

Simon leaned close and said, "You will watch him bleed, sweet Eva. I will not ask again."

Forced to keep her eyes trained on the men exchanging vicious blows, she felt sick. The leopard was merciless now, driving the pole into Sly's side over and over again.

She wanted it to end, prayed that someone would stop it. She thought about pleading with her father to end the madness. To beg Simon for mercy. But she knew her father wouldn't interfere, just like she knew Simon wasn't capable of showing mercy.

The leopard was winning eight rounds to six when Sly knocked him off his feet. The man sprawled onto his back and appeared momentarily dazed.

The music stopped.

The crowd quieted.

Sly straddled his opponent and raised his fist.

"That fist can kill a man. You don't want to kill me, do you, McEwen?"

The words froze Sly's fist in midair, the familiar voice a solid punch to his own gut. "Merrick?"

"Christ, you can fight."

"Why are you here?"

"A couple of Parish's men picked me up in Athens when I got off the plane."

"Where's Bjorn?"

"Bjorn? I don't know. I haven't seen him since he took off for Montana with Jacy Madox."

"What are you doing here? Why aren't you in D.C. where you're supposed to be?"

"You didn't call. I thought you would call. That's why I gave you my private number."

The crowd was chanting, *Kill him, kill him*. They had become a bloodthirsty pack of wolves, Sly thought. He searched out Simon and saw that he'd come to his feet. To keep him from becoming suspicious, he sent his fist into Merrick's jaw with half his strength. "I should kill you, Merrick," he growled. "You set me up. Set us all up."

"Not intentionally," his commander admitted, spitting blood.

"Bullshit," Sly snarled.

"Don't go crazy on me now, McEwen. I have a damn good reason for what I did."

"I know about your reason," Sly said, driving another punch into Merrick's jaw.

Merrick spit more blood. "We get out of this alive and catch the Chameleon, there'll be a bonus in it for you."

This time Sly drove his fist into Merrick's gut. "I don't work for you anymore."

"Sure you do. I tore up your resignation."

"You son of a bitch." Sly got to his feet, dragging Merrick along with him. He threw a right, then a left.

Suddenly, Merrick swore, then stepped back and kicked Sly in the crotch. The blow bent him over, and Merrick followed through with an uppercut.

Sly swore, swung at Merrick and missed. "I figured it out," he snarled. This time when he swung, he clipped Merrick on the shoulder and the older man staggered. Before he toppled off the pedestal, Sly reached out and hauled his commander back.

Black hood to black hood, he said, "I had Bjorn pull

your file. I know everything. I know about your wife. Why you want the Chameleon's ass so badly."

"Then help me, McEwen. Help me catch him."

The raw emotion in his commander's voice gave Sly pause, then he said, "He's here. My guess is the Chameleon's the beak in the crow's nest."

When Merrick turned to search out the crow's nest, Sly drove his fist into his boss's abdomen doubling him over. "That's for ripping the hell out of my side." He grabbed Merrick by the belt and pulled him back, then drove his knee into his groin. "And that's for not staying in D.C. until Bjorn came to get you."

"What the hell are you talking about?" Merrick demanded, sucking air as he tried to fight the low blow.

"I'm going to kill you," Sly said, driving another right into Merrick's jaw, "so stay the hell down this time."

When he let go, Merrick dropped to his knees, then onto his back. Sly reached for one of the wooden poles that lay on the floor and broke it in two pieces. Dropping to his knees, he laid one of the shortened sticks across Merrick's windpipe. With one solid snap, he broke the stick a second time, making it look like he'd crushed the leopard's windpipe.

The crowd gasped, then went still again.

Sly muttered, "If you want to make it out of here alive, stay dead." Then he yanked off Merrick's hood.

As his commander's head fell heavy onto the floor, he glanced up to the crow's nest. The bird man was now on his feet, his fists clenched at his sides. Sly expected as much, but not what happened next.

A wild cry escaped the Chameleon, then he yelled, "Merrick! Don't you dare die! I'm not finished with you!"

Sly felt Merrick tense. He laid a hand on his

commander's chest. "Don't move. It's him, and he's on his feet. He doesn't look happy that you're dead. Why do you suppose that is?"

Suddenly the pedestal began to lower. Sly scanned the room, saw one of the pirates weaving his way through the crowd toward them. He stood, pulled his own hood from his head. The pedestal stopped, and the pirate got on, then it began to rise again.

This pirate was taller than the other two, and when Sly saw the knife sheathed at his hip, he decided that the man had been sent to kill him.

Or maybe not. The sheathed knife that rode the man's hip wasn't familiar, but the man's sudden wicked smile was.

"You're damn lucky I saw Merrick get picked up in Athens, Sly, or I would have flown back to D.C. for nothing." Bjorn looked down at Merrick. "He's playing possum, I hope."

"He is. Pull that knife and let's get the hell out of here," Sly demanded.

Bjorn unsheathed the six-inch blade and when the crowd saw it, they gasped anew. He slashed through the belt at Sly's waist, saying, "I still haven't been to bed yet. You're going to owe me big for this so don't get yourself killed." Then he dropped to his knees and freed Merrick. Giving him a hand up, he said to his commander, "You look like shit, sir."

Sly grabbed one of the cables and swung himself off the pedestal and dropped down onto the ballroom floor. The guests had all gotten to their feet, dazed, they watched him as he charged toward the platform, upending tables as he went.

Simon had dragged Eva to her feet and was trying to escape with her in tow. She was fighting him, and Simon stopped long enough to slap her hard, then continued to drag her along with him. She renewed her fight, finally twisting free. Simon spun around, tried to stop her, but Eva dodged him and started to run.

Determined to cut her off, Sly ran toward her, but when she saw him, she changed directions. He had decided he wasn't leaving without her, and he knocked tables aside as if they were cardboard as he ran her down. Racing past her, he reached out and tossed her over his shoulder.

Simon screamed for his men to stop the zebra and three armed guards rushed forward.

Smoke was filling the air, and Sly realized that the candles on the turned-over tables had lit the linens on fire. Guests were now running for the exits, shoving and pushing to escape the mayhem.

A familiar sharp whistle had Sly spinning around to see Bjorn still on the pedestal. He was pointing upward to the cabled ropes that had been used in the trapeze act. Reading his partner's mind, he started back to the pedestal, dodging stampeding guests, aware that Merrick was racing toward the stairs trying to stop the Chameleon from escaping.

As he neared the pedestal, Bjorn swung a cable toward him. He grabbed it, slid Eva off his shoulder, then said, "We're going up. Climb or ride. Which is it going to be?"

She glanced around, saw Simon's men bearing down on them, then grabbed the cable and began to climb. He followed her up, but only after he plowed his fist into two of Simon's men, and sent the other one flying through the air to land in the middle of a table.

She was just reaching the trapeze swing when he joined her at the top. He helped her onto the swing, then said, "Get rid of the wings."

She didn't make a move to unbuckle the harness

that wrapped her rib cage. Irritated, he was about to rip the damn thing off her, when he saw her knuckles were white gripping the swing. He said, "If you're afraid of heights, I don't want to know about it until later. Just do what I say. Those wings are heavier than they look. Get rid of them."

She took one hand off the swing and slowly un-buckled the harness. A minute later the wings fell to the ballroom floor.

When they were gone, her hand back gripping the swing, Sly pointed to the fourth-floor balcony. "We're headed over there."

She let go of the rope on the swing just long enough to pull the mask from her face and let it drop, too. Eye-ing the distance to the balcony, then the distance back to the floor, she said, "How are you going to get us from here to there?"

Sly was still holding on to the cable that had brought them up to the swing. "I'll come for you."

"You'll come for me?" She raised an eyebrow. "You're joking right?"

"Do I look like I'm in a joking mood?"

"No. You look like you want to kill me. I never con-spired with Simon to trap you on the *Hector*."

"She says, now that I have her life in the palm of my hand."

"I'm telling the truth."

"Do you know what that is?"

"Do you? I found Dr. Fielding's tapes in your room. 'This is about you. This is for you,'" she singsonged. "You used those tapes to deceive me."

She was right. He had used the tapes to get close to her, but this wasn't the time to discuss that now. He said, "Get ready." Then he let go of the swing, and sent the lower half of his body out and away from the cable, swiftly pumping his legs to start the cable swinging.

He would need to get enough momentum going to carry them both forty feet. Moving as fast as he could, he pumped hard and began to swing himself past Eva toward the balcony. Six passes had him almost there. On number nine, he yelled for her to jump, and she answered his demand without the slightest hesitation.

Sly winced as she slammed into his body, but he instinctively locked his arm around her, ignoring the pain in his side as they sailed toward the balcony.

Timing would be everything. If they were off a second they would end up short, and dead.

Seconds before they reached the balcony, Sly let go of the cable and they sailed over it. The speed carried them several feet before dropping them. He rolled with Eva over and over, the force slamming them into a wall. He heard her cry out, and he rolled off her as quick as he could and stood.

When she sat up, he asked, "Are you hurt?"

She got to her feet. "Of course I'm hurt. I just slammed into a wall and had two hundred pounds drop on me."

"Two-twenty," Sly corrected.

She rubbed her lower back. "Why didn't you warn me the landing was going to rupture my spleen?"

He motioned to the ballroom where Simon's guests were still climbing over each other in a panic to reach the exits. "That's a sixty-foot drop. If you're hurting that means we made it and you're alive. Seems to me you should be thanking me instead of bitching me out."

Sly heard a noise behind them and turned to see the man in the panther mask who had shared the crow's nest with the Chameleon step out into the hall from behind one of the hotel rooms and close the door behind him.

Sly pulled Eva against him, and took a step back, wishing he had a weapon of some kind.

The panther said, "Free the woman and I'll let you walk away, McEwen."

The voice was distinct, and Sly recognized it right away. "You're a long ways from home, Reznik. What brings you this far south?"

"I'm here picking up something I've recently acquired." He motioned to the room behind him. "Thank you for bringing her to my door." Suddenly he pulled a smooth black piece of metal from his pocket, and with one quick maneuver a five-inch blade shot out from the end.

Sly squeezed Eva and asked, "Do you want to go with him, Evy? Is he another one of your secrets?"

She hesitated only a second before shaking her head. "No, I don't want to go with him."

Holic Reznik slid the panther mask off and tossed it over the railing. "Sure you do, Evka. I'm a friend of your father's. You remember, we met a few years ago at a similar party."

She never answered. Instead Sly felt her press her body tightly to him. "I don't want to go with him, Sly," she said softly. "Please don't give me to him."

Her voice was rife with fear. Sly said, "I guess you didn't make as good an impression at that party as you thought, Reznik."

"It makes no difference. A deal was made. Promises exchanged. I always keep my promises. Especially when money and women are involved. And of course...killing."

There was an explosion below and it shook the hotel's foundation. Suddenly Bjorn was sailing toward them on a cable. "This place is on its way down, Sly. Let's get the hell out of here. Parish is waving sticks of dynamite around like they're party favors."

He caught the railing with his feet and balanced there as he tossed Sly a second cable. Sly grabbed it, then lifted Eva against him. When he glanced back, he saw Bjorn had locked eyes with Reznik.

"Shit. There's no time for this, Bjorn. You just said this place will be ashes in a matter of minutes."

"There's always time for revenge," Bjorn said, then let go of his cable and leaped to the balcony floor. "Isn't that right, Reznik?"

"Dammit, Bjorn," Sly swore, "not now."

"Yes, now."

"Where's Merrick?" Sly asked.

"Chasing the Chameleon. You go on. I'll catch up."

Another explosion sent the crystal chandelier crashing to the ballroom floor.

"We go together," Sly insisted. "Now!"

Not taking his eyes off his hated enemy, Bjorn shook his head. "I can't do that, and you know why. I'll be along shortly. We'll meet up later."

Another explosion sent several large chunks of the ceiling falling onto the balcony. Eva screamed and buried her face against Sly's chest.

"Dammit, Bjorn, come on!"

"Get going, Sly. Take our Eva, and go."

The balcony groaned, and Sly felt the floor shift beneath his feet.

"Sly!" Eva cried out, and looked up at him.

He swore, yelled at Bjorn to come on, then lifted off with Eva clinging to him just as another explosion sent the balcony supports groaning and shaking.

Spurred into action, Holic Reznik started toward the stairs on the run. Bjorn lunged for him and his momentum carried them both down the steps, end-over-end to the third-floor landing.

The last Sly saw was Bjorn on top of the assassin

giving him an education with his fists when the stairway gave way as chunks of lava let loose from the ceiling and sent all in its wake crashing to the ballroom floor.

Eva clung to Sly as he swung them onto a precarious ledge along the ballroom's cavelike wall and let go of the cable. Her mind was reeling, dumbstruck by Holic Reznik's words.

She had wanted to call him a liar to his face, but she couldn't. Not after he'd stepped out of the exact room where her father had told her she was to meet him at midnight.

Discipline will serve you well in your next life. I have a surprise for you, Evka.

Thank you for bringing her to my door. A deal was made. Promises exchanged.

"Eva? Did you hear me?"

She blinked, felt Sly's body press into her as they shared the same small ledge. "What?"

"I said, we're going to have to climb down from here."

She glanced past him, over the narrow ledge. They were at least thirty feet from the ballroom floor. A floor that was hardly visible for the smoke. An alarm had gone off and she could hear sirens.

She shook her head. "We can't go down there."

"I'll go first. All you have to do is follow me. Take the same route. There are hand and footholds. Use them. If they hold me, they'll hold you."

"And if they don't hold you?"

"Trust me. I'll get you out of here."

"Why would you, Sly? Who do you work for? Who's paying you?"

"We'll talk about this later."

"If you're working for Merrick you would have gone after my father. But you came after me instead. Why? Are you hoping to use me as bait?"

"No."

"Simon told me he killed Dr. Fielding. Did you help him?"

"What?"

"You have the tapes. Are you working for Simon?"

"That lunatic? Not hardly."

"He knows everything. He knows I hacked into his computer…knows I called Merrick."

"Come on. Let's get out of here."

The smell of smoke made her lungs burn. Again Eva sent her gaze back to the ballroom. Hungry flames were devouring everything in sight. A wave of dizziness made her sway and she closed her eyes. Her temples throbbed and she knew what that meant.

She felt Sly's fingers bite into her arm. "What the hell's wrong?"

She blinked open her eyes, her body suddenly cold. She started to shake. "I don't know, but I can't go down there. We have to go up. Not down."

"Listen to me." He gripped her chin. "I'll get us out of here, but you're going to have to do what I tell you."

She shook him off. "No!"

"Eva."

She searched out a handhold above her head and started to climb up the wall.

"Dammit, Eva!"

"Come on, Papa. This way. Up the stairs, Papa. Hurry!"

Chapter 14

Sly didn't believe they were being followed, but he kept an eye out as he sailed the *Hector* up the coast. His mind was working double-time. Something had happened to Eva back at Cupata. She'd looked into the flames and seen something. She'd called him Papa, and then everything had fallen apart. She'd been so irrational that he'd been forced to knock her unconscious to get her out of there alive.

From listening to the tapes he knew that the fire she'd lived through had been traumatic on more than one level. Her mother had died as a result, but more had happened later that same night. She'd said she had fallen down the stairs. Had she? Or had someone pushed her?

She claimed she had heard more than one voice that night, her father's and another man's. That meant someone else was in the house. Tonight, while looking into the flames, had she identified the voice, or finally allowed herself to see his face?

I still believe you're suppressing something from your childhood. Something painful that wants to surface. But you're fighting it, and the headaches are a result.

She'd complained about her head hurting once they were on the *Hector* and she'd come to enough to know where she was and whose bed she was in. He'd set sail soon after that, and he'd checked on her twice since. The second time he'd found the sheer black bodysuit on the floor and her beneath his bedsheet.

He intended to drop anchor when he found a satisfactory hiding place. He was dead on his feet, and he needed some sleep as well.

The word *sleep* turned his thoughts to Bjorn. He had no idea if his friend was dead or alive. He wanted to believe he was alive, but the collapse of the stairway, and the sight of Bjorn and Reznik being buried beneath the rubble, left little hope that either had survived.

Still, Bjorn had spent seven years in the trenches. He'd been shot a number of times, lived through cobra venom in his veins, and damn near being buried alive in an avalanche in the Swiss Alps.

The man was as good at cheating death as he was.

That's why he refused to sell Bjorn short, and would proceed as they always did when a member of the team had gotten separated. He would follow the rules, and in a few days, he hoped, he would get a phone call from Bjorn telling him he was alive.

Damn the Chameleon, he thought. Damn Holic Reznik and Simon Parish, too. And damn Merrick for not leveling with him weeks ago.

He kept on a steady course for another hour and blamed his exhaustion for almost passing the small uninhabited island before he noticed it. He circled back, checked it out, then guided the *Hector* into a maze of sea caverns and dropped anchor.

The cove was quiet, the beach a desolate stretch of sugar sand. And beyond that, the remains of an ancient monastery clinging to the face of a rocky bluff. The one thing Greece had plenty of was monasteries.

Sly went below and checked on Eva again, then returned to the deck and stretched out on the seat that curved the stern, his thoughts going over the night's events. More than once he'd questioned his actions. From the beginning his mission had been to find the Chameleon, learn his identity, then kill him for Sully. He'd had the opportunity tonight to do just that, but instead of going after the enemy, he'd gone after Eva.

If he could believe her, then Simon had lied and had set them both up last night. He wanted to believe that. To believe that she had left him only after finding the tapes. If that was what had happened, then… Then he had no reason to be angry with her.

He had shied away from emotional nooses all his life, but lately he felt as if he was choking from the inside out. And as strong as he was, as disciplined as he was, tonight the facts had spoken for themselves—he hadn't been thinking about the Chameleon when Bjorn had cut him loose. All his focus had been on Eva, and getting her away from Simon.

Sly gave in to his exhaustion, and as he drifted off to sleep he was aware that his entire body ached—for an old guy, Merrick could still throw one helluva punch.

Eva continued to munch on the apple as she watched Sly McEwen sleep. She'd awakened a short time ago to the smell of smoke and had sat up quickly only to realize that she had been dreaming about the fire in Atlanta the night her mother had died.

She'd glanced around, recognizing her surroundings

immediately. The memories of the last time she had been there swamping her emotionally. She had buried her face in Sly's pillow after that, then wished she hadn't, aware that the scent of bay rum made her feel worse.

Her migraine was gone, that was the good news, and she was grateful for that until she had recalled what had happened at Cupata and why she had no memory of how she'd gotten on the *Hector*—Sly had punched her in the jaw and knocked her out.

In the bathroom mirror she'd verified the fact, noting that her jaw was slightly swollen and tender. She had also taken inventory of her appearance and realized that she couldn't go anywhere wearing just a black thong and black star pasties over her nipples.

That had spurred her into raiding Sly's closet. She'd intended to settle for one of his shirts when she stumbled on a small stack of women's clothing: a feminine-looking moss-green shawl in a bottom drawer, along with a black bikini, a pink tank top, a green-and-pink pastel skirt and pink sandals.

She had helped herself to the black bikini, then tied the green shawl around her hips. On her way through the galley, she'd snagged an apple before climbing the stairs.

Eva finished the apple while she slowly sent her eyes over Sly once more. He was still wearing the zebra pants that outlined every muscle on his body, but he'd put a fresh bandage over his bruised side.

Before her brain turned to mush and she started feeling sorry for him, she gently touched her sore jaw. Then she raised her arm and drilled the apple core at Sly's head.

The core smacked him in the forehead and he jerked awake and sat up quickly. Blinking her into focus, he spied the apple core on the deck, reached for it and tossed it overboard.

"You got something against a man taking a nap?"

"I want you to turn around and take me back. I should never have left Santorini with you."

He stared at her, one eyebrow lifting. He rubbed his unshaven jaw, then stood and stretched carefully, wincing as he ran his hands over his black-and-blue chest and abdomen.

"Did you hear me?"

"I heard," he said. "Do you remember what happened at Cupata."

"You slugged me in the jaw. That's what happened."

"I didn't slug you. I skillfully tapped you."

"That was a tap?"

"What did you see when you looked into the fire?"

"Nothing."

"Bullshit."

"I need to speak to my father."

"To ask him if he really did sell you to Holic Reznik?"

"He didn't sell me."

"Reznik said a deal was made. Promises exchanged."

"He could have lied," she offered, knowing she was reaching for something that wasn't there.

"Holic Reznik is a lot of things, but not a liar. If he says you're part of a package deal, then you are. Why is it so hard for you to believe? You've been living with a sadistic freak for four years, compliments of your father. I believe your words were, my father took me with him to a party. It was at Boxwood Estate. Fielding asked you what happened at Simon's party. You answered, if I told you you wouldn't believe me. And if you did, I would have to kill you. What happened that night?"

Eva stiffened. "Did you memorize everything on those damn tapes?"

"What happened that night?"

"That's none of your business." It was as if he could read her thoughts, as if he knew. She looked past him, out over the water. "That night I was introduced to the games. I didn't play, but I…"

"Watched."

"Yes, I watched."

She heard him swear, and she faced him. "It doesn't matter what happened in the past. I survived so one day I would understand. That's what this is all about, under-standing why it all happened. I want to know why my mother had to die. Why my father became someone I didn't recognize after her death. He loved me before that night. It couldn't have all been a lie. I won't believe that. He loved me once. I'll play whatever game I must to learn the truth."

"You think the truth will set you free, is that it?"

"Yes."

"You're wrong. It won't."

"It will. It has to. My father will set me free. I'll get the words out of my mouth this time. I'll make him tell me why it all happened."

"He's long gone from Santorini."

"You don't know that." Again, she glanced around, wondering how easy it would be to escape Sly McEwen and return to Santorini. If there was someone else on the island then maybe… A boat somewhere.

"The answer is no. Escape is going to be damn hard, unless you plan to kill me. The other part of that silent question is also no. We're alone. This island is uninhabited."

"And how long do you plan to stay here?"

"A few days."

"If you're waiting for your friend to contact you, he won't. We watched him die with Reznik."

She saw his jaw clench. He obviously didn't want to believe that.

"Headache gone?"

"Yes."

"Good. We have unfinished business."

The look he gave her sent her body on red alert. An image formed behind her eyes of Sly between her legs, his mouth *there*. She shook her head, forced the image from her mind.

"Your silent question is yes. I want to be there, but not just my mouth." He stepped forward and reached for her, encircled her waist and dragged her against him.

"No."

Eva tried to wiggle free, but he slid his hand over her backside.

"I hate you," she insisted, shoving at his chest.

"You would have given me up to Simon if that was true. You had good reason to. I had the tapes, you felt I'd violated your trust."

She stopped fighting, looked up. "You believe me? You believe I didn't turn you over to Simon?"

"Make me believe you."

As easily as if she weighed nothing, he lifted her off her feet to cradle her against him. She could smell him, feel him, hear his heart. He moved his hips, slid her along his length. She let out a sigh, almost fell under his spell. Almost.

"I can't do this. I won't do this."

"I'll make it good for you."

"No. No!"

"He came quick. I didn't. He was a greedy little bastard. I give you my word, I won't be."

That he could recite passages from the tapes embarrassed her as well as made her angry. She renewed her fight, shoving hard against his chest. Turning her face away, she said, "I don't want you... there."

He released her. "I don't believe you."

His arrogance forced her to look at him. "I don't care what you believe, I won't let you take anything more from me, Sly McEwen. You know too much. I won't let you know my body, too. I won't let you take one more thing from me."

The words were barely out of Eva's mouth and he had her back in his arms, his mouth covering hers, proving to her that he was strong enough to take anything he wanted from her. Anything and everything.

Sly saw her hand raise out of the corner of his eye the second he released her lips. He took a step back, grabbed her wrist before she could strike him.

She tried to escape, but there was no breaking free of his iron grip. He knew that fact registered when he saw fear darken her eyes.

He let her go. "Take it easy. There's nowhere to run. No reason to. I'm not going to force myself on you."

He expected his words to make a difference. Expected that she would turn around and go below. But she tossed him a curve and bolted past him instead. Thrown off guard, she was already past him by the time he reached for her. He came away with no more than the soft green shawl she'd tied around her waist.

He roared in anger as she slipped through his fingers and dived into the water. He tossed the shawl to the deck and followed after her. His anger immediately turned to concern when he popped up and she was nowhere in sight. He dived again. Circled the *Hector*. Surfaced.

The moonlight cast a glow over the calm surface and he could see a long distance. Nothing moved.

Once more he dived, this time going deep, trying to read Eva's thoughts. She knew she couldn't outswim him, so she would try to outsmart him.

He spent the next fifteen minutes diving and resurfacing, and cussing himself for coming on to her too damn hard and fast.

His concern was replaced by cold fear as more minutes ticked by. What if she had tried to swim out to sea instead of into shore? What if at that very minute she was out there somewhere struggling in the deep? The thought refortified his efforts, and he called out to her. Dived, then resurfaced breathing hard, his heart hammering. He called to her again, then again.

He was about to dive another time when he glanced toward shore and saw her standing with her back to him, squeezing the water out of her hair. His first thought was that she was alive. His second was that he was going to kill her for scaring the living hell out of him.

He swam beneath the water toward shore, anxious to get his hands around her neck. She must have heard him as he surfaced, because suddenly she was running toward the rocky trail that led to the shadowy ruins of the monastery.

She was barefoot, half naked. Like an animal on the hunt, Sly started after her, his powerful legs eating up the distance between them. She glanced back once and saw that he'd shortened the distance between them by half. She screamed, turned away from the path, making a wide arch around him as she started back to the water.

It was the mistake that would ultimately get her caught.

Sly changed directions in a flash and cut her off,

tackling her three feet from the water's edge. He made sure he was on top straddling her when they stopped rolling.

"No! Let me go."

She tried to fight him, but he easily pinned her arms. "Dammit, Eva, stop it."

"You stop it," she cried out. "Stop it!".

He understood what she was saying. They had been on the same wavelength since he'd opened his eyes and saw her sitting there on deck watching him.

He shook his head. "I can't stop it, and you know why. What's between us isn't going to go away. Not any time soon. Running from me isn't going to put out the fire, Evy."

"There's no fire. Nothing between us!"

"We'll see."

"No! No, we won't."

"You want me to walk away, is that it? And then what?"

When she didn't answer, Sly released her hands and started to get off her.

She made a desperate noise in the back of her throat. Sly hesitated, stared down at her. Then, quietly, slowly, he slid back, flattening out to bring their lower bodies into alignment.

The contact drove a moan from her. She arched her hips. He angled his head and covered her mouth with his. When he felt her body relax, he kneed her legs open, then settled himself there as he deepened the kiss.

Her heart was hammering against his chest. He raised himself up, locking eyes with her. He unhooked the clasp between her breasts. Sweeping the bikini out of his way, he fastened his gaze on her beautiful breasts. Her nipples were still covered with the black star pasties. He removed one of the stars, sent his lips over the rosy nipple. Once, twice. On the third pass, she released a desperate moan of sheer pleasure.

The other star gone, he laved her second nipple until the areola turned dark red with arousal.

She was smooth as satin, and he loved touching her, tasting her. She arched beneath his mouth, her hands wrapped around his back and tugged at the waistband of his pants.

He rolled off her, shoved the tight zebra pants down his hips and past his thighs. Naked, all he could think about was settling back between her legs when she sat up.

"Stay there."

Sly stretched out on the sand, watching her come to her knees. The sight of her beautiful bare breasts in the moonlight sent more blood into his phallus. He reached out to touch her but she brushed his hand away.

"In your dream I was in your bed on the *Hector*. You never asked me about mine. We're on a sandy beach like this one."

She slid one of her legs across his hips to straddle him.

He groaned low in his throat.

"Am I hurting you? Your side?"

"No…"

She leaned over him. "Then you like me here?"

"I like you," Sly agreed.

"Did I put my mouth on you in your dream? On…*it*?"

He didn't feel like lying to her, but he was reluctant to admit she had.

"If you say no—"

"Yes."

"In my dream your hands were here." She took his

arms and pushed them level with his head. "Pretend you're helpless. That you're staked out and you can't move."

The idea was ridiculous and he was tempted to laugh.

He could reverse their positions in a heartbeat. But why would he? Her soft lips were moving down his chest now, and her beautiful breasts were rubbing over his belly. She shifted, slid herself farther down his body.

He groaned, felt her cup his sac and squeeze gently. He thought about moving then, about rolling her onto her back and driving into her.

He felt the heat of her mouth, then the wet of her tongue graze the tip of him. He knew she was going to go down on him. Felt her sweet mouth cover his mass.

He didn't move. Couldn't.

She had truly rendered him helpless.

She had the power to make him moan and lose control. The realization was as arousing as touching him, and she wondered if that was normal. If other women enjoyed a man *there* as much as she enjoyed tasting and touching Sly McEwen.

Eva couldn't explain what she had become. All she knew was that she wanted this time with him. She was almost twenty-four years old and she had never experienced anything like this feeling.

She refused to analyze what that meant. He had shaken her to the core when he'd put his mouth on her, and ever since she had been wondering if it was possible to do the same to him.

And now she knew it was.

She looked up and sent her gaze over his flat hard stomach, past his corded chest and over his square jaw. His eyes were closed, his breathing rapid. She sat back on her knees and looked him over, her lips wet from loving him.

He was beautifully put together, almost too beautiful. All male and very big. Her eyes locked on his thick penis and it reminded her suddenly of the *Hector*. Architecturally, Sly McEwen was a masterpiece, long and sturdy, built for endurance, with a silent guarantee that he would last and last, and…last.

"Are you wondering what to do with it now that I'm unable to move? Or was that the idea? You plan to sail off and leave me here to suffer?"

"Suffer?"

His eyes were now open and he was scowling at her. "I'm ready to burst. I believe *suffering* is the correct word?"

She glanced down at him…*it,* fascinated when she saw a pearl of moisture glistening on the tip of him. She leaned forward and sent her tongue over the tip, then sampled him with a bit more relish. She sat back, looked again. Watched. Waited.

Everything got bigger and harder.

His breathing had changed. His scowl was deeper.

Eva sent her tongue over the length of him again, licked, then covered him and found a rhythm.

He had done this to her days ago, and the memory of it still burned inside her. She would give him what he had given her, and she wouldn't stop until…

Like a sleeping giant, Sly suddenly sat up, reached for her and pulled her on top of him. One handed, he stripped the black bikini bottoms off her, then set her astride him.

Locking eyes with her, he said, "Normally I'd let you finish that, but I want to be inside you. Now."

It was in that moment that Eva understood how much it had cost him to lie there so still. She felt him pulsing hard against her and a moment of doubt darkened her eyes.

Again, as if he could read her mind, he said, "Don't lose faith, Evy. We'll fit."

Her heart started to pound, then suddenly a warning sounded in her ear like a sixth sense. *Don't do it. You'll never be free of him if you let him inside you.*

The warning evoked a sudden, very real fear. Eva tried to move away from him to give herself time to think, but he moved with her, sliding himself more intimately against her, parting her slightly.

She shuddered, shook her head, fighting the emotions that now seemed to cling to every move he made and every response her body willingly offered in return.

"Sly, wait." She felt his hot flesh start to push into her.

He didn't seem to hear, or if he did, he didn't care.

"Relax your hips."

"Sly, no. I—"

"Come forward." When she didn't comply, he gripped her hips and slid her forward. The movement opened her, allowed him to slip into her tight sheath.

"Sly, please...stop."

"Relax your hips. Here, this will help. Let me..." Suddenly he was moving, rolling her beneath him and at the same time driving himself completely into her. Eva writhed beneath him, thrashed, but it didn't seem to alter anything but her torment.

She cried out as his massive cock sank deeper, stretching her beyond pleasure, making her fit *it*. Making her fit him.

You'll never be free of him if you let him inside.

She wanted him to stop before it was too late. Knew it was already too late.

He was making her fit him, making her want to fit him.

The pain was subsiding, leaving in its wake the beginning sensations of pleasure. And with the pleasure came an unexpected tenderness in his voice as he coaxed her hips into a rhythm, and his hands moved over her curves with loving adoration.

He was concerned with how he was making her feel, and it was that unselfish concern that was going to kill her, she decided. Not today, but later, once he was gone. And he would go; she wasn't fool enough to believe this could ever last.

The wanting, or maybe a better word now was, *craving,* continued to grow. It built on each wave of motion as he slid in and out of her over and over again, the pleasure now so deeply felt that it threatened to steal her breath. Her sanity.

"Wrap your legs around my waist. That's it," he whispered against her lips as he bucked his hips against her pelvis, tripling the sensations between her thighs.

Eva managed a strangled moan. It hung in the night air, a long languid note of desire that had Sly picking up the pace. His powerful body carried her with him toward some certainty that was bound to change who she was forever.

"That's it," he encouraged next to her ear, his hands sliding under her ass to steady her now as the pulsing beat went through her again and again.

She felt herself open more, accept more, need more. She arched up seeking an end to it. Sly responded with a guttural groan. Then she felt it, the agony suddenly turned sweet, and she gasped in reaction to the liquid heat that poured into her.

Several minutes passed before she blinked open her eyes. Sly was staring down at her, saying something about sleep.

She tried to move but he was still buried inside her

hot and pulsing. She felt weak, her body replete, her senses scrambled.

His lips brushed hers, his hands in her hair gently stroking. Her legs were still wrapped around him and she relaxed her hips, let her legs fall away from him. The musky scent of sex mingling with the smell of the sea and bay rum.

Always the bay rum, she thought. She would never be free of it. Not ever. Not now.

So this was the magic women sacrificed everything for—the heaven and hell they chose over survival.

This was what it felt like to love a man.

Chapter 15

The Chameleon boarded the *Ventura* the minute it had pulled alongside the *Pearl*. He had spent hours on the move, sailing a diversionary course in case he was being followed. When he was sure it was safe, he had instructed his captain to double back and run down Simon's yacht.

Standing on the main deck, he ignored the screams. Simon had gone too far, and there was only one way to vent his anger. Someone had to be punished.

"Again!" he insisted. "I want to see blood this time."

The guard nodded, then let the whip fly. The loud crack it made when it bit into Nemo's flesh split his broad back open. Tied to a wooden pole, the guard's body jerked and he cried out in agony.

"Stop it!" Melita screamed.

"Take her away," the Chameleon insisted.

"You're killing him. Stop, please!"

"That's my intent, Melita. Do you and Simon think

I am stupid? You let a guard put his hands on you." His eyes found Simon. "And you, how dare you defy me? How dare you think you can manipulate me. My children, my children…have I taught you nothing?"

"Father, please," Melita begged, tears streaming down her face. She still wore the gypsy costume, her hair wild around her. "I'll do anything you say. I promise. Just please don't kill him."

"You will do whatever I say regardless." He waved her off, nodded to the guard. "Take her below. Lock her in her room." He stared at his daughter in disgust. "As punishment you'll be sent to one of the monasteries. You will live within its walls until I've forgiven you. If that doesn't happen, you had better hope I can find a use for you, other than selling you to someone as a whore."

"Father, please. It's not Melita you're angry with," Simon interjected, "it's me."

The Chameleon turned his attention to his son. "You disappoint me, Simon. All that I have done for you, and this is how you repay me. You disrespect me. Humiliate me in front of a ballroom full of guests. This day you have treated me as an enemy. Betrayed your father."

"Not betrayed. I only—"

"Yes, betrayed. I have sheltered your worthless white ass since the day you were born. I have spent a fortune keeping you alive. And for what? To be disrespected in the end?"

Simon dropped to his knees. "I'm sorry, Father. Very sorry."

"Yes, you will be very sorry. You will remember this day always and be very sorry."

"I should have told you about Eva's activities sooner. Her trips to the psychiatrist over the year. Her phone call to Adolf Merrick. I intended to explain everything the day we met on the *Pearl*. I truly did, Father. But then you announced that you were taking her away from me and… She was a present. You don't take back presents, Father."

"I can take back whatever I wish, Simon. Whatever I wish. You should have come to me months ago when Evka first began to stray. You were given specific rules to follow. Rules you deliberately disobeyed."

"And now I must pay. But not Melita, Father. Be angry with me, not my sister. Don't punish her and Nemo because I didn't play by the rules. Send Melita away if you must, but don't kill Nemo. He is a loyal friend, father. I beg you, spare my friend."

"The greatest lesson is often the most painful. The lesson here is that my rules are nonnegotiable. They have never been, and never will be. Selfish actions carry a high price. Betrayal is unforgivable, and today, Simon, the price for your betrayal will be Nemo's life."

"No!" Melita tried to twist free from the guard, but he lifted her into his arms and carried her toward the stairs that led below deck.

"Get on with it," the Chameleon told the guard. "Whip him to death and make sure my son watches him breathe his last breath. Then throw the body overboard." To Simon, he said, "I'll expect you at the compound in Paros in two days. Bring your sister with you. Someone will be there to escort her to her new home. Be prepared to share all the data you have ferreted on Onyxx, Adolf Merrick, Evka and this agent, Sly McEwen. You say he took Evka with him when he escaped Cupata?"

"Yes."

"Do you think he intends to draw me into a trap using her as bait?"

"It's possible, but…"

"But what?"

"But I don't think that's the only reason he took her. He's interested in her for another reason."

"Another reason?"

"Sly McEwen and Eva… When I captured him last night, it was because I followed her to his yacht."

"Are you saying they are lovers?"

"I don't know when it happened."

The Chameleon swore, his anger turning into rage. "You are a fool, Simon. A stupid fool!" He nodded to the guard. "Give my son the whip. It is time for him to start cleaning up his own messes. Go on, Simon, before the sun comes up and your delicate skin starts to fry."

The guard handed the whip to Simon.

"Take it," the Chameleon demanded.

Simon shook his head. "No, Father. Don't make me kill my friend. Don't make me, please."

"You killed him months ago, Simon, when you decided to take matters into your own hands. You know the rules."

Eva felt something brush the side of her face and she struggled to sit up. An arm draped over her chest made it impossible.

"It's just me."

Sly's voice was rusty and whisper close.

She shoved his arm aside and sat up. The sun was an orange ball on the horizon, and she realized then that she'd spent the entire night naked on the beach in Sly's arms.

"You hungry? I'm hungry," he said.

His words were close again. He'd sat up, too. She didn't turn around. Looking at him would bring everything back. She didn't want to remember. Wasn't able to forget.

Self-conscious of her nakedness in the morning

light, she looked around for the black bikini. The top was within reach. The bottoms weren't.

She could feel his eyes on her, watching her every move. The problem was she wasn't moving.

His hand touched her back as he leaned forward and attempted to kiss her shoulder. She shrugged him off. Heard him swear.

"No remorse. No regrets. That's the way I live. You ought to try it, Evy."

When he got to his feet, she glanced up at him, angry that he had zeroed in so quickly on her thoughts once more. It was true, she was having regrets, but not for the reason he thought. Telling him how she felt, however, would serve no purpose. It would only make her look like an even bigger fool. Still she was angry, and didn't think she should have to take all the blame for what had happened.

He didn't seem to give a damn that he was naked, or aroused. She concentrated on slipping her top on and tucking her breasts into the cups. On her feet, she dusted the sand from her butt, retrieved the bottoms and quickly put them on.

Feeling marginally better, she tossed her hair away from her face and said, "You need to clean out your ears, McEwen."

"What?"

"See, you can't hear worth a damn."

"What does that mean?"

"It means I asked you to stop last night."

"Bullshit. You didn't want me to stop. You came. I felt it. Heard it."

Eva turned her face away. It was true she had climaxed, but before that, if he had been listening...

"You wanted me," he said quietly. Resolute.

Yes, she had wanted him up until the time she had

realized why—that she had feelings for him. Real feelings. Then she had been too afraid to want him. Only she hadn't tried hard enough to get away or he would have let her go. He had already told her he wouldn't force her.

Did that mean the blame was squarely on her shoulders?

Eva went into survival mode. "You're right. I wanted you last night. I wanted to know what it would be like to do it with a man, not a greedy young boy."

She saw something flash in his eyes, but as quickly as it came, it was gone. He glanced around, gestured to the ruins behind them. "That's all that's here. You want to go exploring, be my guest. The closest island is Paros eight miles away. Unless you can swim that far you're here with me until I decide to leave. I worked up an appetite last night. Breakfast will be ready in twenty minutes."

"Sly, come back here. Sly! See, your hearing sucks!" she shouted when he turned away and started back to the *Hector*.

"Oh, I don't know. I didn't have any trouble hearing you moaning last night."

When the water reached his thighs, he dived into the sea. The last Eva saw, before he disappeared into the depths, was his beautiful naked backside in the morning sun.

"Eva. Are you up here? Evy!"

Sly climbed the last step and entered what once had been the monastery's tower. When he saw Eva standing near the window looking out over the sea, relief swept over him.

The day was clear, and the sun's rays outlined her body, giving her hair a golden glow. She wore the pink tank and a matching pink-and-green skirt that had come with the *Hector* at the time he'd bought the yacht. He had thought once about tossing the clothes out, good thing he hadn't gotten around to it.

The skirt, like the top, hugged her body. They weren't meant for a woman with curves, and he decided that when they reached Paros, for his sake as well as hers, he needed to buy her some clothes that fit. Something that didn't make him think of sex every time he looked at her.

He leaned against the wall, his torso bare, his jeans hugging his hips. "You've been gone a long time."

She turned and glared at him. "You said I could go exploring. Are we leaving?"

"No."

"Then go away."

"You need to eat something. You haven't had anything all day."

"I'm not hungry."

"It's midafternoon." Sly was determined to get to the bottom of what was bothering her. She hadn't come back to the *Hector* all morning, and then when she had, she'd taken the clothes and left without so much as a peep.

They needed to talk about her father. He was sure she had information he could use if only she'd share it. That wasn't going to happen, however, until he broke through the wall she had erected around herself since waking up on the beach in his arms.

She had given him the excuse that she'd asked him to stop last night, but that was crap.

"About last night. I—"

"I don't want to talk about it."

"I've given you all the time I'm going to, half the damn day to work through whatever it is that's bothering you. Since you look stuck, I've come to help."

She tossed her head, raised her chin. "I don't need your help, Sly. All I need is to get off this island and away from you."

"If I forced you last night, I—"

"You didn't force me. We agreed I wanted you, remember?"

"And what about now? Do you want me now?"

"What?"

"Answer the question. Do you want me now?"

"No."

Sly shoved away from the wall and started toward her. "You answered pretty quick, but your heart wasn't in it."

She backed away, shook her head. "What are you doing?"

"Playing a hunch."

"What does that mean?"

He kept coming and she kept moving. There was a partial wall that jutted three feet into the room. If she kept moving away from him, she would eventually run into it. He kept tracking her, and she kept moving.

She was going to trap herself if she wasn't careful. If she didn't want that to happen, she would be forced to stop moving, or make a countermove. The only way out of the tower was past him.

She glanced at the door. He guessed she was telling him the truth about needing to get away from him. But the question was, why was the need so strong?

She surged forward, her intention to bolt past him to reach the stairs. She'd done something similar last night on the *Hector,* only today he was ready. When she was almost past him, he reached out, snagged her around her waist and lifted her off her feet.

"No!"

She swung at his head. He ducked, let her fists

bounce off his shoulders as she tried to force him to re-
lease her. In a matter of seconds, he had her pinned
against the stone wall.

"Let go, damn you," she shouted, slamming her fist
into his chest.

He let her hit him, let her have her moment, and
when she ran out of steam, he said, "We're going to do
it again. And this time, I'm going to listen more carefully. But I'm willing to bet I'm going to hear pretty
much the same thing I heard last night."

"No!"

"You're not going to tell me to stop, Evy. You're not
because what's going on between us goes deeper than
just sex."

"You're crazy!"

"Maybe. Maybe I have it all wrong. We're going to
find out. Right here. Now."

"No. I don't need you! You're wrong."

"Prove it."

"I'm not weak. I can survive without feeling."

"Simon's little protégé," he taunted.

She slapped him.

He slapped her back, not hard, but hard enough to
let her know he was through taking her abuse. "It's too
late, Evy. Like it or not, there's a whole lot of feeling
and needing going on between us."

He shoved her skirt up, and pulled her panties down.
Unzipped his jeans. He was fully aroused, and he
braced her back against the wall.

"Tell me no."

When she said nothing he spread her legs wide and
pushed into her hard and fast. She cried out from his
sudden invasion, and it was then that he realized he
should have given her more time, time to say no. Time
to tell him what she was really feeling.

"Dammit!" He slid back and started to pull out of her.

"Wait...."

Suddenly she was clinging to him, pulling him forward and wrapping her long legs around his waist to prevent him from sliding out of her.

Kissing him, she whispered, "Don't leave me, Sly. Make love with me. You're right, it's too late. Much too late."

"I was going after the Chameleon before you came into the picture," he told her, as he flipped the fish fillets onto two plates, then brought them to the table in the galley where Eva sat waiting for him.

The sun had set an hour ago, they both had their clothes back on, and the tower in the old monastery had once again been left to the birds.

Before Sly sat, he poured Eva a glass of wine, then popped the top on a beer for himself. Sitting across from her, he said, "Bread, cheese and grilled fish. It could be worse."

"It smells delicious. I'm starving."

"You should have eaten something this morning."

"I wasn't hungry this morning."

Sly forked a piece of fish into his mouth, watching her as she cut into the fish with delicate manners. When she slid a piece of fish off her fork and into her mouth, she closed her eyes and chewed slowly. Moaning a little as she swallowed.

He grinned. "That good, huh?"

"Heavenly." She opened her eyes. "Simon is a vegetarian. There is no meat allowed in any of his homes. While I'm in Greece, he lets me order fish occasionally at a café, but only when he's feeling generous. As you know, that's not very often. Sometimes I dream about juicy hamburgers and fried chicken," she confessed.

Sly studied her from across the table. She had suffered on every level of her life, and he suddenly wanted to change that for her. He said, "When we get to Paros we'll find a place that serves hamburgers. How's that?"

She stopped chewing and set down her fork. "I would be careful if I were you. If you treat me too well, you might not be able to get rid of me when it's time."

She was looking at him again the way she had after they had made love in the tower. It was a puzzled kind of look, as if she wanted to ask him something, but wasn't sure how to go about it.

"Do you have a plan?" she asked.

He was munching on a piece of cheese. "A plan?"

"You know, what's your next move going to be? I know you're waiting for some word from your friend, but after you don't hear from him, then what?"

Sly scowled. "You don't know Bjorn. Don't sell him short. I've left two messages. One for Merrick and one for Bjorn, neither have responded. But there's still time. I'll try again later tonight."

"And if there's nothing?"

"Then I'll try again in the morning. If I haven't heard something by noon, we'll sail to Paros and buy you some clothes that fit."

"We could sail away tonight like vagabonds. Just you and me. We could disappear."

Her suggestion surprised him. "And you could do that? Disappear? Last night you told me you needed to understand why your mother died, and your father stopped loving you."

"I know what I said. But, maybe… You said it wouldn't set me free, so maybe—"

"Maybe I was wrong."

She leaned back and studied him while she sipped her wine. Finally, she said, "Sly McEwen wrong? Hmm…I was just starting to trust you, and now you say you're wrong."

"I said maybe. I think maybe you need to see this through."

"I think the truth is you need to see this through, and you need me to make that happen."

He reached for his beer, took a swallow, then finished his fish. Shoving his plate aside, he said, "If Merrick or Bjorn don't call, we're going after—"

"I'm not going to help you kill my father."

"Your loyalty amazes me. He doesn't deserve it."

"I know that."

"Tell me what you were hoping to find in your father's file."

She set down her wineglass, then touched her napkin to her lips. "After my mother died my father turned into a man I didn't recognize. He had no time for me. I wanted desperately to fix whatever it was that had driven him away from me, but he left me in Atlanta with Helen and Lida without looking back."

"The minions," Sly supplied, remembering how she had described them to Dr. Fielding.

She picked up on the word and frowned. "Do you have to keep doing that? Reciting every damn word on those damn tapes?"

"Sorry. You were saying?"

"I got to see him once a year, and I used to get so excited. So excited I couldn't eat or sleep for days. It was the same year after year. When I was nineteen, he came to take me to Simon's party. We had never gone out together, and I thought maybe he'd finally decided to take time for me. We walked into Boxwood and I saw all these people wearing costumes. I wasn't introduced to any of them. My father led me down a hall and out a back door to the pavilion. He told me to sit and wait for him to come back. A little while later he returned with Simon."

She stood and turned her back to him. Feeling she needed the distance to get out what she wanted to say, Sly remained quiet.

"I had never seen an albino before. Simon was dressed in a red suit and black cape. He looked like a vampire with his white skin and red eyes." She turned to face him. "My father asked Simon what he thought of his birthday present, and that's when I knew his love for me had died along with my mother the night of the fire. He told me I had things to learn, and that Simon was going to teach them to me. He said I was to learn patience, discipline and survival. After all, you are your father's daughter, he said. Then, he said, living isn't for the weak of body and mind. Those who master the game, master their own fate. Make your father proud. That was all, then he left. You can't know what it felt like when he walked away from me and never looked back."

Sly worked hard to control the overwhelming urge to reach for her. He had thought his stepfather had been the lowest scum on the earth, but the Chameleon had LeRoy beat hands down.

"I had no idea that Simon couldn't... That he'd been castrated. A few months after his party he became ill. An infection attacked his delicate immune system. He spent several days in the hospital, and when he came home, he was quarantined in his bedroom. One night, he asked for me and I went to his room and found him lying naked on a cotton sheet. I saw what had been done to him, and...and I was shocked, but mostly I was re-lieved. Since I had come to live at Boxwood I had worried day and night that part of my lessons would be Simon violating me. After that night, I settled into my new life. I played Simon's games, learned the lessons and vowed to survive all of them, so one day, when my father was ready to tell me why he had thrown me away, I would be alive to hear it. But then…"

"Then?"

"Then a year ago I started to have the dreams. Or maybe I should call them nightmares. I kept seeing my mother lying on the floor while the fire came closer, and I could hear the voices. I decided to see Dr. Fielding. Her office was close to the pharmacy and health store. I devised a plan to go there when I had to pick up Simon's vitamins and oddities. When I became comfortable with the doctor, I let her hypnotize me. It never really worked on me. Except that it gave me recurring headaches."

"What about the voices?"

She returned to her chair. "One of the voices is my father's, but I still don't recognize the other one."

"A man's voice, or a woman's voice?"

"It's a man's voice."

"So you hear him, but can't see him?"

"In the dream his head is turned. I can see that his hair is dark like my father's, with gray temples."

"Where is your mother when you hear the voices?"

"She's lying in the TV room dead."

"How do you know she's dead?"

"I can see her. She's on her side by the couch. She's not moving. The couch is on fire."

"So she was killed before the fire started." It wasn't a question. Sly's mind was sifting through the pieces, trying to fit them into the puzzle. "Where were you when your mother was killed?"

"I don't know." She closed her eyes. "I was upstairs.

After supper my mother always spent an hour with me before bedtime. We were sitting together in the TV room downstairs and I remembered a picture I had drawn in school. I went to get it and when I started back downstairs I smelled the smoke. I stopped halfway down."

"Because of the smoke?"

"Yes…no. Because my father was screaming at the other man."

She started to rub her temples.

"Headache?"

"The start of one."

"Don't try to force it."

"The smoke is coming up the stairs and I'm worried about Mother. She's just lying there and Father is crying and yelling at the man. The man's laughing. No, maybe my father's laughing. No, he wouldn't be laughing. I don't know. The smoke is burning my throat and I'm scared."

She shoved the plate of food aside and laid her head on the table.

Sly reached out and stroked her hair. "That's enough. Don't try to remember any more."

"It always stops there," she muttered. "My head starts to hurt and I smell the smoke, and then nothing."

"Forget it for now. We're done talking. You're going to make yourself sick if you don't think about something else for a while."

He left her at the table, urging her to eat some more while he cleaned up the galley. She joined him a short time later, and he was glad to see that her plate was empty when she brought it to the sink.

She helped him finish the last of the cleanup, then excused herself and went into the bathroom. While she was gone, he stepped into the utility room under the stairs to turn on his computer and check his message board. Seeing that neither Merrick nor Bjorn had responded, he sent a second coded message, then went into the sitting room to wait for Eva.

He was seated on the couch, resting his head on a plump pillow that curved his neck, when he heard the music. Eyes closed, he blinked them open. Eva stood in the doorway barefoot, a look of indecision on her face.

He said, "Come here."

"I thought you said we were through talking?"

"We are."

"There's a guest bedroom and bathroom in the bow. I went exploring before dinner."

"If you think you're going to sleep in there tonight you're wrong."

She smiled, walked toward him, stopping a few feet away. "I'm not tired. You?"

"No."

"What should we do?"

His eyes traveled the length of her thinking of a couple dozen things he would like to do with her.

"If you want me, Sly, unzip your jeans."

Sly couldn't remember a time when he hadn't wanted her. Even when he'd wanted to strangle her, he had wanted her. It was something he'd come to accept even before they had met, when her smoky voice had turned his nights into a playground of hot fantasies and heavy breathing. He unsnapped his jeans and slid the zipper down. Waited. Watched as her hands moved down her hips and her fingers caught the fabric of her skirt along her thighs. Slowly she began to slide the skirt upward until he could see that she had removed her panties. He let the air out of his lungs along with a moan, his eyes fastening on the cinnamon curls forming a narrow V between her thighs.

"You do know how to get a man's blood pumping, Evy."

"Am I going too fast?"

For an answer, he reached for her and she let him lift her astride his hips. A little shifting, and she was there, guiding him into her moist heat while she looked him in the eyes.

Slowly she leaned forward and kissed him using her tongue.

He took the kiss. Gave one back just as wet.

When she settled around him on his lap, he arched his hips and moved deeper. It clearly told her that fast or slow, he was up to playing whatever game she had in mind.

"This afternoon, in the tower," she whispered, "I was afraid you wouldn't come looking for me, and then when you did, I..."

"Shh..."

"I don't want to need anyone, Sly. Needing is dangerous." She kissed him again, then leaned her forehead against his as she slid forward, then rocked back, working him slowly in and out of her.

He settled his hands on her hips. "Get rid of the top," he said, then watched as she slid the tight pink tank upward along her rib cage and off over her head.

Her beautiful breasts spilled forward, filling his vision. He leaned forward to rub his cheek over the sweet fullness of her. He loved the smell of her, and the taste. He captured a ripe nipple and suckled it, savoring her and the sound of her sighs of pleasure. He gave the other nipple the same attention, and on a moan, she arched her back and began to move on him with more urgency.

The music became distant, their rapid breathing finding a companionable rhythm with their bodies. He slid his hands under her skirt and cupped her butt, encouraging her to move faster.

"That's it," he groaned, then he closed his eyes and let her take him on a ride that filled him up and drained him at the same time.

They made love on the floor and against the wall in the companionway before they found the bed. At midnight, he woke her and loved her again.

She snuggled against him after that, and just before she drifted off to sleep, she whispered again, *"We could sail away like vagabonds."*

Chapter 16

Eva woke to the sound of the *Hector's* engine turning over. She sat up, then slipped out of bed. She found one of Sly's shirts in the closet and pulled it on, then went looking for her underwear.

She had just found them when the door opened and Sly stepped into the room. Feeling self-conscious, she had no idea why—he had seen her naked more than dressed over the past twenty-four hours—she said, "I hope you don't mind if I borrow one of your shirts."

His eyes drifted over the white shirt, then to the black thong in her hand. "You're not going to need either this morning."

Eva angled her head and studied him. His hair was wet, and he wore a pair of black diving pants.

"And why would that be?"

"I found a coral reef I want to show you. We'll suit up and take the tanks down."

"What's the matter, tired of sharing your air?"

His smile was generous. It was perhaps the most relaxed smile he had ever offered her. He crossed the room and snagged her around the waist and lifted her off her feet. Pulling her against him, he kissed her, then said, "Mornin', Evy."

"Good morning…Slayton."

He arched a black eyebrow. "Where did that come from?"

She shrugged, ran her fingers through his short black hair. "You're wet."

"That's a fact. You sleep all right?"

"You know I slept like a slug. I didn't even know you had gotten up until I rolled over and…"

"And what?"

He was searching her eyes. She'd hoped he would want to make love to her again. Maybe they wouldn't get out of bed until noon.

She asked, "Any messages?"

"No."

"I heard the engine start up."

"Just turning it over. Making sure everything is working all right. Come on. Let's take a swim."

They explored the coral reef together, and Eva vowed she would remember this day forever. She loved the underworld, the marine life and the mystery of the deep, but today it was twice as enjoyable seeing it with Sly. At times she found herself more enchanted and distracted watching him, and marveling at how powerful and graceful he was in the water.

His diving equipment was high-tech, and his knowledge seemed endless. He had given her a crash course in the science of diving, essential equipment, and let her drive one of his aqua gliders. She had been surprised to know that he had two on board, that she'd had the means to escape him all along.

But today she had no wish to escape him. The past two days had been the happiest of her life, and she hated to think of it ending. Yet she knew it would. Must.

She prayed for one more day. One more day to discover all that she had been missing over the years.

It was strange, but at times she felt like an innocent just discovering what it felt like to be a real human being, to feel like a real woman.

It was late morning when they surfaced. While Sly stowed the equipment, she went to take a shower. She had just left the bathroom with a towel wrapped around her when Sly entered. She looked up, prepared to flash him and knew immediately that something was wrong.

"What is it?"

He walked past her and retrieved a pair of jeans and a gray T-shirt from a drawer beneath the berth. With his back to her he said, "A message came in."

He stripped and dressed quickly while she stood frozen in the middle of the room, knowing this was what he'd been waiting for, knowing that her prayer for one more day wasn't going to happen. He was on his way to the door, when she reached out and touched his arm. It was enough to at least stop him. He turned around and finally looked at her. Really looked.

"What?"

His voice was anxious. She shook her head. "Nothing."

"Get dressed, Eva. I want to set sail as soon as possible."

Eva. Not Evy. She dropped her hand, sensing the change in him already. His beautiful blue eyes were now distant, and she knew why. He was again Sly McEwen, a man on a mission—one of Onyxx's elite— and she was the Chameleon's daughter. The woman who stood between him and the success of his mission.

She raised her chin, went into survival mode. Forced a smile. "Who made contact?"

"Merrick. He's in Paros at a place called Christos. He wants to meet."

Christos was a dockside bar with rooms to rent upstairs by the hour or the week, or any combination in between if you had the money. Sly entered the seedy taverna with Eva on his arm, wishing he'd taken the time to buy her some decent clothes first. Or better yet, a nun's robe. The men covering the barstools were a crusty lot. Some were fishermen, but most appeared to be independents looking for a piece of action, or a piece of ass.

Sly was in no mood for a confrontation. He wished he could have trusted Eva enough to leave her on the *Hector*, but then trusting her hadn't been the only reason he had elected to take her with him. He'd spied the *Ventura* in port. That meant Simon Parish was also in Paros. A coincidence? He didn't believe in them.

He nodded to a waiter as he steered Eva toward a table along a back wall. As she moved ahead of him, he could feel the men at the bar shift to watch her.

It wasn't her fault she had a beautiful body, or that the clothes she wore fit a little too well. But dammit, a little less attention would have suited him better.

He put her in the chair that wouldn't allow anyone but him to ogle her cleavage, then took the seat next to her.

"Are we going to eat? I'm hungry," she said.

"We're not going to be here that long." He flagged a waiter, and when he arrived, Sly said, "The lady will have a glass of wine. What do you have?"

"Lagaria."

Sly eyed the waiter who was tapping his foot to the

disco music and grinning at Eva. He shifted, brought his-leg a bit forward from beneath the table and covered the waiter's sandaled foot with his boot. The waiter's grin died as he sucked in his breath.

Sly said, "Lagaria, then, and for me a *mia bira.*"

"Right away," the waiter said, then quickly hobbled away the minute Sly removed his boot from his foot.

"Wine? My stomach is empty and you order me wine?"

Sly narrowed his eyes. He knew she hadn't appreciated his ill mood since Merrick's message had arrived. As a result, she had countered his mood with one of her own, picking a fight with him every chance she got since they'd left the cove.

He wanted to explain to her why he was feeling the way he was, but he didn't know how to tell her the news. It wasn't good news, and he'd been looking for the right time to tell her, knowing damn well there was no right time.

"When is Merrick going to get here? I'm hungry. If you weren't going to feed me you should have at least let me fix something on the *Hector.* If you remember, I suggested it, but you—"

"Enough, Eva. I don't like Merrick's taste in bars any more than you do."

A different waiter brought them the Lagari and beer.

As Sly scanned the dingy room, he noted a table of five men playing cards. They had been there awhile. Beer bottles littered the table, and they were laughing and enjoying the game, and...watching Eva. He worked on the beer, tried to keep himself relaxed. Eva leaned back in her chair, and his eyes went straight to her chest.

"Do you have to do that?" He grumbled.

"Do what?" She followed his gaze. Attempted to adjust the top.

It made things worse by Sly's estimation. "That helped a lot."

"You didn't seem to mind how little it covered last night," she reminded. "You know, Slayton, if I wasn't sure you didn't own a jealous bone, I'd say that you were letting yourself get worked up over nothing. Those men over there are just being men."

Before he could tell her she was right, that he didn't own a jealous bone, just a permanent hard-on where she was concerned, he saw Merrick enter the bar.

He had to look twice to be sure, but it was Merrick all right underneath a beat-up hat and ragged clothes he must have stolen off a drunk.

He crossed the room and headed for the stairway. Sly, watched him disappear, then flagged the waiter who had taken their drink order. The man slowly limped back to the table, a wary look on his face.

"I'd like a room," Sly said.

"A room…upstairs?"

"That's right. How much?"

The waiter glanced down at the floor, then took a step back. "Twenty dollars an hour."

Sly pulled two twenties and laid then on the table, and in return the waiter pulled a key from his pocket, handed it to Sly, then curled his fingers around the money. "Anything else, *amerikano*?"

"That'll do."

When the waiter left, Eva said, "Why do we need a room? I thought we weren't staying here long?"

"We're not, but I need you out of the way while I speak to Merrick."

"Out of the way? Why can't I go with you?"

"Because you can't," he said, not wanting to get into it. He finished his beer, then stood. "Come on."

They climbed the stairs. Sly glanced at the number

on the key, stopped in front of room eight and unlocked the door. Ushering Eva inside, he noted that the room wasn't clean, but it was better than he had expected.

"You're leaving me here?" She turned around, then around again. "You're kidding, right?"

"It's just for an hour."

"You paid him forty dollars, That's two hours."

"It's not going to take that long. Come on, just take a seat, and I'll be back as quick as I can. Maybe Merrick brought the file on your father."

That brought her turning quickly to face him.

"Do you think so?"

He didn't. He had only mentioned it hoping it would be enough to keep her in the room anxiously awaiting his return. He warned, "Don't leave the room, especially dressed like that. Those men downstairs aren't used to hearing the word *no*. Lock the door when I leave. I'll keep the key and let myself in. I'll be back as quick as I can."

He waited outside the door until he heard her lock up, then walked down the hall to number eleven. He tried the door and found it unlocked. He pulled a knife, then slipped inside the dark room. Closing the door behind him, he stood with his back to it ready for anything unexpected that might come his way.

A small light came on, and he saw Adolf Merrick seated at a small wooden desk. "They call this the executive suite," he said. "You weren't followed, were you?"

"No."

"I hoped you'd be able to decipher my code. Find this place and the room. Left the same message for Bjorn, but I haven't heard from him."

"He was taking Holic Reznik apart at Cupata when one of the balconies collapsed. I don't know if he made it," Sly admitted, sliding his knife into the sheath at the small of his back.

Merrick pulled off his hat. "Where have you been?"

"Laying low, trying to get a message to you and Bjorn. You?"

"On the *Ventura*. I missed the Chameleon. He got away on a yacht named the *Pearl*."

"And for two days you've been on the *Ventura*?"

"Yes, I have. I kept myself out of sight. You beat the hell out of me pretty good. Took me a day to get my strength back."

"In your message you said you watched Simon Parish beat a guard to death. You sure the guard was Nemo?"

"It was. The *Ventura* left Santorini thirty minutes after the *Pearl*. When I saw Simon and his sister, Melita, board, I slipped over the side and hid. The yacht set sail and didn't stop until just before dawn. I understood why when I saw the *Pearl*. They were having a little rendezvous at sea. By the way, the Chameleon *is* Paavo Creon. I watched him board the *Ventura*. Parish and his sister met him on the upper deck where I was hiding in an air vent. I couldn't hear what was said. I was too far away."

Merrick uncorked the bottle of whiskey and motioned to the sofa. "Sit down, McEwen. A drink?"

"No, thanks. So Simon and his sister work for the Chameleon."

"That's what it looks like."

Sly took a seat. "You set me up. All of us weeks ago."

Merrick rubbed the back of his neck. "I had started to give up hope of ever finding the Chameleon. The Agency suspected Paavo Creon after they investigated the fire at his home. It was all hush-hush, but there was an evaluation, and a possible explanation—Paavo hadn't died. I went over the data on the Chameleon. The Agency suspected he was restoring Greek monasteries and turning them into compounds to aid his illegal activities. When Eva called and told me about Castle Rock I had to check it out. Of course, I now have the proof I need. I've seen Paavo with my own eyes. He is the Chameleon. It's been fourteen years and he's aged, but it's him."

"You should have told me. Told someone. The mission to Castle Rock never smelled right from the beginning. You offered me that crap job afterward, knowing I wouldn't accept it."

"I needed you out of Onyxx. To be my eyes and ears. I didn't plan on Sully dying, but after he did, I knew who I could depend on to go after the Chameleon. You're a predictable son of a bitch, McEwen."

"So you sent me that information on Eva, put me on her scent, and waited for me to call."

"Only you didn't call, so I hopped a plane, and that's when Simon Parish picked me up. I'm sorry about Sully. Truly sorry, McEwen. And if Bjorn is a casualty, I take full responsibility for that, too." Merrick took a sip of his whiskey, his silver hair almost white in the lamplight. "The birth of Onyxx was supposed to solve the world's problems, not create more debauchery. The NSA poured billions into the project. The agents hand-picked from an elite few. Five years later one of those elite goes rogue. Do you know what that did to the project, and to those of us who were caught in the middle? We had everything at our disposal. Nothing was off-limits to the agents at Onyxx. We had access to the darkest secrets on the continent. International clearance on every level. We collaborated with the CIA and the NIA, and every organization in between. We even had men who worked in the underworld."

Merrick took another sip of whiskey. "I'd been a government assassin for three years before I was inducted into the Onyxx program. Paavo Creon was recruited because he was a mastermind strategist for the military. Both our records were spotless. Both married. Both happy with our lives. At least I was until hell came knocking and blew up my world. Today Onyxx inductees are required to be single. That was brought forth after Johanna was killed. How much has Eva told you?"

"She doesn't remember the details of the night her mother died. She says someone else was there in the house, but she doesn't know who."

"Do you believe her?"

"Yes. Was it you? Were you in the house that night?"

"Me?" Merrick stood and shrugged off his tattered shirt, revealing the bruises Sly had inflicted on him at Cupata. "Why would I have been there?"

"You said you and Paavo were friends. Eva says you used to bring her suckers when you visited."

"I was nowhere near that house when it burned to the ground. Actually I think I was at my country home with Johanna when I got the call that it had happened."

"So your wife wasn't killed until later that year."

"Three months later."

Sly studied Merrick, searching for the truth, but like before, his commander's face was masked by his facial hair and cold gray eyes.

"I'd like to talk to Eva and ask her some questions," Merrick said. "You brought her with you, didn't you?"

"No," Sly lied, not willing to hand her over to Merrick until he was sure he could trust his boss, and his motive.

"She's our bait, McEwen. Paavo will want what is his. I know how she's lived, and I don't understand why Creon has treated her the way he has, but he'll still want her back."

"Maybe not."

"It sounds to me like you've let your emotions affect this mission, McEwen."

"I don't work for you or Onyxx anymore, Merrick. My reason for being here is personal, that means I don't have to follow Onyxx procedures or policy."

"You're sleeping with her, aren't you?" When Sly didn't answer, Merrick swore. "It's worse than that, isn't it? You've let yourself care about her. That's stupid, McEwen. If you think I'm going to back away now, after I'm this close, you're mistaken. I want to talk to Eva Creon, tonight."

"You're the one who's stupid, Merrick, if you think I'm going to let you sacrifice her to ease your conscience over a tragedy that happened fourteen years ago. You can't bring your wife back."

"Sully, either. So why are you here?"

"We both want the Chameleon. That isn't up for debate. But I'm not going to jeopardize Eva so you can put another notch on that legendary belt of yours."

Sly stepped to the window. It was dark outside, and the sound of violin music in the street mingled with rowdy laughter coming from downstairs. Anxious to get back to Eva, he said, "Are there any other members of your team still alive? Any of the original six?"

"Me and Briggs."

Sly turned from the window recognizing the name. "Briggs? The man in records with no legs."

"That's right."

"And the others. Who were they and how did they die?"

"Parnel and Krizova were killed outside of Prague

in a scrimmage three years into our tour of duty. We were on a classified mission and we were ambushed. Ray Parnel and Cyrus Krizova were casualties. In the explosion, Peter Briggs lost his legs. Me, Paavo and Sid Nolles escaped. Nolles died ten years later in a plane crash. Bad weather traveling from Moscow to London."

"No body?"

"No. The plane crashed high in the mountains."

"And Parnel and Krizova?"

Merrick shook his head. "The same. Their bodies weren't recovered, but that's not unusual, Sly. Sully's dead. We don't have proof of that, but we know he's gone. About Eva, I still want to talk to her about the night of the fire. You going to let me?"

"Questioning Eva is a waste of time. I've already tried to get her to remember what happened that night. If you had Paavo's file there might be a chance for her to remember something, but—"

"What do you mean?"

"She believes that something in that file might trigger her memory. She hasn't shared what that might be, but that's why she contacted you weeks ago. The psychiatrist called it memory rejuvenation. She tried hypnosis, but that didn't work."

"If the file is what you need, then I can help out with that."

"Not unless you brought it with you."

"But I did." Suddenly Merrick was striding into the bathroom and turning on the light. Sly followed, and watched as his commander opened his mouth and popped the crown off one of his back teeth. Turning around, he pulled out a miniature data chip the size of a tooth filling.

"Paavo's file?"

"Paavo's file," Merrick confirmed. "Where is your computer?"

"On the *Hector*," Sly said, holding out his hand.

Merrick shook his head. "I think I'll keep it until we reach the *Hector*. Let's get going."

"Not together," Sly said, wishing he could talk Merrick out of the chip, knowing he wouldn't be able to. "I'll leave first. Wait two hours, then come. Make sure no one follows you."

Merrick turned to the mirror and popped the chip back into the perfect-size hole, then replaced the crown. When it was back in place, he said, "A good field agent doesn't let himself get tailed. You know that, McEwen. In two hours."

Sly pulled the key out of his pocket as he strode down the hall. He reached room eight, but didn't need to use the key. The door stood open and Eva was gone.

He swore, took the stairs three at a time, and came to a sliding halt at the end of the bar. She was seated at the table across the room with the five card players who had been ogling her a long hour ago. Someone had bought her a drink, and there was food in front of her, too.

He studied her a moment, and decided she was unharmed. She no longer wore the tight skirt. Where she'd gotten the jeans he had no idea, or the white shirt she'd slipped over the tank top.

Angry that she'd left the room after he'd told her not to, he strolled across the room, moved behind her and jerked her chair away from the table. Then drew her off the seat by taking hold of her arm. "Say good night, it's time to go."

"*Perimenete amerikano!*" one of the men said, coming to his feet.

Two others stood. Then a third, and fourth. They were definitely laborers of some kind. Probably fishermen—all of them tough lookers, used to ten-hour days building biceps and attitude.

Sly said, "I don't want any trouble."

"Then you should not have touched the pretty lady. Let her go, and we will think about letting you live," said the long-haired Greek who was still sitting.

"I thought I told you to stay in the room," Sly muttered.

"I told you I was hungry," she said as if that was a good enough reason to put her life in danger, and now his.

"And I told you I would feed you later."

"Meat," she reminded. "But now you don't have to. Look—" she pointed to the table "—it's called *bifteki*. A Greek hamburger."

Sly glanced at the half-eaten hamburger left on her plate.

"They knew what I was talking about," she continued. "Well, after I explained."

From behind the bar, the waiter called out, "American Mac. *Ne.* We make good."

"Actually, I think it's goat," she whispered, leaning into him, "but it's tasty, just the same."

"Let the pretty lady go, *amerikano*. She amuses us and we are not yet tired of her company. She has promised each of us a dance to pay for the *bifteki*."

Sly arched an eyebrow, and Eva responded with a shrug. "It seemed like a good idea at the time. A pain-free proposition. Food for fun. I haven't had a chance to dance much on this trip."

Sly dug into his pocket and tossed a fifty-dollar bill on the table. "That should cover the burger."

"I don't think so," said the man who had appointed himself spokesman for the rest of the crew.

The sound of a knife being flipped open told Sly that things were about to get ugly. He looked down at Eva, put his hand on her ass, and squeezed. "Where did these come from? Who else will be looking to collect for these?"

"No one. I found them in the room. The jeans are a little tight, but the shirt fits well, don't you think?"

Her beautiful breasts were still on display and her comment had every guy in the place taking another long hard look at her sun-kissed cleavage.

Suddenly the long-haired Greek stood, flashing his knife—a six-inch switchblade. "We don't want your money, *amerikano*. We want the woman."

The crew nodded, then laughed.

Sly didn't laugh, didn't crack a smile.

The men were blocking the exit, so running was going to be difficult. Then, too, he had never thought much of tucking tail and running unless the odds were double-stacked, as Sully used to say. That meant ten to one odds.

He glanced at Eva, gave her a cold smile, then spun her away from him toward the bar. "Don't disappoint me, friend. Keep her safe."

The bartender's eyes widened, but he shook his head. "*Ohi,* no disappoint. Come, *kyria.*"

While Eva scurried behind the bar to join the bartender, Sly raised his knee and hooked the edge of the table. It flew up into the air, knocking over two of the men who were in agreement to take his head off. Spinning right, he kicked out and planted his foot into another's gut. A second later, he grabbed the long-hair and head-butted him before he could use his knife. As the man wilted to the floor, the two who had landed on their asses first were on their feet again. Swearing at Sly, they rushed him. He deflected a number of blows, exchanged swings, taking their punches as good as he gave back.

He lunged forward and snagged one of the men by the shirt. Lifting him into the air, he tossed him into the other man and the two went down together again.

Eva screamed and Sly turned away for a split second to make sure she was all right. But she hadn't been screaming because she was hurt. He realized then that she had screamed as a warning to him. Too late, he felt the knife cut deep into his forearm. He winced at the pain, then whirled around and grabbed the barrel-chested man's hand and gave it a hard jerk, then twisted. The switchblade went clattering to the floor. The man stood there howling, his expression a mixture of pain and admiration for Sly's superior strength and natural ability.

Just before Sly's fist knocked the man to his knees, he said, "You shouldn't play with knives unless you intend to stick it where it counts."

It was all over in a matter of five minutes. When Sly strode to the bar, the bartender gladly handed Eva over to him. Seconds later, they were out the door, sprinting past two violin players who continued to serenade an old couple holding hands on a bench.

As they left Christos behind, taking a different route back to the *Hector,* Eva said, "You're losing a lot of blood. We should stop and—"

"Keep moving," Sly said slowing their pace to a fast walk. His tone was hard as nails, and he glanced behind them to make sure they weren't being followed. Relieved when he saw no one, he muttered, "So much for a pain-free proposition."

Chapter 17

Merrick came over the side of the *Hector* dressed in black, moving as quietly as a cat burglar. A *young* cat burglar, Sly decided, more than a little impressed with his commander's field ability.

He hadn't seen Merrick outside of Onyxx headquarters in seven years, and never once in field attire. He had to admit that the data he'd read on the mighty legend had been hard to swallow—until two days ago when he'd faced him at Cupata on the pedestal.

The data had claimed that Adolf Merrick had been the deadliest Onyxx agent ever recruited. He still held several top-ranking stats, and was still on record as the most accurate government assassin ever. Not even Holic Reznik had been able to top Merrick's skill for masterminding the perfect kill. And by the way he had arrived tonight, it looked like *Icis*, the legend, had been keeping his talents polished just in case there was a good enough reason to get his hands dirty.

Sly had searched the *Hector* from top to bottom once he and Eva had returned to the yacht. Seeing nothing amiss, he had accepted her help with his arm wound, then let her fix him a meal of scrambled eggs since he had been the only one who hadn't eaten something at Christos.

They hadn't talked much, and he had decided not to tell her that Merrick was bringing her the file. He hadn't wanted to make any promises in case something unforeseen happened.

He was seated in the wheelhouse having a smoke when Merrick entered.

"Nice yacht, McEwen."

Sly nodded. "Always wanted to get myself one of these."

"Then it's yours?"

Sly nodded, then blew out a stream of smoke. "You sure you weren't followed?"

"I'm sure. But I'm surprised you weren't. What the hell was that all about at Christos? They were still mopping up blood when I went down for a bite to eat."

"That was my blood," Sly admitted.

Merrick eyed the bandage on his arm. "You getting soft or slow?"

Sly offered him a cold smile. "Everywhere she goes, she can't help but turn heads."

"It's been years since I've seen her. She was nine, I think. Slight, with big green eyes and lots of red hair."

"She's still got lots of hair, and those same big green eyes, but I'd say you're in for a memorable experience, old man, when it comes to the rest. Come on." Sly tossed the cigarette overboard, then led the way downstairs.

Eva was making coffee in the galley when they entered. She turned around at the sound of their voices, a look of surprise on her face when she spotted Merrick behind him.

Sly turned and grinned when he saw the look on Merrick's face. "Like I said, memorable." He looked back, said, "Eva, this is Adolf Merrick. Merrick, meet Eva Creon."

She didn't say anything for a moment, and neither did Merrick. Sly watched as the two of them assessed each other for several awkward minutes. Then Merrick reached into his pocket and pulled out a sucker. "I brought this for you. I went to five shops before I found the right flavor."

When he held the sucker out to her, Eva took it with a smile. "Strawberry."

"It's my favorite too, remember? I thought it was appropriate, even though I can see you're no longer a child with a sweet tooth."

"She's graduated to meat now," Sly said. "Hamburgers."

Merrick looked lost, and Eva gave Sly a don't-go-there look that made him chuckle.

Sobering, he said, "You have something else for her, too, right, Merrick? Show her what else you brought her while I get things set up."

Merrick glanced at Sly. "You didn't tell her?"

"No. I wanted to make sure you showed up before I started making promises."

To Eva, Merrick said, "I brought you the profile on your father. I know you gave me a deadline, and it's past, but McEwen says you've been trying to piece together the night your...the night of the fire, and that your father's file might help."

Eva raised her chin in an effort to keep from looking too hopeful. Merrick missed it, but Sly didn't. He figured there was a good reason for that. He'd spent days with her, and nights, too. He'd watched her sleep, held her when she'd dreamed, heard her climax and felt her shudder with the force of it. He knew her inside and out.

"I'll get the computer turned on," he said, then left the galley.

He was in the small room behind the stairs getting things set up when he heard footsteps and turned to see Eva standing in the doorway. She was holding the data chip in her hand.

"He took it out of the inside of his tooth," she said. "It's so small. Are you sure there's a file in there?"

Sly grinned, then held out his hand. "It's in there."

He took the chip from her, dropped it into a small well on a disk, then slipped the disk into the computer. It took only a matter of minutes and the file had been converted and downloaded into the computer.

After Sly hit a few buttons, he glanced over his shoulder to see Eva chewing on her lip. "You all right?"

"Yes. I'm just wondering what I'm going to find."

"I'll hang around."

"You don't have to. In fact, if you don't mind, I'd like to read it in private. Is that okay?"

He nodded. "Still unsure what you're looking for?"

She stepped close, laid her hand on Sly's chest. "Still unsure, but hopeful." She patted his chest. "I left Merrick in the galley with a cup of very black coffee. Why don't you go keep him company for a while?"

Sly swung the chair around and gestured for Eva to take a seat. "You want me to bring you anything?"

"No. Sly?"

"Yeah?"

"Merrick looks almost the same. His hair's all gray now, not just his temples, but he looks like I remember him."

* * *

Eva closed her eyes and said a prayer before she sat in the chair. She had waited so long for this day and now... Now she was afraid. Afraid that she would read the file and nothing would happen. Her memory would fail her and she'd still be left in the dark.

She suddenly wished she hadn't asked Sly to leave, but she was getting too used to having him around, too used to relying on his broad shoulders to lean on.

She pushed that aside for now and placed her fingers on the keypad and began to read and scroll, scroll and read.

Paavo Karol Creon, born March 7, 1948. Deceased, August 3, 1990. Only child of...

The file wasn't lengthy—a few pages was all. It highlighted her father's birth and childhood, his education and military years. His marriage to Muriel Gallo had come about while he was stationed in Italy. In his five years with Onyxx, he'd been shot nine times, and lost his index finger on his right hand. For identification purposes the file listed the permanent scars on his body, and where each was located. There was also a complete health record. The last page of the file was dedicated to the fire at their home in Atlanta, resulting in his death, as well as the death of his wife and daughter.

Eva sat back and went over the material in her mind once more. She felt like crying when nothing stood out as odd or enlightening. She closed her eyes determined to revisit the night of the fire, and this time, force herself to stay with the nightmare long enough to see the face of the man with her father in the hall.

She put herself back on the stairs, a small nine-year-old girl with long red hair and curious green eyes. She smelled the smoke, and heard the voices. She saw her mother still and lifeless. Fear swelled inside her with the knowledge that her mother was dead. She took a deep breath, accepted the smoke into her lungs. Let it burn as it climbed back up her throat.

She looked farther down the hall. She could see them, her father and the other man, the mystery man who had haunted her dreams. She was crying and they must have heard her. The man turned and…

Eva leaped out of the chair. When she turned around she bumped into Sly. He reached out and pulled her into his arms. She went willingly, shaking fiercely, as she buried her face in the warmth of his chest.

"What is it?" He asked. "What did you see?"

For a long minute Eva didn't speak, then she looked up, tears clouding her vision.

"Eva, what did you see?"

"My father," she answered. "My father laughing. Laughing, Sly. Mother's dead on the floor and he's laughing."

Eva went looking for Adolf Merrick after she had pulled herself together, and assured Sly that she hadn't seen anything more. She found Merrick asleep in the guest bedroom. She had wanted to talk to him, had convinced Sly that she needed time alone with him.

She stood over him now holding the sucker he'd given her. She had always thought her father's friend had been handsome. Even more handsome, perhaps, than her papa. Merrick had a sophisticated look about him, mixed with a ruggedness that would appeal to any woman.

He had a clear complexion, a sleek nose and beautiful thick hair that had turned completely gray over the years, with one dramatic streak of silver slashed through it. His jaw was covered with a short gray beard

a shade darker than his hair, and a silver mustache covered his upper lips.

He wasn't as tall or muscular as Sly, but he had a
solid frame that guaranteed his survival on the pedestal
at Cupata hadn't been all luck.

Evy, come see what Adolf brought you. You two have
something in common. Strawberry suckers. Come, Evy.
Come to your papa.

The words came to her with affection, her papa's
voice full of love for her. She had always believed he
loved her, and warmed to the name Evy. She understood
now why she had liked hearing it so much when Sly had
used the name as well—it had made her feel special. It
had reminded her of her papa when he had loved her.

She stared at the sucker and realized that it wasn't
the file that was making her suddenly remember. It was
Adolf Merrick. He had unlocked the door to her memory the minute she had seen him in the galley.

She continued to stare at him as conversations un-
folded in her head, and key words began to piece the
puzzle slowly together. They fell into place one by one,
and with each piece a clearer picture began to form in
her mind.

Quietly, she sank to the floor next to where Adolf
Merrick slept, tears streaming down her face. She had
no proof to validate what she believed to be true. Nothing but a gut feeling.

It wasn't enough, she realized. Not enough to go to
Sly with what she suspected. But the night was still
young.

Eva unwrapped the sucker, stuck it into her mouth
and closed her eyes. She was nine again, and she'd
come home from school to find her father there. He'd
been away a while and she'd been so happy to see him
that she'd run to him and hugged him. And he had

hugged her back, and then... And then Mother had come out of the kitchen saying it was time for dinner.

Eva felt suddenly cold and she hugged herself where she sat on the floor. How could she not have known? she wondered. How could she not have sensed the evil in the house? Sensed the evil within him?

Sly found Eva on deck staring off into the star-studded night. He came up behind her and wrapped his arms around her.

"Don't ask me anything," she whispered. "Just hold me."

The words trembled in her throat, and Sly drew her against him. Lowering his head, he said, "You need to trust me. Trust that I want what's best for you."

She turned in his arms. "Best for me, or best for you and Merrick?"

"It could be the same thing. Let me help you."

Sly studied her face. She was hiding something, something important. For her own good she needed to share it with him.

He'd just finished going over the file for a second time, but like Merrick, he hadn't found anything alarming, or that would explain why an Onyxx agent with a family, who appeared to be happy, had killed his wife, then faked his own death, along with his daughter's, to become the Chameleon.

"I need to tell you something," he said. "I need to share something with you."

"What?"

"I never told you how Merrick got to Paros, but I think you should know that the *Ventura* is here in port, and it's likely that someone has reported to Parish that we're here."

"The *Ventura*'s here?" She turned away from him to search the harbor.

She was looking in the wrong direction and he said, "Over there," then took her by the shoulders and turned her a quarter-turn to the left. "A hundred yards. See it?"

"Yes, I see it."

He turned her to face him. "I need to tell you something else. Merrick was hiding out on the *Ventura*. He jumped on board after he saw your father leave Santorini on a yacht called the *Pearl*. He told me that early the following morning the *Pearl* and the *Ventura* rendezvoused at sea."

"And?"

"And your father boarded the *Ventura* to speak to Simon and Melita. Merrick said the Chameleon appeared angry, and that he wasn't able to hear the exchange. Only watch."

"Watch what?"

"Nemo beaten to death."

"No! Oh, God. Did my father do it?"

"No. Simon did it."

"How could he!"

Sly pulled her into his arms when she started to cry, but she quickly jerked away from him.

"When did you learn this?"

"Earlier today."

"It was in the message Merrick sent you when we were at the cove, wasn't it?"

"Yes."

"Why didn't you tell me then?"

"I don't know. I—"

"'Trust me, Evy. I can help you,'" she mocked.

Sly wanted to reach out to her, but instinct told him she wasn't about to let him touch her right now. She was far too angry. "I didn't tell you because I knew it would upset you and I was trying to spare you."

"Spare me?" She laughed. "Spare me because you care about me, right?"

"You know I do."

"You're good, Sly McEwen. Very good at lying. Almost as good as..." She shook her head. "For the record, I never trusted you. Trust is like friendship. It's an expensive luxury. A fool's luxury."

"Your father—"

"No more! I have nothing else to say to you. I'm tired and I'm going to bed."

Eva heard the bedroom door open and she sat up quickly and looked at the clock. It was twelve-thirty, and she had been sleeping soundly for at least two hours. "You don't really think I'm going to let you share this bed with me, do you?" she asked the minute Sly turned on the light next to the bed.

"This is my room."

"Go sleep with Merrick tonight."

"This is my bed."

"Fine. Then I'll sleep on the couch." She tossed back the sheet and climbed out of the berth. Aware that she was topless, wearing only the black thong she had worn beneath the sheer bodysuit in Santorini, she reached for the white blouse on the end of the bed that she'd taken from the room above Christos. But before she could pull it on, Sly grabbed it out of her hand and tossed it behind him to the floor.

Eva attempted to retrieve it, but he quickly hauled her off her feet. One second she was in his arms, and the next she was airborne, landing on the mattress so hard she bounced.

"Don't move," he warned when she started to sit up.

"I'm not sleeping in this bed with you," she promised. "You're not touching me."

"I'm tired, and my arm hurts. This is my bed."

"Whine to Merrick, maybe he'll give you a sucker."

He swore, unsnapped his jeans. "Whether you like it or not, we're sharing this bed. Odds are, sometime during the night you'll get needy and want to snuggle." He offered her a smug smile. "Care to make a bet?"

Eva grabbed one of the pillows and covered her breasts at the same time she shoved herself into the corner of the berth. His words stung and she tried not to let it show. Feeling his eyes on her, knowing he knew her far better than anyone, she said, "I can live through a night of torture. I'm used to cruel and unusual, remember?"

He frowned, his voice softening. "Yes, I remember. You've hung by your wrists in a clothes chute for ten hours at the end of a belt, and…"

"…lived to tell about it," she finished. "A real survivor. That's me."

"Well, tonight, Evy, you're going to have to survive my sleeping next to you. And if you feel like snuggling you won't have to make too much noise to get my attention. I'm a light sleeper."

With that, he slid his jeans to the floor, turned off the light, then climbed naked beneath the sheet and gave her his back.

It wasn't long before Sly's body began to heat up the bed. Not long after that, the scent of him wrapped around Eva and she began to remember…and ache.

She struggled with the carnal need burning between her thighs, with the ache in her chest. She battled both demons, determined to win.

She had known her time with Sly McEwen would end soon. Had known there was no way to prepare for it.

Against her better judgment, she slid beneath the

sheet and curled her body against him. She waited to be humiliated, sure he would toss cruel words at her soon. She would suffer whatever he deemed fair, she told herself, as long as he didn't deny her his arms tonight, or his body.

He never spoke when he rolled over and pulled her close. Nothing before or after he kissed her. He just continued to overwhelm her with his warm lips and gentle hands as he made love to her.

Made love to her as if he knew it would be the last time.

Chapter 18

"What time did she leave?"

Sly finished pouring himself a cup of coffee, then turned to see Merrick standing in the middle of the galley rubbing his left temple. "Around four. I've been in contact with Bjorn. He tailed her to the *Ventura*, It doesn't look like they intend to sail."

"Then maybe the Chameleon is here," Merrick said.

"Or somewhere close by," Sly offered.

He hadn't been crazy about Merrick's idea to use Eva as bait. At first he'd refused to listen—but then just before midnight Bjorn had sent him a message that he was alive. That he'd survived the balcony collapsing on him at Cupata. Holic Reznik hadn't fared as well. No, the assassin wasn't dead, but he had been injured. His arm had been broken and his hand crushed. Possibly some internal injuries. Bjorn said Reznik was now in a safe place awaiting transport back to Onyxx headquarters in D.C.

Sly had asked him how soon he could get to Paros. When Bjorn had given him the right answer, he'd agreed with Merrick that when Eva attempted her escape—which he knew she intended—he would let her. But on one condition, that they bug her, *and* put Bjorn on her tail in case something went wrong before they located the Chameleon.

Sly poured another cup of coffee and placed it on the table for Merrick, then sat. "I don't like having to wait," he said, "but I agree that this is the fastest way to force the Chameleon's hand."

"Got any cream?" Merrick walked to the fridge and opened the door to have a look inside. As he bent forward, he lost his balance and dropped to the floor. Sly leaped to his feet, and when Merrick made no attempt to get up, he pulled his boss to his feet, slung him over his shoulder, and carried him back into the guest room and laid him out on the bed.

Once Merrick opened his eyes, Sly said, "So how damn bad off are you? I know about the tumor, so tell me, are you going to be in any shape to back me up today? Or is the Chameleon going to win again like he always does?"

Before Merrick could answer, a light flashed on Sly's Suunto watch telling him Bjorn was sending him another message. He flipped open his phone and hit a button to receive the message.

It read, "The time is 7:10. Our Eva has left the *Ventura* with Parish. She left on her own power. She looks well. Melita not so good. They were picked up by a black Altima. I'm following. They're headed south."

Eva had boarded the *Ventura* before dawn with a story prepared—part lie, part truth. She said Sly had kidnapped her at Cupata, and that she'd been held on the *Hector* for two days. She told Simon she hadn't had a chance to escape until Sly had sailed into Paros, and she had seen the *Ventura* docked in the harbor.

Simon seemed to believe her, but she couldn't be sure. She never mentioned hacking into his computer, or the fate of Dr. Fielding. She truly didn't want to think about Simon killing her psychiatrist, or Nemo.

She was back in the lion's den and was afraid, but she had no choice. She now knew the truth, and the only way to face it was head on. She couldn't run away. She wouldn't.

She was worried about Melita. Her eyes were lifeless, her skin deathly pale, and she wore bandages on her wrists. Had Melita tried to take her life after Nemo had been killed?

She prayed it wasn't so, but feared it was true. When she'd asked Simon what had happened, he had simply said Melita had an accident, then told her that she needed to shower and change. That they had a morning engagement, and they couldn't be late.

She'd stepped out of the shower to find a pale green blouse on her bed with a matching skirt and shoes. She'd dressed quickly, followed Simon's instruction for her hair to be worn down, and her lips painted pale pink.

She met Simon on the upper deck at seven sharp. She had no idea where they were going, or why they were taking a car, but when she had climbed into the back seat Melita was already there.

She never spoke to Eva or Simon, and after thirty minutes of silence, the car pulled off the road, and Simon got out, urging her to follow. The guard who had driven them helped Melita.

Simon said, "Take my sister to the boat in the lagoon. They are expecting her." Then he kissed his sister's cheek and started to hike up the narrow path to a large monastery high on a rock overlooking the sheltered lagoon.

When the guard started to lead Melita away, Eva panicked. Afraid she was never going to see her friend again, she hurried to Melita and pulled her close. Hugging her, she scrambled for something to say, knowing she had only seconds to say it.

She settled for the one word that had saved her years ago, the one word Melita needed to hear. Kissing her cheek, she whispered, "Survive, Melita. Endure the demon and survive."

That was all there was time for, and then the guard took her away, down a rocky path to the crystal-blue water, and the boat waiting there.

"Come, sweet Eva, we are also expected," Simon called out. "Come now."

She wiped her tears as she followed Simon along the trail, and eventually through an iron gate. Inside she counted sixteen guards on the grounds. They passed through a private courtyard that had a sturdy post dug into the ground with heavy iron rings bolted into it, and entered the monastery.

A short stairway later, then down a windy passageway that was poorly lit, Eva heard moaning. Her stomach knotted and fear climbed her throat. She wanted to turn and run, but Simon was behind her and there was no escape. The passageway narrowed, then turned sharply, and that's when she saw them—men caged like animals.

A chamber of horrors, she would later come to think of it—the men battered and beaten, some wearing ragged clothes, some naked and huddling in corners, clearly defeated.

Eva felt sick, and she quickened her pace through the passage, tears stinging her eyes.

From behind her, Simon said, "Don't waste your tears on them. They are all criminals, and if they had the strength, and could get their hands around your neck, they would kill you as quickly as they would me."

She spun around. "Why, Simon? Why am I here? What is this place?"

"It's the hall of justice."

"You're crazy, Simon."

He laughed. "What is crazy, sweet Eva, is your expecting me to buy that stupid story about being forced to leave Cupata with Sly McEwen." He shoved her toward a pair of wooden doors. "Because of you, Nemo is dead. Because of you, Melita no longer wants to live. Because of you, I will forever live with my friend's blood on my hands. Yes, I must be crazy, because after all of it I still love you."

"You don't know what it means to love someone," Eva snarled. "You don't hurt the people you love, Simon. You're a coward. A coward and a freak."

He slapped her. Slapped her so hard Eva flew back into the door.

"You stupid bitch. Now look what you made me do. In all the years we've been together, I never once made you bleed. That was one of the rules."

Eva locked her knees, unsure if he would hit her again.

But he didn't, instead Simon pulled out his handkerchief and stepped forward to wipe the blood from her nose. Eva knocked his hand away, then raised her knee to his groin and sent him staggering backward.

"Bitch!" Simon screamed. "You bitch! You'll pay for that. You have no idea who I am, or you would never have done that. I am—"

"Simon, get yourself under control. I will tell Evka

all she needs to know when the time is right. Take her into the game room and put her in *the chair,* then send a message to Merrick and McEwen. Give them this location, and tell them not to keep me waiting. I grow weary of this game and wish to end it."

Eva watched as the Chameleon stepped out of the shadows, and for the first time in years, she was no longer blinded by a child's need for her father's love. Yes, it was her father's face, but not her father. Her father was dead. He'd died fourteen years ago.

She said, "You killed them. You killed my mother and my father."

"Yes," the Chameleon admitted. "I killed your mother quickly because she was unimportant. Paavo..." He shrugged. "Simon, take her inside, then send the message."

"Yes, Father."

Eva looked from Simon to the Chameleon, then back to Simon. "Father?"

"That's right, sweet, Eva." Simon smiled wickedly, then stepped forward and wiped the blood from her nose with his handkerchief. "The Chameleon is my father. Mine and Melita's."

The room Eva was taken to looked like a medieval torture chamber. There was a dunking machine operated by an indoor windmill, a wall of nails and what looked like an old-fashioned rack.

There were more grisly-looking torture devices, but she refused to contemplate what they might be used for.

Simon had ordered her into the chair in the middle of the room, and had tied her wrists together at the back of it, and then he tied her ankles. She had no idea how long she'd been sitting there, but it was long enough for her hands and feet to go numb.

She hadn't lost hope, however. She'd seen Sly McEwen in action, and if he hadn't heard her leave the *Hector* in the middle of the night, the man needed to invest in a hearing aid.

At first she'd planned on facing her father—correction, the man impersonating her father—alone. He had killed her parents and cheated her out of fourteen years of her life. Selfishly, she wanted to be the one to kill him—for he did deserve to die. But she knew she couldn't do it alone—the odds were against her; even if she was willing to sacrifice herself.

The door opened and Eva saw the Chameleon walk into the room with that confident swagger she had once admired. How could she have ever thought this man was her father? Yes, he looked like her papa, and talked like him…almost. He was even missing the forefinger on his right hand, and had the documented scar on his chin. The silver lighter her mother had given him for Christmas one year was a nice touch, too.

It made sense now. He'd known that as much as he had cloned himself to look like her father, he could never pass as Paavo for long periods of time. That's why she'd seen him only once a year after the fire, on Simon's birthday—his son's birthday.

The Chameleon walked into the room feeling an odd sense of relief. He'd played the game so long he had wondered if he would ever know when it was time to end it.

But Simon was right. Evka had outgrown the game. She had changed this last year, and he could see that she had. Now they would move on to another game. A more productive game. He still would give her to Reznik if the fool ever contacted him to tell him he was alive, and in the meantime…

In the meantime there was always another lesson to be learned. A very important lesson. Melita had learned it a few days ago—if you couldn't afford the price of betrayal, you had no business playing the game.

Of course it would pain him to punish Evka, but children needed discipline. She was not of his blood, but she was his creation—all that she was and had become was because of him.

"I have come to speak with you," he said, stopping before her. "I'm sure you have a number of questions for me. I feel it is my duty to reward you for your courage. I honestly didn't think you would come back on your own. Simon tells me you've been fornicating with one of Merrick's agents. Sly McEwen, the impressive rat fighter at Cupatra. So what's on your list, Evka? What do you want to know first?"

"You stole my father's face. Surgery?"

"Yes, of course. Several, in fact." He smiled and turned so she could study his profile. "It is a nice face, don't you think?"

"Why?" Eva asked softly. "Why did you need to kill them? What in this world could be so important that it would be worth so such trouble? Why my father's face?"

"That is more than one question, but I'll do the best I can. When a man is betrayed, Evka, he is inclined to seek revenge. It is the only way to reclaim his honor. Paavo and Merrick betrayed me years ago, and Onyxx embraced them for it. They took everything from me, so I in turn took everything from them. I stole their lives, like they stole mine. I found out what they loved most and took it from them. For Merrick it was his wife, and for Paavo…it was his sweet young daughter. You, Evka, you were the love of your father's life."

Chapter 19

Sly paced the deck, envisioning all sorts of scenarios, none of them good. Eva had ditched the tracking device. That meant she'd changed clothes. All they could do now was wait for a message from either the Chameleon or Bjorn.

Had he made a mistake by letting her go? He knew why she wanted to go back, knew what it was like to live with unanswered questions.

"I survived so one day I would understand. That's what this is all about, understanding why it all happened. I want to know why my mother had to die. Why my father became someone I didn't recognize after her death. He loved me before that night. It couldn't have all been a lie. I won't believe that. He did love me. I'm prepared to play whatever game I must to learn the truth."

"You think the truth will set you free, is that it?"

"It will."

"You're wrong. It won't."

"It will. It has to."

"McEwen, the waiting's over. You received a message from Parish. You've been invited inside one of the Chameleon's compounds. Simon says if you care enough about Eva to die for her, you should accept the Chameleon's offer. But if you want to live to fight another day, you should go home. I've also been invited to tag along. It seems that Eva either told them I'm here, or the past two days I haven't been as invisible as I thought."

Sly listened, but he had already made his decision last night when he had allowed Eva to leave the *Hector*. The game he was about to play, however, was the most unorthodox of any he had ever contrived. He would be walking into an armed camp without any weapons, under the guise of total surrender.

"Let's get moving," Merrick said. "Eva's been in their hands too long already."

"I thought you wanted revenge at any cost. You saying she's gotten to you, too?"

"I'll admit she's special. I'll even admit that I understand why you let your professional training take a back seat for one short pleasure ride. But you and I know in the end, if we're successful today, the best thing for Eva is if things go back to the way they were and she disappears. We're in agreement, right?"

"We're in agreement," Sly said. "I'd say she's earned her wings."

"Then let's go get this son of a bitch, so she can fly," Merrick said. "Let's send him to hell once and for all so we can all be set free."

Sly strode across the deck and into the wheelhouse to start the *Hector*'s twin engines. "Where?" he asked, as Merrick joined him.

"Head south. Parish says we'll get an escort once we pass the red-and-black tower on Andiparos."

In a matter of minutes they were underway, heading south along the eastern coast of the island. As Simon had promised, two fishing boats joined them after they passed the tower. The crew, however, didn't look like they had fishing on their minds unless the plan was to shoot their prey out of the water with Uzis.

"Contact Bjorn," Sly said. "Tell him we're—"

"Already done."

Sly looked over his shoulder at Merrick. He still looked pale. "You feel all right?"

"I feel great. I've waited years to feel this good."

The comment had nothing to do with Merrick's immediate health and everything to do with his need to face the man who had stolen his life.

A few miles farther down the coast one of the fishing boats swung wide and started into a narrow channel. There was a strip of beach ahead and behind it a rugged outcropping of rocks that partially concealed a monastery.

The channel was shallow, preventing large boats from coming in too close. At anchor a trideck monster yacht rode the gentle tide, the name the *Pearl* on its stern.

"We're going to be walking into a trap," Merrick said. "At least that's what it's supposed to look like. We'll play it that way, and hope the Chameleon's luck—"

"Luck." Sly glanced at Merrick. "The Chameleon's got more on his side than luck."

"He doesn't have you spooked does he?"

"Spooked? No. But what keeps me humble is that he's been able to slip through the Agency's fingers too many times."

"Why the hell did you agree to this game plan if you don't think we can beat him?" Merrick asked.

"I didn't say we can't beat him."

"You could have stopped Eva from leaving last night if you had doubts."

"I wanted to," Sly admitted. "But we both agree that Eva deserves a future of her own choosing. That won't happen while the Chameleon is controlling her every move. A part of Eva wants her father back. The man who once loved her. He doesn't exist any longer. She needs to see that with her own eyes. The good news is, I haven't seen him piss on the run yet. If he can't, the odds might swing in our favor once the noise starts."

"Noise?"

"That's Bjorn's department, getting the noise started."

"And when will he know when it's time for the cavalry to start shooting?"

"He says I should trust him. Says he'll be able to read my mind when the time comes."

"He's been hanging around Jacy Madox too long. Bjorn called him a shaman once."

Sly shrugged. "All I know is Jacy should have died on the Rock. He was out of blood and out of time, and he still survived."

They took the submersible aqua gliders into shore, joined by an escort of four of the Chameleon's men driving similar water toys. On shore they were searched, then led up the path. At the iron gate they were greeted by Simon Parish.

The albino dismissed Merrick, and faced Sly. "So you have chosen to die for her. Or maybe, you think you are invincible, and can save her? I assure you that will not be the case today. You made a mistake when you touched her. You broke the rules. Players who break the rules are eliminated from the game. It's going to be a pleasure watching you die, McEwen."

"That's right, Evka, your father loved you. That's what you've wanted to hear all these years, isn't it? I could have killed you that night. Killed you along with your mother, but what would that have accomplished? Dying is easy, Evka. As my enemy, your father deserved better. In death, we suffer only once. But alive... Alive a man can be made to die countless times. Just ask the men in my prison. They beg me to let them die."

The Chameleon was as crazy as Simon, Eva thought. Like father, like son.

"I know what you're thinking, but I'm not mad. I'm a genius. Look at what I've accomplished in fourteen years by taking your father's face. My face... I lost it in an accident and was in need of a...facelift." He chuckled at his own joke. "It was fate. I've come to accept that. It took over a year to copy Paavo's likeness, but it was worth every painful surgery. And they were painful. At times I— Well...that isn't important now."

"Tell me about that night," Eva asked, needing to know how she and her mother had been fooled so completely.

"I arrived at the house while you were at school and your mother was out buying groceries. I drove into the garage, and even waved at the neighbor. He waved back. I closed the garage door, pulled Paavo from the trunk, and took him into the house and put him in a closet just off the kitchen. I wanted him close enough so he could hear his family welcome me home. When Muriel returned we hugged and I kissed her. She kissed me back. Paavo, or should I say I, had been away several weeks and she was in need of her husband. She had no reservation when I..."

Eva closed her eyes, could only imagine the torment her father had suffered in the closet listening to her mother make love to another man.

"Afterward she made chicken for supper. You came home, and you ran to me and hugged me. Do you remember?"

"Yes, I remember."

"After supper you went downstairs to watch TV with Muriel. I went to the closet and cut Paavo loose and took him downstairs into his office. I told him I wanted him to watch me kill you both. He begged me to let you live. You, not your mother. We went into the room, but you weren't there. You should have seen the look on your mother's face when she saw the two of us. I let her look, and remember what had happened in the kitchen before supper. In that moment she knew she had betrayed her husband with a stranger. A stranger with the same face. She was more willful than I thought she would be, and she tried to fight me. That's how the fire started. She knocked over a candle before I killed her. I had planned to set fire to the house anyway, only not before my work was done. I dragged Paavo out into the hall and pulled down his gag to ask him where he thought you had gone. You started downstairs just then, and stopped halfway when you saw us."

"At first I thought I was seeing double," Eva remembered. "Then I wasn't sure about anything. You looked exactly like my father, only you were laughing. I saw mother lying so still and I started to cry."

"Paavo swung and hit me, then told you to run. I overlooked his determination to save you. You fled back up the stairs while I staggered back to my feet. I thought I'd have to chase you down, but then you stumbled and fell, rolling down the stairs. You hit your head. Paavo thought you were dead, and he started screaming and crying. He went to you and dropped to his knees. That's where he made his mistake—turning his back on me. A man who loves deeply often feels before he thinks. That's when I realized my revenge had just started. Stealing what Paavo loved best and keeping it was the perfect way to right the wrong. It was the same with Merrick. He also let his emotions rule his head. It's what lost him his wife. That's why he lives in the past. He hates himself, not me."

"And now what?" Eva asked. "What's going to happen to me? How can I be set free?"

"You will never be free. You will do whatever I say regardless of what you now know. Just as Melita will do what I wish in the days to come."

"Where are you sending her?"

"Melita's attempt to kill herself shows me that she is weak, and needs supervision as well as discipline. Children." He sighed. "I admit to earning every gray hair on my head enduring their flaws. Take Simon, for example. He's been a father's nightmare. You, however, have been a refreshing diversion. That is until lately. I admit the rat fighter, McEwen, is quite a specimen in male testosterone, but you should have used restraint, and trusted me to provide you with what you needed at the appropriate time.

"Where will Melita live?" Eva asked again. She couldn't help her friend if she didn't know where to look for her once she escaped. And she *would* escape. Sly would come after her and together they would kill the Chameleon.

"Melita knew the rules. She was instructed to save herself for a suitable husband, and when the time was right, she would marry a man of my choosing. Someone—"

"Is that what you had in mind for me when you sold me to Holic Reznik?"

"I didn't sell you. I made an arrangement. And it didn't include marriage, though I wouldn't have minded. But the truth is Holic already has a wife. No, you were to be his mistress. He has several, but he assured me that he would treat you well."

"He won't be treating anyone any way any longer," Eva stated. "I watched him die at Cupata. A balcony crushed him."

"That is distressful news. I hope you are wrong, but it's true I haven't heard from him since that evening."

"Melita loved Nemo," Eva said.

"Yes, so it seems."

"He was a wonderful man."

"He was a simple guard. A man of little importance."

A vision of Nemo dancing with Melita at Popeo's Taverna flashed in Eva's mind and tears stung her eyes.

"If it grieves you to think of his short life as a waste, don't. With Nemo Owin's death my children have learned a valuable lesson. Thus his life had value. Now then, let's discuss Sly McEwen. I thought I should meet him so I invited him and Merrick to pay us a visit. You do need to be punished for your disobedience, and like Melita, you must understand that I say who and when in all things."

Eva twisted her arms and tried to fight the rope that bound her. Knowing it was useless, she was too enraged to sit there any longer and do nothing. She felt the ropes cut into her wrists, and still she fought them.

When she heard the door open, she whirled her head, hoping it was Sly with an army of Onyxx agents. And she was right, it was him striding through the door. Only something was wrong with the picture.

He was being ushered into the room, along with Adolf Merrick, at gunpoint.

* * *

A needle was driven into the back of Sly's neck. He felt a stab of pain, then nothing. He woke up later to the sight of Merrick a few yards from him stretched out on a table, his legs and arms shackled. He was shirtless, his body covered in bruises, and blood dripping from the soles of his feet.

Sly wasn't sure of much at that point, but he knew Merrick wasn't dead. The Chameleon hadn't toyed with him for fourteen years to kill Merrick quickly.

He scanned the room and found Eva still seated in the center of the room. Her eyes were red from crying and they were fixed on him as if she'd been watching him for a long time. That made him wonder just how long he'd been out.

"Good, you're awake. See, Evka, he's not dead. Simon didn't overdose him. Mr. McEwen, it is a pleasure to finally meet you. I always enjoy a good game, and I can see that you do, too. Not too many men would have accepted my invitation to a death party."

"Let me kill him, Father. Let me do it," Simon insisted.

Sly frowned. *Father?* The Chameleon was Simon's father? Had he heard right?

"As you can see, my son is eager. I had a certain agenda he was required to follow for the past four years where Evka was concerned. She was to remain untouched, and he obeyed the rules. Only now he feels you stole what he was ordered to protect. His anger is justified, but it is my outrage you should be worried about. Only I don't believe you're worried at all. What kind of man are you, McEwen? What kind of man has no regard for his own life?"

The Chameleon opened the file Simon handed to him. "I'll tell you what kind of man. You are an expert in diving rescue and marine navigation. You're listed as the Agency's leading wreck diver, with a top secret recovery in Molonkini Crater, a rescue in the Galapagos Islands, another in Nova Scotia, and a two-week stint diving in Antarctica. It also says here you own the record for holding your breath underwater longer than any man alive." The Chameleon looked up and smiled. "I believe you have an opportunity today to break your last record, McEwen. Shall we see how well you do?"

While Sly listened to the Chameleon, he was busy assessing his surroundings. He'd been stripped down the same as Merrick, leaving him in his water pants and nothing else. He was tied in an iron chair that jutted out from a long metal arm. Suddenly the floor below him began to move—open up—and he understood the meaning behind the Chameleon's words. The torture machine he'd been strapped into was an elaborate version of a dunking machine.

It was clear what game they would be playing, but Sly refused to think about what was coming up. Or, a better word would be, going *down*. Bjorn should be starting to make some noise damn soon if they were all going to get out alive. Where the hell was he?

"I haven't survived all these years to believe that you would have come here without some kind of backup, McEwen. If you're wondering where Odell is, and if he's going to be able to save your ass, the answer is no."

The Chameleon gestured to a guard, and the man flipped the switch on the wall across the room. The wall parted—much like the floor had—and there, stretched spread-eagle, was Bjorn manacled in iron. He looked like hell, tortured and bloody. But alive.

Of course. The Chameleon didn't believe in anyone dying too quickly.

Bjorn raised his head, and to Sly's surprise, managed

to speak. "Reminds me of that time in Roatan, Sly. We were going to die, then, too. Remember?"

Sly felt the iron seat jerk as the arm swung him sideways and began to lower him into the water. He heard Eva cry out just as he was plunged into the depths. His arms and feet were strapped down, and he had no way of breaking free. He conserved his air, sure the Chameleon wouldn't drown him yet. He waited out the minutes, trying to decipher what Bjorn was trying to tell him by mentioning Roatan, the mission from hell. The vertical dive in the Caymans had him and Bjorn marked for death until they had escaped through a narrow cave that had led to the open sea.

Vertical dive...open sea...

Suddenly Sly knew what Bjorn meant. There must be a cave somewhere below the compound that led out to the sea. By the temperature of the water, he could tell that the dunking hole was fed by the sea, which meant that there was an escape route if he could get free of his ropes.

Sly came up gasping for air after a long five minutes. Eva was screaming now, begging the Chameleon not to kill him.

"See that the *Pearl* is ready to sail," the Chameleon said to one of the guards. "Simon, your job will be seeing to it that Merrick is transferred to the *Pearl*. The bastard will not die before his time. We sail within the hour."

"What about Eva?"

"She'll be coming with us, I'll bring her with me. I wouldn't want her to miss Sly McEwen taking his final breath."

Sly heard the iron arm grind as he was swung over the water again. This time he was nearly unconscious by the time he was hoisted from the water. He sucked air, isolating the pain in his burning lungs. He could see that Bjorn was still shackled to the wall, and that Eva was still restrained on the chair, but Merrick had been taken away.

On the third dunk, Sly felt a strange presence around him. It would be just like a sadistic bastard like the Chameleon to toss in a reef shark or a stingray to add a little more sport to the game, he thought. He waited to see a pair of jaws open and start sampling his flesh, but instead of a hungry animal, he saw a light. And, as the high-powered beam came closer, Bjorn's words came back to him once more.

Reminds me of that time in Roatan, Sly. We were going to die then, too.

Yes, they would have died if Pierce Fortier hadn't shown up to rescue them from their watery grave. Suddenly, Pierce swam into vision and quickly offered Sly the extra clip regulator on his air tank while he cut the ropes at his ankles and wrists, then handed him a gun and a knife.

A few hand signals, and a wicked grin later, and Pierce motioned to the chair and they silently settled on a plan. The rat fighters had worked together for seven years, and as if they could read each other's thoughts, the air tanks and BC vests that Pierce had brought were stowed, then they each grabbed onto the iron arm as it began to lift.

They broke the water, guns raised. Sly shot three guards while Pierce knocked off four. As the guards were caught by surprise and fell one by one, the Chameleon took cover. Pierce pulled himself out of the water and raced to the wall to cut down Bjorn, while Sly sprinted to Eva. Dropping to his knees behind the chair, he cut through her ropes.

"There are men in cells in a passageway, Sly. We have to get them out," she told him.

"Later. Where's the Chameleon?"

"There," Eva pointed as he began cutting the ropes that bound her ankles.

Sly looked up just as the Chameleon made a mad dash for the water and dived headfirst into the black hole. He swore viciously, then yelled, "Get Eva out of here, Pierce, and take Bjorn with you. I'm going after the Chameleon."

Sly dived into the hole and swam hard for the wall where they had stowed their gear. When he reached the spot where they had hung the BC vests and tanks, he saw one set was gone and the others had been destroyed.

Without knowing how far the cave extended before dumping out to the sea, Sly had no way to assure himself that he could make it without an air tank. But tucking tail had never been his style, and so with the determination that had earned him the title as one of Merrick's elite, he swam fast and furious into the blackness.

When he saw the beam of a headlamp, or what could have been an underwater flare, he pushed himself faster, believing he might be able to catch the Chameleon before he reached open water. But before that could happen, the cave opened up and Sly saw a man on an aqua glider pick up the Chameleon, while two others turned toward him.

He pulled hard, kicked his legs, not wanting to get trapped underwater. He was nearly out of air when he surfaced. While resupplying his lungs, one of the gliders shot out of the water three feet away from him. He was near an outcropping of rocks, and he quickly climbed out of the water. When the glider came at him the man wasn't expecting Sly to lunge off the rock. He struck fast, drove his knife blade between the man's ribs, then knocked him off the glider to take control of the machine. He shot the second guard off the other glider, then sped toward the *Pearl*, which was now on the move, sailing for the open sea.

Sly maxed out the glider, worried now that he might not be able to rescue Merrick. He was sure the Chameleon was already on board, that the *Pearl* had a secured underwater hatch that had allowed him to enter the yacht on the aqua glider from some pressurized chamber underwater.

It occurred to Sly at that moment that the Chameleon could indeed piss on the run. But then why not? The man was an ex-Onyxx agent.

Gunfire on board the *Pearl* had Sly raising his eyes to the upper deck. He had no idea how Merrick had managed to get himself free, but he was armed. Within a matter of seconds two guards went over the side, then his commander pitched himself overboard as well.

That he would abandon ship without the Chameleon told Sly that something was amiss. He turned the glider, searched the water for Merrick, and when he surfaced, Sly opened up the glider once more. One handed, he pulled his commander onto the machine behind him as he sped past.

Merrick motioned for him to send the glider into the deep. Sly didn't question the request. He cut away from the *Pearl* and started down, just as an explosion sent the yacht out of the water and into an orange fireball. A geyser of water went up, then rained down as the water churned and the earth around the lagoon shook. The force of the C4 sent debris spraying the perimeter, littering the sea for a half a mile in all directions.

Sly blacked out and when he came to, Merrick was swimming toward a fishing boat, with an arm locked around him. It occurred to him at that moment that his injuries must be serious, since he couldn't move. Then that the men on board the boat Merrick was swimming to looked familiar—Onyxx agents.

He heard Bjorn's voice, then Pierce's. He had trusted his comrades countless times with his life, and in that moment he felt confident that Eva was safe on board, too.

It was only then that he gave in to his injuries and slipped into unconsciousness.

Chapter 20

Three weeks later Sly strolled down the hall at Onyxx headquarters and, without knocking, stepped into Merrick's office.

"McEwen, I was told you were in the building," Merrick said from behind his desk.

Sly studied his commander. It was the first he'd seen Merrick since they had both been airlifted to a hospital in Athens, where he'd spent five days and Merrick had spent less than twenty-four hours.

It was during those days that Bjorn had explained how he had called Pierce and Ash back in D.C. and asked them to fly to Greece. Stating his reasons, they had hopped a plane as quickly as they could. While Ash had stayed behind in Santorini to stand watch over Reznik until they had made arrangements to fly him back to the States, Pierce had been elected to follow Bjorn to Paros and play a game they called double-tag.

Bjorn had allowed himself to be captured by the Chameleon's men in order to fool them into thinking they had captured Sly's backup. Since they had seen only Bjorn at Cupata, Pierce had been able to wire the *Pearl* with explosives, then enter the monastery through the back door. At that point, Pierce had reminded Sly that with so many sea caves in the Greek Isles he had figured the Chameleon's back door would be an underwater tunnel of some kind.

Within hours of the explosion, the Agency had dispatched a mop-up crew to Paros to sweep the mission, and tie up loose ends. They had found a number of bodies, and on hearing the news, Sly had insisted that Bjorn and Pierce break him out of the hospital. Together, along with Ash Kelly, they had supervised the recovery of the bodies, and Sly had identified the Chameleon—or rather Paavo Creon—along with Simon Parish.

"You look good, McEwen," Merrick said. "I was wondering how soon I'd see you. Does this mean you're ready to start back to work?"

"I resigned two months ago, remember?"

"Yes, I do. But I told you that I tore that paper up."

Sly shrugged, wincing a little. He was still sore from the shrapnel that had been dug out of his shoulder and back. "I just came by to tell you I'm taking some time off. An extended sabbatical. And to give you this."

He tossed a file on Merrick's desk.

"Is it all here? Everything?"

"Everything. Including pictures."

Merrick opened the file, thumbed through the many pages. Glanced at the gruesome pictures of several bodies. He located the one identified as the Chameleon. "I see in your report you've confirmed the Agency's suspicions."

"That's right. The Chameleon is…was Paavo Creon."

Merrick looked up from the file. "Do you believe that?"

"No." Sly handed over the neatly written letter Bjorn had given him in the hospital from Eva. "In that letter it says the Chameleon surgically copied the face of Onyxx agent Paavo Creon fourteen years ago after killing Creon and his wife in Atlanta." Sly paused, then said, "Eva's father…your friend didn't betray you, Merrick. Paavo never killed your wife."

"If what you say is true, and I'm inclined to believe you, then we still don't have a positive ID on the Chameleon's body, and it'll take weeks, maybe months, to positively ID the remains."

Sly hoped so. Merrick needed time to deal with his own health issues before he discovered the truth.

"We're still looking for the Chameleon's daughter, but there's no sign of Melita. We haven't been able to get much out of those eight prisoners that we found at the compound, either. But we're still working on both." Merrick peered into the box. "Bjorn mentioned some tapes. At least a dozen from a Dr. Fielding concerning Eva. Where are they?"

"Gone."

"Gone?" Merrick looked up. "Those tapes are evidence."

"I can't say for sure, but I think Simon Parish stole them off the *Hector* the night I was captured by him." Sly's lie was believable. He said, "Bjorn says Reznik is refusing to talk."

Merrick grunted. "There's a rumor that the Chameleon gave him a kill-list. That they made a deal of some kind. Know anything about that?"

"Some. It's in my report. Where is she?"

Merrick was back flipping through the file. He looked up. "Eva's fine. You don't need to concern yourself about—"

"Where?"

"Signing the *Hector* over to her was a nice gesture. She told me to thank you. We did agree that when she was free, she should fly and things would get back to normal. I mentioned to her what you and I had talked about and she agreed that disappearing would be the best for everyone. I told her you'd be coming back to work, and… Well, you know as well as I that as agents we do a lot of things that we normally would never think of doing otherwise. Our lives here at Onyxx force us to role-play and use people. We—"

"Where is she?"

"Listen, McEwen, nothing can come of this. As your commanding officer, my advice to you is to— Hold on, where are you going?"

Sly's hand was on the doorknob. He looked over his sore shoulder. "I'm taking off."

"Then I'll see you tomorrow?"

"No. I told you I'm taking a sabbatical."

"Dammit, McEwen. For how long?"

"Can't say."

"What are you going to do?"

"A little fishing." Sly opened the door.

"But you gave away your boat."

"Yes, I did."

"Don't you want to know where she is?"

Sly turned to face his commander. "I know where she is, Merrick."

"You do? Then why did you ask me?"

"To see if anything had changed."

"Changed?"

"You're an asshole, Merrick. You still have an ice

chunk where your heart should be." Sly started out the door again. "Oh—" he spun around "—get that operation. You're going to need to be in shape in a few months."

"What's that supposed to mean?"

"Trust me, get yourself fixed up and in shape."

"In shape? Who saved whose ass in Greece?"

The door was pushed open and in walked Bjorn. "I believe I saved both of your asses." He sauntered past Sly and took the chair in front of Merrick's desk. "You wanted to see me, Merrick?"

"That's right."

"You're really taking off, Sly?" Bjorn asked.

"I'm really taking off."

"When can I expect you back to work?" Merrick asked.

"When there's something worth coming back for." Sly stepped through the door.

"How can I reach you?" Merrick yelled.

"You can't." Sly started down the hall. "When I want to be found you'll be the first to know."

Eva angled her head and let the warm sea breeze touch her cheeks and lift her hair. She had sailed the *Hector* to the private cove weeks ago expecting Sly to follow her within a week.

She'd seen him briefly just before he'd been wheeled into surgery. She hadn't been able to speak to him, not even to thank him for…everything.

She'd been interrogated for five days before she'd been allowed to disappear. That's the word Merrick had used when he'd come to talk to her that last day. When he'd described her relationship with Sly as an encounter during a dangerous mission.

He'd said, "I know you and Sly became close…

friends, Eva, and that's why... Sly signed over the *Hector* to you. Here's the deed. It's yours. A gift. A way of saying thanks."

A way of saying thanks.

She hadn't wanted to believe Sly could be so cold about what they'd shared, but after the week had turned into ten days, she had started to have doubts. Now, twenty-one days later, she could no longer keep pretending that he'd just been delayed.

The truth was, he wasn't coming. Merrick, as gently as he could, had been telling the truth. She and Sly had had an encounter during a dangerous mission, and the *Hector* was her consolation prize.

She felt like a fool for thinking that he had cared about her over and above job level. That he would want to spend some time away from the *job* with her.

When Merrick had handed her the deed to the *Hector*, she had thought that Sly was sending her a silent message. A message to meet him here where they had fallen in love. Correction. Where she had fallen in love.

He wasn't coming.

Eva felt the lump in her throat swell as tears stung her eyes. She wanted to cry, but that would really make her look like a fool.

It was actually generous of him to give her the yacht considering she had no money or home. Nothing now but her freedom.

She should be thrilled. She'd always wanted to be free to go anywhere her heart wished. To sail away with the wind and never look back. It was all possible now. No more rules, no more games.

She could disappear and she would.

She would leave tomorrow and go...where?

East, west, north or south.

One thing for certain was her food supply was running low and she would need money to restock the galley. That meant she would have to find a job. She wasn't qualified to do anything. Anything but survive, and at the moment she had no idea who would hire her with that one word written in the skills column on a job résumé.

It was late afternoon when she heard the motor, then saw the fisherman in the distance. He waved and she waved back. Her heart had sped up for a moment, had allowed her to hope for a brief few seconds.

She went below, and had a good cry. Feeling better, she went back up on deck ready to enjoy another beautiful sunset alone. Curling up on the cushion along the stern, she drew up her legs and stared out over the blue water.

She couldn't blame Sly for not coming. Tomorrow she would leave this beautiful place and never return.

"It's over," she whispered. "It's finally over."

"Is it?"

She whirled her head around to see Sly standing in the doorway of the wheelhouse. He was soaking wet, as if he'd come straight out of the sea. He looked…tall, and too good for words.

"The fisherman…" she said, absently pointing in the direction she'd seen the boat.

"Nice guy. Says you've been out here awhile. A few weeks."

"Soaking up a little sun," she said. "You know me. I love the sun. I found your underwater cameras and went exploring. So what brings you out here? Did you finally wrap everything up?"

"The Agency is still looking for Melita."

"I wanted to help, but Merrick told me that you… They preferred I just disappear. Did you find his body?"

"Yes. Simon Parish's, too. When did you finally remember?"

"That the Chameleon wasn't my real father? I suppose deep in my subconscious somewhere I always knew. That's what Dr. Fielding would say. My father was never the same person after my mother died because he, in fact, wasn't that person. My papa died that night."

"So it was just a hunch you were playing when you called Merrick?"

She had hoped he had come to see her, but he'd come to tie up the loose ends. That was all.

Eva settled back on the seat cushion and raised her chin. "Since I was a little girl I felt something wasn't right, but how could I dispute what was staring me in the face? He looked like my papa. Had the missing index finger on his right hand. The scar on his chin. He even carried the silver lighter my mother had given him. Still, I couldn't believe that my papa would abandon me like he did. We were so close when I was little."

"Because you believed he loved you."

"He did love me. The Chameleon admitted that to me at the compound. When you started calling me Evy, I didn't know why I liked hearing it so much. But later I remembered my papa used to call me that. I'd forgotten that, just like I had forgotten that I called him Papa, not Father. The Chameleon always said to me, 'You are your father's daughter.' Not, you're Papa's little Evy. That's what Papa used to say. I didn't remember that until Merrick brought me the sucker. The Chameleon gave me this ring." Eva raised her hand. "It's my mother's wedding ring. He must have taken it from her before he killed her because after the fire started he was too busy getting out of the burning house and taking me with him. At the Chameleon's compound he told me about that night in Atlanta. He helped me remember why I was so frightened, and confused. I saw him and my father together in the hall, and they had the same face, only one of the faces was—"

"Laughing. I remember you telling me that after you read the file the night you left."

"You let me leave so you could follow me."

"Yes. And you left knowing I would follow."

Eva nodded. "Yes. My father told me to run that night in Atlanta, and I did try to get away. That's when I fell down the stairs. I think when I came to I wiped out everything because it was too bizarre and frightening to believe."

"So you've been here all this time putting all these pieces together while sitting in the sun. Is that right?"

Eva sucked on her lower lip. "That's about it."

"Really?"

She could no longer look at him and so she sent her gaze over the water not knowing what to say. She sucked in a breath, hoped he hadn't heard her below deck crying.

Finally, she said, "I'm free now, and it feels good. I can go anywhere I want."

"Yes, you can."

"I can be a vagabond, if I like."

"Come here, Evy."

That name on his lips sent a shiver down her spine and she wrapped her arms around her legs. Shook her head, still not wanting to look at him. "I don't think— Merrick told me you two had talked. He said—"

"Come here."

She didn't know if it was the need she heard in his voice that made her look, or her own need to fill her senses with the sight of him. But she did look, and when she saw his hand outstretched to her, she let out a strangled cry, and came off the leather seat in a solid, fluid motion. She raced to him and he scooped her up in his arms and pulled her close, burying his face against her neck.

"I've missed you," he whispered into her hair.

They were the simplest of words, and yet they sent tears flowing down Eva's cheeks. "I thought you weren't coming," she confessed on a sob.

He squeezed her tight and she rejoiced in the feel of his arms so strong around her. She raised her face and searched out his lips. They kissed, a long, heartfelt kiss full of warmth and sweet desire.

Suddenly remembering his recent surgery, she pulled back and asked, "What about your back and shoulder?" She checked him out, studied the vivid scars.

"I'm fine. Scratches, is all."

"Scratches that required six hours of surgery."

"You were there?"

"Yes."

"I didn't know. Merrick never told me."

"He doesn't like me."

"I'd say he likes you a lot. So much he's appointed himself your parental protector."

"I don't want to be protected from you." Eva wrapped her arms around Sly's neck and kissed him again, then again.

He carried her to the seat and sat with her in his lap. "So where should we sail?"

"You want to go somewhere with me? But I thought... Merrick told me you were going back to work as soon as you were well enough. What about Onyxx?"

"I'm on a sabbatical."

"I thought you said you were feeling fine."

"I am. You complaining?"

No, she wasn't. She just wanted to know where things stood. "How much time?"

He drew back and studied her face, brushed a tear from her cheek. "Can't say. I suppose I'll go back when you get sick and tired of me and kick my sorry ass off your boat."

Eva sucked in her breath. "What are you saying, Sly?"

"I'm saying I'm in love with you, Evy."

Sly watched her open her mouth, but unsure what was going to come out, he quickly added, "You don't have to say anything. I know what you think about that word, and that's okay. I just wanted you to know that I don't usually seduce beautiful women out of their panties during a mission."

She was sitting very still, and he wondered what she was thinking.

She said, "So you liked me from the beginning. Is that it?"

"From the first time I heard your voice," he agreed.

She touched his cheek, brushed her fingers over his lips. "I was wrong. *Love* is a beautiful word, and the most wonderful feeling in the world. To love and be loved. To need someone, and have that person need you, too. You need me, right?"

"I need you, Evy."

"What happens after I say, I love you, too, Slayton?"

Sly hadn't let himself hope that she might feel the same way he did. He'd told himself on the entire fight from D.C. to Athens not to expect too much. That he could have read her wrong those times they had been intimate.

What would a beautiful woman like Eva Creon see

in a man like him, anyway—a rat fighter with a past as black as the Mississippi mud where he'd been born?

God, he loved her. Had missed her. He'd been so damned relieved when he'd seen the *Hector* in the cove. He'd almost kissed that grinning fisherman.

He had told Merrick he knew where she'd be, but it had been a bold statement. The truth was, he'd given her the *Hector* in hopes that this place had meant as much to her as it had to him. Hoped, no prayed, that she'd want to return.

"You meant for me to meet you here, right? I didn't read you wrong, did I?"

Sly grinned. "You didn't read me wrong. But the mop-up at Paros took longer than I'd planned, and then I had to go back to D.C. for a few days to file my reports."

He drew her to him and kissed her, then glanced over her head to the sandy beach where they had first made love weeks ago. Heart-stopping, blood-pumping, all-or-nothing love.

"That stretch of sand over there looks lonely. What do you say we go keep it company for a while?"

She followed his gaze, and when she looked back at him he saw mischief in her eyes.

"I had another dream," she confessed.

He ran his fingers through her hair, slid them down her back. His gaze lowered to her parted red lips, then to her sun-kissed cleavage straining her black bikini. "So damn beautiful," he muttered.

She blushed. "You really like me...love me."

"Every inch," he promised.

He could hardly believe she'd waited here for him for three damn weeks. Twenty-one days.

"You really like me," he mimicked.

"Love you with all my heart."

Feeling oddly emotional, he said, "You want to tell me about the dream, or show me?"

She pulled him close and kissed him. Against his lips, she whispered, "We were *doing it* underwater along the reef."

He raised a black eyebrow. "Doing what?"

Her smile opened up. "Stop teasing. Have you ever made love in the deep, Sly?"

"No," was his answer, but it looked like that was about to change. Whatever time they were given, he intended to use it wisely.

He slid her off his lap so she was standing between his legs. The little strings that kept her bikini clinging to her trim hips were easy to untie, and so he did.

"Let's make a memory, Evy." He lifted her into his arms and kissed her with all the passion and care of a man who knew just how lucky he was. Then, he tossed himself over the side of the *Hector*, plunging into the azure water with Eva's sweet body clinging to him.

There were a thousand islands and islets in the Cyclades. Two thousand more scattered from the Aegean to the Ionian Sea. Together Sly was confident he and Eva would find their own paradise in this magical place. And for a time they would be as carefree as the wind, sailing from port to port. They would love like vagabonds, and live each day as if the world might end tomorrow.

For who really knew what the future would bring? Or how soon the truth would surface and the Chameleon would rise up out of the sea, and it would start all over again?

What follows is an excerpt from

THE SPY WORE RED

by Wendy Rosnau,
a sequel to A THOUSAND KISSES DEEP,
coming soon from Silhouette Bombshell.

Chapter 1

Winter smog hung thick over the city of Prague, as well as a fresh layer of snow. Both, however, couldn't be blamed for Nadja Stefn being late. Twelve minutes, to be exact.

Red wool swirled around her as she dashed up the stone steps to the Vysehrad Museum. Inside, she kept moving as routine and familiarity took over. She pulled off her black leather gloves, her booted feet clicking out a hurried tempo on the slate floor as she made a right down the corridor, then a hard left.

In a narrow passageway Nadja stopped and faced a small mirror next to an elevator. Once the retinal scanner identified her, the doors opened and she stepped inside and placed her right hand into the fingerprint identification mold on the wall. An electronic charge tingled her fingertips, a computerized voice welcomed her by name, and then the elevator took off, descending into the underworld beneath the museum.

Polax would be having a hairy cow by now, Nadja thought as she checked her watch, then buried her gloves in the outer pocket of her slim black briefcase. He would be cursing her in ten languages for holding up his all-important morning meeting.

Today a Quest agent would be selected to accompany an Onyxx agent on a mission into Austria.

A milestone mission, Polax had promised when he'd called her yesterday with the news that she was one of the candidates being considered. He hadn't offered her the particulars, and no more would be shared unless she was the agent packing a bag at the end of the day and flying out of Ruzyne Airport at midnight.

That's how it worked at Quest; everything was done on a need-to-know basis. Nadja was ranked number one in sanctioned assassins at EURO Quest. She had a special technique that set her apart from the others, and it had successfully kept her on top of her game for the past four years.

It was safe to assume that this particular mission required her expertise, or she wouldn't be a candidate. Normally she didn't do handstands to get noticed at Quest. Contrary to the rumors—and the stats—she didn't live for her work. But this case was the exception to the rule. It opened the door for her to return to Austria. A week or a month—the mission's term didn't matter. All she needed was an excuse to make a stop in Innsbruck, and an hour of Ruger's time.

Her past three letters to her brother had been returned unopened. She didn't believe that he'd moved. Why would he? He loved his work. He certainly hadn't changed professions.

She was desperate to make contact with him. Now that she knew what she really wanted out of life, she was anxious to tell him. Anxious to move forward. Anxious for him to become her ally and point her in the right direction.

The elevator continued on its way into the underbelly of the Vysehrad Museum. That's where EURO Quest had been conducting their secret intelligence operations for the past ten years. Where femmes fatales such as herself were utilized to their fullest potential.

Nadja shrugged off her wool cape, and that's when she saw the fat wrinkle blazing a path across the front of her skirt. How it had gotten there she had no clue. She studied it for a moment and decided it made her look as if she'd slept on a bar stool all night. She hadn't. She'd gone to bed on time—she just hadn't fallen asleep until dawn thinking about returning to Austria, and how Ruger would take her news.

She must have fallen asleep harder than usual, because she'd slept straight through her alarm. When she'd opened her eyes to learn that she was late, she'd raced through her apartment in a frenzy to get ready.

She must have grabbed the wrong suit out of her closet, she decided, slapping at the wrinkle. When the wrinkle didn't budge she dismissed it and made a quick assessment of her white blouse and black jacket. Her blouse looked good, her jacket…was missing a gold button.

This was the suit she'd planned to take to the cleaners.

"Shit."

Nadja dropped her cape to the floor, chanting her frustration into the air three more times. She pinched the briefcase between her knees and peeled off the jacket. Briefcase back in hand, she draped the jacket over her arm and studied her appearance in the mirror along the elevator doors.

"Better," she muttered softly, "but…"

She turned her head side to side, then gathered her long blond hair into one of her small hands and pulled it back from her face. Wishing she hadn't overslept, disgusted that she had no clip to make even a bare-bones improvement, she released her hair and peered at her bloodshot eyes.

Glasses would disguise her lack of sleep, and lack of makeup.

Again she pinched her briefcase between her knees in search of the reading glasses she kept in her jacket pocket. Of course they weren't there—she was wearing the wrong suit. Frustrated, Nadja grabbed the briefcase from between her knees, unaware the metal clasp had caught on her silk stockings. She looked down too late to do anything but gasp out loud as one by one the delicate threads parted company with one another.

In a matter of minutes the elevator would stop. The doors would open and Nadja would be greeted by two in-house agents. Kimball and Moor had squarish faces, pug noses and no sense of humor. But then, why would agent hopefuls who had fallen short be in a good mood? Ever.

The "Butlers"—as she called them—would flank her as she left the elevator and doggedly escort her to the conclave where Pasha Lenova and Casmir Balasi, the other two agents vying for the Austrian assignment, would already be waiting.

As stringent as Polax was about being punctual, he was twice as neurotic about professional neatness. Which meant she could easily be skipped over in favor of Pasha's promptness, or—she glanced down at the *fat* wrinkle tracking her thighs, then the hole that had targeted her knee—Casmir's flair for always looking like she'd just stepped off a Paris runway.

Three more times shits bounced off the elevator ceiling, as Nadja dropped her briefcase to the floor and quickly pulled off her boots. Standing with her belongings scattered around her, she jerked her skirt high and began unhooking her stockings from her garter belt.

The sexy garter belt was red, the flat screen monitors in Polax's office recreational size.

After studying the first two Quest agents on the monitor as they entered the elevator, Bjorn Odell had slid his ass onto the corner of Polax's desk to watch the third, and final, candidate. She'd been late, and Polax had pissed and moaned about that for the entire twelve minutes.

Arms crossed over his chest, Bjorn now watched as the brown-eyed blonde peeled off her silk stockings and dropped them to the floor next to her briefcase. He put to memory every detail of her performance. Studied every move she made, every article of clothing on the floor, and left on her body.

Her garter belt was the same fire-red color as the Italian-leather holster strapped to her thigh. Inside the custom-made holster was the prettiest pearl-handle minicompact .45 Springfield he'd ever seen. The Springfield was a dandy—a one of a kind, just like the femme who owned it.

She had long legs and beautiful thighs. The sweetest ass in Prague—Bjorn would wager his own concealed .380 Beretta Cheetah on that.

"As you can see, the logical choice is Pasha Lenova. It's not hard to see who is who here at EURO Quest. Or more to the point, what specific role these top three operatives play. Lenova is our endurance agent. She can match any man she's put up against. My personal favorite for a physical mission such as this. Balasi is our actress-slash-model. She was recruited not just for her pretty face and amazing body, but because her role-playing skills are flawless.

"Stefn… Nadja appears a bit scatterbrained today, and I can't explain that. She's my cream. She always rises to the top."

Polax chuckled, the words obviously tickling his funny bone.

Without conscious thought, Bjorn fit people into three categories—the doers, the watchers and the talkers. Polax was without doubt a watcher. And with what appeared to be a limitless expense budget, he'd outfitted his office with the latest in gadgets to enhance his obsession—keeping a very close eye on the women who worked for him.

The wall-size monitors were equipped with pulse-sonic sound and a state-of-the-art zoom feature that could find a grain of salt in a sugar bowl. The chair behind his desk was motorized and voice sensitive. It had been following Polax around the room for the past thirty minutes like a pet puppy. And on the chance he felt like taking a load off on a second's notice, all he had to do was plop.

"Here at Quest," Polax began, "Nadja's our candy queen. She's got a sweet body, and she's not shy when it comes to sharing her treats. I guarantee that the men who find themselves in Q's bed end up with one hell of a toothache. But then if my number was up, and I had a choice, I'd elect to die high on sugar, wouldn't you?"

With a hearty laugh Polax pressed the zoom button on his remote and brought Nadja Stefn's sexy ass into the room in a big way.

Bjorn glanced at his boss. Adolf Merrick was leaning against the wall with his arms crossed over his chest. His interest wasn't on Q's ass, however. He was staring directly at Bjorn, watching him with an intensity that would have made a lesser man squirm.

Bjorn didn't squirm. He didn't even flinch. He turned back to the monitor at the exact time Polax zeroed in on a chocolate mole on the candy queen's inner thigh.

What it came down to was that the commander of EURO Quest enjoyed his job a little too much. He had paraded through the Agency corridors like a sheik who owned his own private harem. A sheik with itchy fingers and a fetish for electronic gadgets—he was now fiddling with the supersensitive sound control, tuning in to Nadja's rapid breathing as she worked quickly to strip off her naughty red garter belt. Bjorn raised his eyebrows just as Polax looked over his shoulder.

"What's wrong, Agent Odell? You did ask to examine the candidates. I thought a profile expert such as yourself would appreciate my willingness to cooperate to the fullest with your demands."

It was true he had requested a sneak peek, but this wasn't exactly what he'd meant—playing voyeur with his boss on his left and a stranger on his right.

"We aim to please here at Quest." Polax sent his drab green eyes over Bjorn's broad shoulders, down his solid chest and athletic long legs. Taking his measure, noting the obvious differences in size and height, and possibly the importance of keeping the bigger man happy, he added, "I've read your profile, Odell. It's impressive. You're a damn hard man to kill."

"You say that as if it's a flaw."

"On the contrary. I respect you and your ability to survive seven years in the hot seat. But then, I'm not surprised. Only the best are commandeered to become 'rat fighters.' Merrick's Onyxx elites are simply the best there are anywhere. That's why it's important for you to have the right partner at your side on this mission. All my agents are top-notch in their own unique way. As I said, they each serve a specific purpose. Quest trains only the top two out of every hundred that make it to the evaluation stage. Stefn…" Polax motioned to the monitor. "To be honest with you, I interviewed her as a favor to an old colleague. I never believed for a minute she'd meet my criteria."

"Meaning?"

"Her injuries automatically made her ineligible. But then I read her profile and… Well, it was simply amazing that she was even alive, let alone back on her feet. More amazing was the fact that she showed no signs whatsoever that she'd been in a physical rehab facility for three years, a good share of that time in traction in between surgeries. She doesn't even limp. What I've learned since is that Nadja has an incredible tolerance for pain. It's unbelievable. As you know, the number one obstacle agencies face when finding suitable operatives is their tolerance for pain and their desire to endure it on a level ten."

"What were her injuries?" Bjorn asked.

"She was in a skiing accident."

Bjorn picked Nadja Stefn's file off the desk and opened it. "It says here that she was born and raised in Austria. That she was an Olympic gold medal hopeful."

"She comes from a line of Olympic champions. Both her mother and father were professional skaters. Her grandfather won a gold medal in alpine slalom. Nadja was expected to do the same the year she had her accident. She crashed during a race in Zurich. I don't think there was a bone in her body she didn't break."

Polax walked closer to the monitor—his pet chair on his heels—and cocked his head as if searching for something. "At this angle you can't see her scars, but there are a few the plastic surgery couldn't make disappear."

He ran his hand over the screen, touched Q's right knee, then moved it up her thigh, stroking her leg like a man who knew her intimately. Or a man who had lain awake nights contemplating the idea.

"She also has a tattoo that is quite spectacular." He turned and looked from Merrick to Bjorn, then plopped down on his chair. As his pet took off and rounded his desk, he said, "It's in an area I call the *dead zone.*"

Bjorn waited for Polax's chuckle to wear out before he asked, "These old injuries—do they limit her in any way?"

"Not in percentages. But that's because I've tailored her missions. That's what it's all about, you know. Finding a niche. If a woman wants to work at Quest she must be special. We like to think we're in the made-to-order intelligence business here."

"You said you recommend Agent Lenova," Merrick injected. "Why?"

"I do feel strongly that she would be your best choice. If you look in Stefn's file, you'll see that she hasn't been sent on too many endurance assignments. Physical missions, as well as cold weather, can affect her performance. Her medical file reveals that her blood circulation isn't a hundred percent. The scar tissue that has developed due to her many surgeries is the cause. To be blunt, Q does her best work on her back. She's a first-rate bedroom assassin. Since this mission will be a chilly affair, a manhunt of sorts, and will likely prove to be physically strenuous, I recommend Pasha Lenova. Rain or shine, desert heat or arctic cold, she will match you every step of the way."

"It says here Stefn trained for the biathlon. She shoots

ninety-six percent." Bjorn scanned the file for more data.

"Pasha also shoots over ninety-five percent," Polax quoted from memory. "Casmir Balasi, ninety-eight."

Bjorn looked up at the monitor. Nadja was now wiggling her skirt back over her satin-smooth thighs. He lowered his head to the file once more, thumped through the data.

He had arrived in Prague late last night, accompanied by his commander. They'd flown in from Washington, D.C., and that's when Merrick had informed him that an agent from EURO Quest would be accompanying him on the mission.

Three days earlier, when he'd learned that Holic Reznik had successfully slipped through the NSA's fingers and escaped his well-guarded prison cell, he'd been so angry he had walked out of Merrick's office in a rage. How in the hell had Holic managed a jailbreak with a twenty-four-hour guard on duty, and a prison cell built better than Fort Knox?

It had been two months since Bjorn had apprehended Holic in Santorini, Greece. In a do-or-die fight during a hotel fire, he'd managed to capture the country's most wanted assassin. It would have been better if he had just killed him. Instead, he'd pulled Holic from the fire and debris after a balcony had collapsed during the chaos—his orders from the Agency demanding that he take the bastard alive.

Normally he was an even-tempered guy. Reasonable, even during upsetting news. After an hour of walking off his anger, he had returned to Merrick's office to discuss what the Agency intended to do now that Reznik was once again a free man.

Seated in front of his commander's desk, he'd asked, "Has the Agency issued a new objective?"

"They have, and your name was mentioned for the assignment. It's yours, if you want it."

"I'm not a field agent any longer."

"Reinstatement would be a simple formality. You've got the experience. You've studied Holic Reznik's habits, and know his weaknesses. That makes you the most qualified for the mission. I want you on the job, Bjorn. That is, if you'll take it."

It was true. He and Holic "the butcher" Reznik had a history. Bjorn had listened while Merrick detailed the situation. Holic had been seriously injured in Santorini when the balcony had collapsed and he'd fallen thirty feet. Because of Holic's many injuries, the Agency believed he would return to Austria to heal and grow strong again. They hadn't been able to pinpoint where exactly, but they felt confident it would be someplace familiar to him. Someplace remote.

"We know that before the Chameleon died he contracted Reznik to do some work for him. He was given a kill list, and promised ten million dollars, as well as—"

"Eva Creon as his mistress," Bjorn had finished.

"That's right. Since that portion of the contract fell through, we're not sure what Holic's next plan of action will be. There's a good chance that someone within the Chameleon's criminal enterprise has already taken over for him. The league is too large to crumble. That means they will be expecting Holic to fulfill the contract, or renegotiate it. We suspect there are at least fifty names on that list. NSA and CIA agents, as well as many of our own Onyxx operatives. If you should decide to take the assignment, your mission will be to infiltrate Austria, uncover Holic's hideout, seize the kill-file, then assassinate the assassin."

Bjorn liked the new objective. Currently Holic

Reznik was the most reliable killing machine for hire on all seven continents. He had hundreds of kills to his credit. Grisly kills. After all, Holic enjoyed his work.

Ranked in the top ten most wanted at the NSA, the man had become a bloody pain in the ass.

Polax was still tossing out reasons why Pasha Lenova was the best choice for the mission. Bjorn listened while he watched Nadja Stefn slip her tall black boots back on her pretty feet.

When Merrick cleared his throat, he glanced at his boss. "You say something?"

"I asked you which one you've decided to take along to Austria with you?"

"You're giving me the choice?"

"You're the profile expert. It'll be your back she'll be watching, and vice versa. The question you've got to ask yourself is which woman do you want to share your days and nights with for the next month or two. I don't care who or why, as long as she can keep up. So do you fancy the brunette, goldilocks, or the bedroom blonde with the candy-cane legs and cotton-candy ass?"

"My recommendation—" Polax began.

"*Ja,* we know," Bjorn turned his piercing blue eyes on the Quest commander. "Your choice is the brunette. You've made that clear. A little too clear."

Polax climbed out of his chair and puffed out his chest. "As I said before, my job is to match the mission with the best possible agent. If I need an actress, I send Balasi. If I need a seductress, I send Q, and if I need a ball buster who chews ice cubes in place of gum, I send Lenova. Quest is a young agency. The only way we can earn our stripes in the intelligence world is if we come back a winner every time. It's how you get noticed. It's how your 'rat fighters' got noticed, Merrick. With Pasha Lenova at your side in Austria, that win is inevitable."

"What you're forgetting is it's not your choice," Bjorn reminded. "It's mine."

He glanced back to the monitor. The elevator had stopped and Nadja was now greeting the two men waiting for her in the corridor. She stepped out of the elevator and handed her red cape to the shorter man, then, like a resilient cat who had just landed on her feet, she started down the corridor. Her briefcase in one hand, and her jacket draped over the other, so that the Quest insignia was visible and the missing button was hidden from sight.

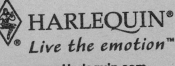

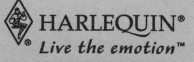

Forrester Square

LEGACIES . LIES . LOVE .

A story not to be missed…

In July, Forrester Square comes to a
gripping conclusion!

ESCAPE THE NIGHT

by top Harlequin Intrigue® author

JOANNA WAYNE

Returning to Seattle
after many years,
Alexandra Webber meets
Ben Jessup, who now lives
in her childhood home.
When recurring nightmares
and memories of a long-ago
night begin to haunt and
endanger Alex, Ben vows
to protect her.

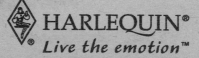

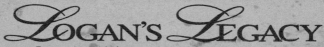

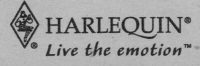